LORI CONNELLY

I was born and still live in Oregon. Despite being a good student, my teachers complained about my tendency to daydream. The tales dancing through my imagination were frequently far more entertaining than real life! As far back as I can remember I made up stories, to calm my sister after a nightmare, entertain myself in boring classes and write in countless notebooks, many never again to see the light of day. I earned a BS from Eastern Oregon State College and married my best friend almost twenty years ago. I have three brilliant, handsome sons, one amazing daughter-in-law, a grand baby to be and two spoiled dogs. When not writing I love to read, hike, camp, rock hound, and take long walks with my husband just after it rains. You can learn more about me at my blog http://loriconnelly.blogspot.com/.

The Outlaw of
Cedar Ridge

LORI CONNELLY

Harper*Impulse* an imprint of
HarperCollins*Publishers Ltd*
77–85 Fulham Palace Road
Hammersmith, London W6 8JB

www.harpercollins.co.uk

A Paperback Original 2014

First published in Great Britain in ebook format by HarperImpulse 2013

Copyright © Lori Connelly 2013

Cover Images © Shutterstock.com

Lori Connelly asserts the moral right to
be identified as the author of this work

A catalogue record for this book
is available from the British Library

ISBN: 978-0-00-755972-5

This novel is entirely a work of fiction.
The names, characters and incidents portrayed in it are
the work of the author's imagination. Any resemblance to
actual persons, living or dead, events or localities is
entirely coincidental.

Automatically produced by Atomik ePublisher from Easypress

Prologue

The saloon doors slammed open. "That yellow-bellied, four-flusher," a tall man complained loudly as he staggered out of the Bucking Pony, "needs to be taught a lesson."

The breeze carried the sound of stomping feet and more raised voices through the night. Benjamin Rolfe, only a few yards away, took a prudent side step off the boarded sidewalk. From where he hid, in-between two dark, empty buildings, Ben could only make out snippets.

"Low down dirty cheater."

"I warned the boss not to buy that horse from Rolfe."

Curious, Ben peeked around the corner. *Talbert's men.* He counted the figures of at least six men standing by the horses tied in front of the saloon.

"If the Sheriff won't do his job, then someone needs to do it for him."

Ben moved back into the deeper shadows. He didn't care what some drunken ranch hands thought of him and wasn't about to risk his hide defending an already ruined reputation. With his back against a rough wood wall, he let their tirade drift past him, waiting for them to leave.

Minutes passed with aggravating slowness. His mouth dry, thirst nagged by the time the men finally mounted up and rode out of town. Ben lingered out of plain sight a short time to be certain they were gone then continued on his way to the saloon.

Inside the batwing doors, the place was almost full. Ignoring the brief lull in conversation as he walked in, Ben crossed the room to stand at the bar and dropped his saddlebag to the floor. The bartender stared at him for a couple of seconds before slapping down a glass and filling it with cheap whiskey.

His hand curled around the glass, but instead of taking the long drink he'd been craving for hours, the cowboy stared down at the golden brown liquid. He should be happy, celebrating. His share of the take would at least half fill the jar he'd emptied at home. Evie wouldn't even have to know he'd broken another promise.

Ben tilted the glass slightly from one side to the other, watching the alcohol flow. He should go home. It was late and he needed to talk to his wife. The image of blue eyes filled with disappointment flashed through his mind. A muscle worked along his jaw and he tossed back the drink.

The whiskey burned his throat and he put the glass down with a hard thud. Familiar with his routine, the bartender moved over, poured him a refill and left the bottle. His fingers tightened around the glass but before he lifted it to his mouth again, the noisy room quieted.

Braced for a fight, Ben released his grip and turned to face the door, expecting to see that the group of Talbert's ranch hands had returned. The sight of only two men standing by the door caught him off guard. *Damn.* He would've preferred a fight.

The Nash brothers strode across the room, cocky, confident, as if they owned the place. His decision to hook up with these lowlifes for this last con was one he'd regretted from the moment he made it. They had no good reason to follow him back to Cedar Ridge.

"Rolfe, what a surprise," Billy's smile was more like a coyote barring his teeth than anything human.

"Yes, it is." He offered them an equally insincere smile of his own. "Have you lost Byron?"

"He's getting patched up."

"So what brings you out this way?"

"Seth and I were bored," Billy's over pleasant tone set his teeth on edge. "I thought we could find a game here."

A two hour ride at night for a game? "Is that so?"

"If not, we'll start our own."

Billy chuckled and shouted to the bartender for a couple of bottles as he and Seth sat down at the empty table. Ben reached back, grabbed his glass and lifted it in a mocking toast. He drank then slowly turned his back to the outlaws, a deliberate act to show them he wasn't afraid. With a hand steady through sheer force of will, he refilled his glass.

The fact that Billy hadn't bothered to offer a believable explanation didn't bode well. They were here either to rob him or kill him, possibly both. His options were few. Most of the townspeople wouldn't spit on him if he was on fire and the one man who'd likely help was the one man he couldn't ask.

Please protect me from the other lowlifes, Sheriff. Yeah that would go over well.

Ben finished off his drink and poured another. He nursed this measure of whiskey and listened to the brothers persuade a few men to play poker with them while he waited for the chance to slip away. A band of pressure coiled around his chest when they started to brag about the robbery. With them running off at the mouth, the Sheriff would soon have more than suspicion about his 'jobs'. And then meant leaving town sooner rather than later.

Ben cursed under his breath. He'd thought he'd have time to break the news about the move gently, to make Evie see that this would be the best option for them. Now he wouldn't have that luxury. From the slurred speech of his fellow conmen, he knew that escaping the Nash brothers tonight would still be possible. But, with these scumbags in town, it wouldn't be long before their loose lips would have the law on him or, and his gut clenched at the thought, they'd find out where he lived.

He'd endangered his wife.

More whiskey poured into the glass. Yesterday he'd cut her off when she tried to encourage him to tell her what was wrong. If she knew the truth about his family, about him, Evie wouldn't have wasted her breath. Ben downed a few drinks in a row then paused, noticing the bottle was now half empty. Shame bled through him even as he filled his glass again.

Ben shifted so he could watch the Nash brothers out of the corner of his eye. He'd never meant for it to go this far. It was just going to be the one time, one job so they could have a home again. After that, for a time, he'd worked damn hard to stay on the straight and narrow and play by the rules. Only he was kicked in the teeth for it.

The whiskey no longer burned going down. It barely numbed the pain. He'd been a fool to think he could be a better man than his father had been.

Ben squared his shoulders and straightened away from the bar. He needed to go home. He had to explain. His fingers tightened on the glass again. He didn't know where to start, what to say. He'd lied to Evie about so much, for so long.

Instead of walking away, Ben loosened the glass, grabbed the bottle and turned around. Both Nash brothers were red in the face drunk. He picked up his bag and moseyed over to stand by them. Neither man looked up from his cards. He could slip away without a fight now, that would be the smart thing to do, but the pile of coins on the table captured his attention.

It was enough money to build the home he'd always promised Evie. Ben took a swig from the bottle then pulled up a chair, joined the game. *Maybe this time...*

Chapter One

Cedar Ridge, Idaho – Spring 1891

Her eyes popped open. In the darkness that enveloped her, Evie Rolfe swallowed hard. Sometime during the night, her lamp had died and left the young woman alone. Her fingers tightened into a white knuckled grip around the rifle while she listened for anything unusual. She didn't dare move, waiting untold minutes, locked in fear until light trickled through the cabin's only window.

While the ebony grayed and the shadows faded, she gained a measure of courage. Evie scanned the modest room in search of what had woken her. A simple chair sat beside her in front of the stone fireplace. Cast iron pots and a frying pan were stacked on the hearth by short rounds of pine. Along the walls was a long low bench with towels folded neatly on top, a four-drawer dresser, a metal pail then a bed in the corner. Nothing appeared out of place so far.

Nervous, Evie twisted so she could look at the wall behind her. A gap in the window curtains allowed a glimpse of the crimson sky. Against the door, a crudely made wood table remained snug with the oil lamp in the center. To the right of that, her cloak and a large tan wicker basket hung side by side. A rough broom she'd fashioned stood propped in the corner. Relief seeped through her, and the breath that she'd held released.

Evie sagged against the chair her grandfather made. Her left hand lifted, rubbed over her face, then lowered to slide palm down over a scarred, oak arm. Loneliness, a muted ache, haunted. The worn rocking chair was all she had left from her family. She sighed softly, almost soundless.

A distinct thud carried through the log walls. Her short-lived calm vanished. Blood raced through her veins. Heart in her throat, Evie gathered the edges of the quilts close around her. Slow, cautious, rifle cradled to her stomach, she pushed up to her feet then turned to face the window.

A minute passed. Then another. Evie heard nothing, saw nothing. She drew in a breath and stepped close to the glass pane. With the rifle muzzle, she pushed the washed out material aside. Her gaze found the source of the sound, what had likely woken her, right away. Fear evaporated.

Drained, her grip loosened. The blankets slipped, sagged around her waist. Anger whispered. Evie turned around and, jaw clenched, stalked to the fireplace. She hung the weapon back on the hooks above the mantle where it belonged. The hard packed dirt floor chilled her bare feet, hastened her pace as she moved to the corner.

Beside the empty bed, Evie stilled, stared at it for a few seconds, her lips compressed into a hard thin line. With a snap of her wrists, she spread the thin patchwork quilts over the mattress. Sadness, resentment and frustration crashed over her in waves as she pulled her nightgown over her head, tossed it on the covers. Goose bumps soon dotted her skin. In quick, jerky movements, she donned stockings, undergarments, a faded blue long sleeved shirt and a brown ankle length skirt.

Another thud sounded. Evie ground her teeth. She sat down on the bed and pulled on well-worn black boots. Her hair fell across her face in the process. Exasperated, she plucked her hairbrush off the wall where it hung by a leather thong.

With the ease of long practice, she swiftly tamed her waist length dark brown hair into a single thick braid that hung down her back. Evie stood and slapped the brush back in place. Her hands shook as she stomped over, shoved the table away from the door.

Orange and pink stained the clouds on the horizon when she stepped outside. Tall pine trees populated the landscape to her right, a sea of green as far as the eye could see. On her left lay the road to town and a couple of small cleared fields. Daisy, her cow, called out, impatient. Four hens scratched the grass for bugs. Evie noted it all, but focused on what brought her out at dawn.

A mare, all black except for a short white stocking on each leg stood just outside the barn. Its open door swung in the gentle wind. It hit against the wall, and again created the sound she'd heard while inside. Evie hissed through clenched teeth, irritated, as she moved with swift steady strides to the horse.

Her temper simmered as she led Sugar into the fenced area attached to one side of the barn. Evie stripped off the mare's tack, propped the saddle against a fence post. With bridle in hand, a pat and promise of oats later, she headed to the barn.

Evie stepped into the shadowed interior of the weathered structure. While her eyes adjusted to the low light, she took a couple of hesitant steps forward, one hand on the interior wall for assurance. She hung the bridle where it belonged then moved on.

It didn't take long before she found him near Sugar's stall, sprawled face down on some loose hay.

For a second, intense emotion seized her. Evie shook with the force it. Although the desire to turn around and leave held strong appeal, she just couldn't do that. She knelt down beside him, leaned in and whispered his name. He didn't react. With both hands, she shook him, called his name with force. As she half expected, Ben still didn't respond.

Evie got to her feet and with some effort, rolled him onto his back. Shaggy brown hair fell across his face. She crouched down, reached out and swept the mass to one side. His familiar features stirred up a storm of conflicting emotions.

Tears burned her tired eyes. It'd been some time since they'd been affectionate, intimate and, unable to resist, her fingers ran down the side of his neck, a light caress. Scratches and purple bruises marred his skin. Her hand came back up to rest her palm on his cheek. As upset as she was, Evie savored this simple physical contact.

Caught up in the moment, his groan startled her. She gasped. A hand came up, covered hers. His eyes opened and sorrow pierced her. The amazing forest green eyes that had captured her fancy years ago were so bloodshot that it was painful to witness. A crooked smile spread across his face.

"Hey doll," His voice low, rough, almost playful.

Strong whiskey fumes slapped her and Evie reared back as if physically struck, sparking her temper. His hand dropped to his side when she pulled away. Words she'd mulled over for months were on the tip of her tongue, about to explode from her when she noticed he'd passed out again. An incoherent sound of pure frustration passed her lips.

Fuming, Evie started to rise, and then noticed a small bag at his side. She leaned over, picked it up and the weight made her stomach churn with nausea. Her hand opened, dropped it on the ground, its contents spilling over. There was no honest way for him to have that amount of coin.

Evie Rolfe sat back on her heels and looked at the mess that was her husband.

Ben's shirt, ripped and stained, offered further evidence he'd been in another fight. It was hard to believe her husband had become this man. As she watched the steady rise and fall of his chest, her mind drifted to the past and longed for the man of her memories.

One hot August night five years ago, a stranger had walked into a dance at her church. His stance radiated confidence. A crooked nose sat in a face of raw, rugged features that intrigued her. And as soon as he saw her, the man strode directly to her.

Easily towering over her by several inches, with broad shoulders and a wide, well built chest, he instantly made her feel protected.

"Dance with me," his eyes, the deepest of green, charmed her. Her heart pounded. Without even asking his name, she'd given him her hand, captivated. In his arms, from the first moment, she'd felt a profound sense of belonging.

Daisy voiced loud displeasure, snapping her back to the present. Frustrated, Evie ignored the cow, instead reached out to shake Ben awake and then stopped herself. She knew from experience that a few hours rest increased the odds that her husband would actually listen to her and last night's events had made it clear that she needed him to hear what she had to say today. Terrifying memories snaked through her mind. Her hand shook as it hovered between them for a moment then dropped. The day had just begun. She'd let him sleep.

Evie stood, grabbed an old grey wool blanket they had for the horse, covered Ben with it and took one last look him before going off to care for Daisy. Sun streamed in through the doorway and warmed her while she milked. She had a difficult time focusing on the task though as her gaze kept wandering back to Ben.

The bond between them, frayed and strained, was not yet broken. Their damaged relationship left her emotions in a mess, and she couldn't stop her thoughts from circling around the conversation to come.

When she turned the cow out to graze, the cloudless sky for once failed to boost her spirits. She continued with her chores, checking on Ben occasionally, but misery dogged her. The morning hours passed slowly. Desperate to stay busy she grabbed some laundry and headed down to the creek.

A pair of ravens glided in the cool breeze above her to perch on the upper branches of a maple tree. Evie knelt by the water and as she reached into the basket and drew out a red and black checked shirt, the tears began to well. Eyes closed, she buried her face in the flannel, breathed in the scent of pine and Ben.

She wondered how it was possible to miss a person with every fiber of your being when that person shared your home, your bed.

After a moment, Evie set the shirt aside and pulled out the rest of the washing. Her fingers, soon reddened from lye soap and aching from the icy water, brought painful but welcome distraction. Faint sounds of movement carried towards her on the breeze as she wrung the excess water from heavy wool. She looked up toward the cabin and caught a glimpse of her husband's familiar form before he disappeared into the cabin. Although she wasn't looking forward to his reaction, her conviction remained solid. The time had arrived for a tough discussion.

Nerves stretched taut, she waited for him to come to her.

Clear blue sky peeked through tree boughs that provided a generous amount of shade. She had rinsed her last item for several unnecessary minutes when the dull thuds of footsteps broke the peace. When he sounded close, she glanced back. The sight of him walking through the shadows of the trees caused a sweet flash of memory.

Ben had coaxed their wedding party outside that glorious spring day, with everything green or blooming. His good humor infectious, he'd claimed that nature's beauty would bless their marriage. Eager to take on the world, life to him had been a grand adventure. As she walked to where he waited with the minister, beneath a canopy of branches, she'd fallen in love with him even more.

Ben stepped out of the shadows. The bittersweet echo of what had been faded. The years had fashioned clear changes. Scarred by hardship, his current expression was typical of the man she lived with now, hard and defensive. Pale from a certain hangover, his steps slow and measured, the contrast to the past wasn't kind.

"Hey," his voice low, tense, as he stopped about a foot away.

Her fingers curled up in the soaked material she'd been washing. Ben stood so close if Evie stretched out an arm, she'd touch him. Emotions twisted in a knot, each breath shallow, painful, her head throbbed. She felt every inch of the small but deliberate distance he placed between them. The wounds of recent years raw and her anger at his absence the previous night fresh, for a second she had a childish urge to ignore him.

Instead, knowing that would solve nothing, she lifted her chin. "Benjamin," she acknowledged, his name stiff, formal.

"I'm sorry."

His gaze focused past her, his tone flat, the muttered apology didn't move her. Evie looked down at the shirt in her hands. She twisted it, wringing out water. "No you're not."

"You're upset."

"Shouldn't I be?"

Silence, heavy and expectant, hung between them. She didn't offer her standard angry accusations or tearful pleas. They hadn't made a difference before. The pattern remained the same. Her husband refused to alter it. She looked back up at him. Now, for better or worse, things would change.

Ben shrugged. He shifted his weight from one foot to the other. "I mucked out the stalls."

"Good."

"And put the saddle in the barn."

"Fine."

"Brought in some firewood."

"Okay," Impatient, irritation crept into her voice.

"What do you want from me?" His gaze met hers for a split second before looking off into the distance again. "You want me to say I'll stop drinking?"

"No." Ben looked back at her, eyes wide, shocked. Pleased to have his complete attention, Evie was blunt. "I want you to not drink yourself into a stupor whenever life gets a little hard."

"A little hard," Ben bit out.

"Yes, like when we lost—"

"I'm not talking about our son now."

Evie held his gaze, silent, until the ache in her chest subsided. "I wasn't referring to James."

"Good."

"I meant when the Blakes'—"

"Stole my horses."

"Well you did catch them on their ranch and—"

"I didn't know I was on their land."

She gave him a soft-spoken reassurance. "I know."

"Months of hard work gone."

"I know."

"Then you should understand." Anger made his words harsh.

"I know it'll be a struggle to recover but it's doable."

Ben snorted. "Impossible."

"As long as you continue down the path you've chosen, I agree."

"What do you mean?" Tone wary, his eyes narrowed.

"Well, for one thing, you shouldn't cheat our neighbors."

"Excuse me?" His face a study of outrage but in his voice notes of defiance and satisfaction rang clear.

Evie stood. "You sold Spice."

"We needed the money," his gaze shifted, wouldn't quite meet hers.

"You didn't say he was only green broke and needed more training. That horse was nowhere near ready for a young rider to handle."

He lifted one shoulder. "Let the buyer beware."

A sick feeling settled in her gut. Evie shook the shirt she held out hard. To have a moment, steady her thoughts, she moved over to where the rest of her wet clothes hung and threw it over a free branch to dry. She drew in a breath then turned to face him again.

"Eddie Talbert was thrown."

His face impassive, Ben didn't say a word, showing no remorse. Her heart sank, but hope died hard and Evie prayed that some remnants of the man she'd married lay hidden under that brittle shell.

"He broke his arm."

"He didn't die."

Stunned, she couldn't hide her shock. "Ben."

"What? I should feel sorry some little rich boy took a tumble?"

"Yes you should and accept responsibility for your part in it."

"I didn't put him on the horse."

"No but you didn't tell—"

"Drop it," His tone stone cold.

Evie held her temper in check, just. Her fingers curled so her nails bit into her palms. "Some of Talbert's hands were here last night."

"Oh?" He angled his face away. "What did they want?"

"A pound of flesh? I don't know exactly but I think you should return Mr. Talbert's money."

"Too bad."

"Ben they were six men - angry, armed, men. Nothing I said satisfied them. I went in the house, shoved the table in front of the door while they rode around outside shouting threats."

"Just trying to frighten you," Ben dismissed her words with a wave of his hand.

Her jaw dropped. She'd been scared out of her mind with good cause. Their homestead was a good hour from the town of Cedar Ridge, the nearest neighbor miles away, unspeakable things could happen to a woman alone out here. Ben knew that.

"Well it worked. I was terrified long after they left, sat up all night with the rifle in my lap."

"So you were fine."

Her body went rigid with indignation. "I was not *fine*." She spoke slow, precise, each word distinct. "You should have been home. I needed you."

"I can't be here to baby you, all the time."

"I don't expect that," Anger as bitter cold as the snowmelt fed creek she stood beside knotted her insides. "But when you kick up a hornet's nest, you should face the consequences."

"Fine, you made your point," The cold, hard word shook her to the core, no trace of regret in his voice. "I'm leaving, have work to do."

"Like you did last night? And what sort of horse training is done after dark?" Bitterness, sharp and painful, seasoned her words, crafted to provoke him.

"Don't start in again," His gaze locked on hers. "I have to support us."

"There are other ways."

"Which I tried, and they earned me a tiny cabin and an almost empty barn. There's no reward for being good, doll."

"How about honor and self respect?"

"I'd rather have the coin."

"If you're so pleased with this way of life why do you need to soak yourself in whiskey?"

"I need a drink or two to unwind."

"You were full as a tick when you finally came home."

"That's my business."

Her jaw clenched. Evie looked down, brushed a bit of dust off her skirt. A breeze caressed her face, brought the scents of moss and recent rain. "I don't want to argue."

"Good."

"But—"

"Evie for the love of—"

"But," Her tone unyielding, she paused, looked up, met his gaze squarely then continued. "Things have to change."

"Like?" His voice sounded dangerous, a confrontation itself.

"No more lying, cheating and—"

"That's the way of the world, Sweetheart."

His sarcasm stung. "It's wrong."

"I do what I need to do and I will again," He growled with conviction.

The day after Evie married, her brother and only living relative, Henry, had taken off in search of gold and she'd never heard from him again. Ben was all she had. It took no small measure of courage to stand firm.

"I won't stand by and watch it anymore, you're hurting these people."

"Well you don't have to."

"You'll stop?" Hope laced her voice.

"Of course."

His voice, silky smooth, disturbed her. "That's a sudden change of heart."

"Maybe," Ben moved close. "I only want," His hand reached out, played with a loose strand of her hair, "to make you happy."

The gesture reminiscent of their early days, when simple, affectionate touches were common, made her heart ache. Evie blinked back tears. The back of his fingers left a trail of tingling nerves across her cheek. She allowed it, savored the moment then stepped back.

"I get the feeling you don't believe that." His voice sounded hoarse, shaded with mockery. She shook her head, unable to speak. He'd traded on her love too many times before and her trust was frail.

"Fine, you won't have to worry about our poor neighbors any longer because we won't be here. It's time we moved on."

Anxiety made it hard to breathe. The thought of starting all over yet again was almost unbearable. "No."

"What?"

"I'm not moving."

"Don't be foolish."

"I'm not."

His head tilted slightly to one side, he studied her. "Do you want to see me arrested?"

"For gambling?"

Ben held her gaze but didn't say a word. The sick feeling she'd tried to ignore for so long threatened to overwhelm her. She sensed he was waiting for her to ask, to bring things out in the open.

"The sheriff suspects you of something?"

"After last night, it's just a matter of time."

"What did you do?" Disappointment tasted like ashes in her mouth.

"Don't worry your pretty little head about it."

His tone set her teeth on edge. "Of course not."

"Good then—"

"If this is how you want to live then it'll be without me. I want no part of it."

"But I'm your husband." His expression incredulous, he stared at her as if she'd grown horns.

"Yes I know."

"Do you know what would happen if I abandoned you? Do you really want to find out how vulnerable a woman alone is?"

"I already have." The dreadful pressure around her chest increased. She crossed her arms over her stomach, "last night."

Silence stretched between them. For a long moment, the only sound came from the wind blowing through the branches of a straggly oak tree near her. Despite the warm spring day, she shivered.

"Look, Evie I... I'm sorry about that."

Though his words felt sincere when he stepped toward her she put one hand in front of her, palm out. "Please don't."

"All right," Ben stilled. "Just hear me out. We'll start fresh. We'll—"

"Own land as far as the eye can see and you'll build us a grand home? I've heard this before."

"It'll be different this time."

Evie fought the urge to cry. "Like it was supposed to be when we lost the boarding house in Montana, the saw mill in Salmon or the little farm right outside Cedar Ridge?"

"I've learned from my mistakes."

"You were passed out in the barn a few hours ago."

"What do you want me to do?" His hands clenched at his sides and his voice sounded edgy.

"Stop lying to me. Stop cheating people. And please, please stop doing whatever it is you're doing that has the sheriff asking questions and is driving you to drink. Remember your dreams? Riding the range in the Wild West? You could make that happen. We have good land. We could have a good life here if you'd just—"

"I can't chase those dreams here."

"You won't know unless you try," her tone fierce, Evie scowled at him.

"We have to move."

"Don't give up, please Ben."

"We don't have a choice anymore."

"Yes we do," tired and cranky, Evie snapped. "I do."

"I sold it."

Her vision blurred. A headache pulsed to life, pounded behind her eyes. "You did what?"

"I sold it."

"Our home?" Her voice trembled, a whisper, barely audible. Dazed, she stared at him. "How could you do that?"

"I did what I thought was best."

"Without even discussing it with me?"

"It had to be done and I didn't want to argue."

Tears clouded her vision. "You knew I wouldn't agree."

"Doesn't matter, it's done." The note of finality in his voice made her stomach clench. "We're moving as soon as possible."

Her poise precarious it took her a second to respond. In a voice soft but clear, she forced words out. "You are. I'm not."

"You can't stay here."

"Yeah, you made sure of that." Sick at heart, she averted her face, looked away.

"Evie—"

"I guess that explains the money," A short burst of ugly laughter escaped her, "I should be relieved it came from a lawful source, shouldn't I?"

"Sweetheart I just—"

The gentle coaxing tone caused tears to spill down her cheeks. "No excuses," she choked out; his attempt at softness now made her want to hit him. Pride kept her upright but she couldn't take anymore. "Just go."

Ben stood, studied her silently for a long moment then turned and walked away. Evie stiffened when she heard him pause for a few seconds a short distance up the trail. "I do love you."

His words sparked a heated response. As the sound of his footsteps faded, Evie kicked the basket hard and sent it flying over the rocky bank. She snatched the flannel up and threw it in the creek with a hoarse cry. Her chest heaved. Tears streamed down her face. She collapsed on the ground and wept until it hurt to breathe.

When the emotional storm passed, Evie got to her feet, slow like an old woman. Her hands rubbed her temples as she tried to ease her vicious headache. She shuffled over to the creek and bent down to splash water on her hot face and her swollen eyes. As she straightened, she noticed the shirt she'd flung, tangled on a fallen log some distance downstream. She made no effort to retrieve it. The sweet connection she'd felt moments earlier had soured.

Dread stalked within as she headed back to the cabin. Her steps dragged. The steady breeze chilled her despite the bright sun. She swayed on her feet, exhausted, though it'd been a short walk to the simple log structure. Still and quiet, it seemed to reflect her loneliness.

Her gaze swept the area. As she'd expected, the pasture appeared empty. He'd left. Arms crossed, her hands rubbed over her upper arms.

Ben wasn't coming back.

Worn, weary, she felt hollow inside.

All of a sudden, Evie heard shouting in the distance from the direction of the road. Her heart raced. She gathered her skirt up enough to run, dashed into the cabin, grabbed the rifle then peeked outside. No one had ridden in.

An ominous feeling settled in her gut. Warily, Evie stepped outside. Normal day sounds greeted her as she slowly scanned the surroundings. Nothing looked out of the ordinary. Though she knew it wasn't wise, she headed down the road.

A few hundred yards from the homestead, Evie stopped just around the first bend. Shock rooted her to the ground. Sounds evaporated, until only her heartbeat remained. Ben's flattened hat rested in front of her boot next to a patch of new spring grass, splattered with blood.

Chapter Two

The low rumble of several horses soon became thunder on his heels. His fingers tightened on the reigns. Ben twisted in the saddle and looked behind him. The number of riders who approached him at a fast pace didn't bode well. As he straightened in the saddle, his gaze swept the area.

Flat grassland stretched for miles to his right. A thick stand of pines sat an impossible distance from the other side of the road. His only hope rested in the direction he chosen just moments before, down the road toward Evie. Although his gut warned him to put his heels to the mare, race around the bend for home, Ben refused. He'd been a poor excuse for a man but whatever trouble was about to descend upon him, he wouldn't endanger his wife.

Edgy, he pulled up then hunched forward to hide his actions from view. Ben fumbled, his fingers clumsy, to open the hidden pocket his friend Henry had fashioned in the saddle after they'd been robbed one too many times. He stuffed coins out of a small bag in quickly, gauging how long he had to work by ear. When the riders sounded close, he fastened the flap and tossed the last of the money into his saddle horn bag.

Ben turned to face the danger head on. He didn't have to wait long as within minutes several men rode up and surrounded him. The stench of stale sweat and rotgut whisky filled the air. The man right in front of him with greasy blond hair and bloodshot eyes glared at him for a second then all six of them dismounted.

"Is there a problem?" Ben strove for calm.

"Yeah," A man to his left cocked his revolver then responded in a low, lethal tone. "Get down."

"Why don't we just talk for a while?"

Ben heard movement behind him, turned to face it a second too slow. Rough hands pulled him from the saddle. He hit the ground hard, pain radiated from his shoulder, side and hip.

A man stood over him, his expression fierce. "Shut up."

With effort, Ben got to his feet. "Look guys let's—"

"You cheated our boss," A fist slammed into his face. His nose cracked. Blood, warm and metallic, streamed down into his mouth. He staggered back. "And cost us our jobs."

Talbert's men. "I can make this right. I—"

Another punch landed on his jaw, jerked his face to one side. Ben remained upright through sheer stubborn will. In rapid succession, punches slammed into him. He tried to defend himself, landed a couple blows, but the pummeling continued unabated. Outnumbered, overwhelmed, he soon collapsed.

With him flat on the ground, barely responsive to the most vicious kicks, their attack started tapering off. A heated exchange erupted. Disoriented, Ben struggled to focus. It took some minutes before he grasped the meaning of their words. Raw terror struck his heart. They were arguing over which of them would comfort his widow first once they finished him off.

His fingers curled, formed a fist. Ben lifted his head off the hard packed earth. Anger burned. They had gathered to one side and focused on each other, paid him no heed. His gaze found Sugar about a yard to his left. Seconds felt like hours while he crawled to his horse. He painfully pulled himself up into the saddle.

Ben clutched the reigns along with a good hunk of mane and slumped forward. He pointed Sugar toward the trees and put his heels to her flanks, his only thought to get the men as far from Evie as possible. Each stride jarred and sent shards of pain through him. He heard angry shouts then the sounds of pursuit. Desperate, he urged the mare on, faster.

Blood roared in his ears, drowned all other sound still he sensed the men were closing in. Sadness filled Ben. There was little hope of survival. He'd never get to hold Evie again or tell her he was sorry. She'd never know that he'd turned around and headed back home, that he'd wanted a second chance.

Dear God, I want a second chance.

Pain eroded the remnants of strength. Ben started to slip off one side and barely caught himself. For only a moment, the world came into sharp focus then his thoughts clouded. His grip weakened. The mare started to slow. A moment later, he lost his hold, toppled off her.

Ben rolled for some distance over rocky ground before he at last came to a stop. He ended up flat on his back, stunned. It took several seconds for him to remember how to breathe. Limbs leaden, he tried to get up but could hardly move. A shadow fell over him. He looked up to discover the blond man beside him, a smirk on his face.

A boot slammed into his side and his body exploded in pain. The man kicked him a couple more times. Ben felt ribs snap and moaned, a raw animal sound.

White-hot pain pierced his shoulder then rough hands seized him, pushed hard. He had no strength to resist. They rolled him over an edge and Ben tumbled down a hillside, battered by brush and stones. His misery ended when his head hit something with enough force that agony consumed him and he lost consciousness.

Fingers pressed against the rifle stock hard in a painful, numbing grip, she took a couple steps forward. Evie moved past the hat that she couldn't bring herself to pick up. Her gaze studied each stump and bush for any sign of her husband. Minutes passed like an eternity. Reality pressed upon her, ruthless. The land that surrounded her appeared empty of all but small wild creatures.

By the distant tree line, a couple of deer meandered along. Some small brown rabbits played by a rotting log. A turkey vulture flew by so close her nose wrinkled at its stench. Unsure of what to do next Evie started to turn around to head back home, and then stopped cold.

Out of the corner of her eye, she spotted distant puffs of dust on the previously deserted road. Rhythmic beats of horse hooves against the earth soon disturbed the quiet. Wind swayed tall blades of roadside grass on either side of her. Evie brought a hand up, shaded her eyes and spotted a rider. The image roused hope. She wanted to believe it was Ben, safe and sound, on his way home.

Apprehension swept over her when it became clear the rider wasn't alone. Evie could make out three, none with a mount that had Sugar's coloring. With the realization that Ben wasn't one of them, another possibility occurred to her.

It could be the men from yesterday.

Alarm rooted her to the ground. Her mind screamed run but her feet refused to move. Nausea churned her stomach. Her legs threatened to buckle. Yet Evie stood, a statue, the entire time it took for them to reach her.

As they neared, it became clear she'd never seen these men before but the sight of strangers brought little relief. They slowed then stopped only feet in front of her. Evie kept a calm façade even as her heart raced. Expressions serious, they didn't look lost and the only destination on this section of the road was her home.

"Gentlemen."

"Mrs. Rolfe?" The stocky older man in the center wearing a dusty dull white hat moved his horse slightly forward.

Evie cradled the firearm against her mid-section. "Yes?"

"I don't believe we've met. I'm William Talbert."

"Mr. Talbert," her tone sharpened by nerves. "Did you know some of your men harassed me last night?"

"I'm aware of that ma'am." He dismounted with the ease of a

man who'd spent a lifetime in the saddle. "And I don't hold with craven behavior. I let those boys go as soon as I found out what they'd done. It won't happen again."

Evie inclined her head, acknowledged. "Thank you."

"It was the right thing to do."

"And you rode out here just to let me know?"

"No." Anger threaded into his voice as he stepped away from his horse, "I've business with your husband."

His long strides ate the distance between them. With each thud of footfall, her anxiety intensified. Evie inched back, kept space between them.

"Please stop."

"If you'll just—"

"I said," Her stance wide, Evie brought the rifle Ben had insisted she learn to shoot, and shoot well, up to brace against her shoulder. The firearm wobbled in her hands for a second then steadied. "Stop."

Mr. Talbert stilled. He raised both hands chest high, palm out. His tone pitched to soothe, "Ma'am there's no call for that. Put it down."

"Not another step," Evie issued a firm command.

The other men started to protest. Mr. Talbert made a sharp gesture and they fell quiet. "Easy now, there's no need to get upset. I just want to talk to him."

"Not today," Evie stalled as she bore the weight of his steady gaze. Like a cornered animal, she felt trapped. Her grip on the smooth wooden stock tightened until her knuckles gleamed white, a finger hovered over the trigger. "Come back tomorrow."

"No, he will explain himself today," his tone firm.

Her lips parted but no words emerged. Evie couldn't admit she didn't know where Ben was, that would reveal she was here alone and she couldn't ask them for help. These men had reason not to wish her husband well. Seconds stretched into almost a full moment of silence while she tried to decide what to do.

Unexpectedly the sound of another rider interrupted the tense standoff. Evie flicked a glance in the direction of the noise. On a dappled grey horse, a lanky man, the tallest she'd ever seen, wearing a battered black hat, was easy to identify even at a fair distance.

"You asked the sheriff to ride out."

"I just want to keep things civil ma'am."

"By threatening me?"

"I haven't," his words clipped, jaw tight, "nor will I."

Evie wasn't certain she believed him but with the lawman closing in fast, she made a gesture of good faith. She lowered her weapon, pointed the muzzle to the ground. They waited the few moments in awkward silence until Jim Green joined them.

The sheriff positioned himself between Evie and the other mounted men. His fingers tugged the brim of his hat, "Mrs. Rolfe."

"Sheriff Green."

"Though it's a fine day for a walk," his voice studiously polite, "perhaps we should head back to your place. Mr. Talbert and your husband can then settle matters."

"I'm afraid that isn't possible."

"Ma'am?"

"Ben isn't home. In fact I'm worried he—"

"Where is he?" William Talbert demanded.

"I don't know. He—"

"Do you know what that horse he sold me did?"

"He threw your son." Her face stiff and hot, Evie spoke in a soft tone. "I'm truly sorry. I—"

"Your husband conned me."

"I—"

"My son could've died."

"Again I'm so sorry but Ben—"

"I've no tolerance for lies."

"Mr. Talbert I don't—"

"Mrs. Rolfe—"

"Kindly have the good manners to let me finish a sentence."

He jerked his hat off to hit it against his thigh, "Ma'am."

"Thank you." Slow, even breaths eased agitation. "I don't know where Ben is," She said, holding up her free hand when Mr. Talbert started to open his mouth and shaking her head. "I don't but with the sheriff as my witness I give you my word, if it's possible, I'll make things right."

"He should face me like a man," the older man's contempt a barb, she flinched. "Not hide behind your skirt."

"I think you should accept the lady's offer," the sheriff's calm voice of reason entered the exchange.

Seconds passed then, "fine."

"I need to speak to the sheriff first." Without waiting for agreement, she looked up at the lawman and at last gave voice to her gut-wrenching fear. "Something happened to Ben. I..."

Her throat closed. Evie couldn't continue. Her emotions reactive and raw, tears threatened. She bit down on her bottom lip, struggling to keep control. Sheriff Green dismounted, put a hand on her shoulder. She drew in a shaky breath.

"Ben rode off and I... " Evie pulled away. "I... "

"Easy ma'am, take your time."

"After a time I heard," Evie paused, drew in a breath. "I thought I heard an argument out here. I came out and..." She shook her head unable to continue, stepped back and gestured to what she'd found.

His face a blank mask, Sheriff Green studied the scene for a moment. "You go on home now and I'll take a look around."

"But I—"

"Can you settle things peacefully with Mr. Talbert?"

"Ah yes but—"

"Trust me ma'am, I'm good at my job." As he walked past Mr. Talbert to his horse, the sheriff addressed him. "Would you escort Mrs. Rolfe home?"

"I will."

"I could use the help of your men."

Mr. Talbert frowned, his tone dry. "Of course."

Evie watched the three men fan out. She trusted Sheriff Green. He'd tried to work out a fair resolution when the Blakes' claimed the wild horses Ben had caught and trained were theirs all because he'd been mistaken about the property boundaries. It wasn't her husband's fault the judge, a relative of Daniel Blake's wife, ruled against him.

Her chest ached with intense pressure. Ben didn't share her good opinion. He blamed everyone who worked with the law as much as the crooked justice for his loss. And for some reason he believed that he was about to be arrested. Time would tell if she'd done the right thing sending the sheriff after him.

"Mrs. Rolfe?"

Her eyes burned with unshed tears. Evie knelt down, picked up Ben's hat and pressed it to her stomach. Although she wanted to believe he was fine, the bad feeling in her gut persisted.

"Yes," her tone calm, perhaps a little flat.

"Shall we?"

Evie nodded then turned, started back toward home without waiting for a response. "What do you want?" She winced as her question emerged sharp bordering on rude. "Sorry," she took a breath then tried again. "What would make us square?"

His tone terse, "I return the horse. You return my money."

"How much would that be?" The sum he named caused her heart to skip a beat. A lump formed in her throat. "I'm not sure I have that."

"I understand your husband spends a lot of time at The Bucking Pony." His tone held a note of pity.

Her cheeks heated. "What if you kept the horse?"

"It's not worth what I paid."

"I wasn't suggesting that it was," Evie cleared her throat, swallowed the urge to cry. "I was thinking we could work out something for the difference?"

They walked without speaking for a couple minutes. The quiet undisturbed save for sounds from the horse Mr. Talbert led. Leather creaked, metal jingled and hooves delivered soft thuds against the ground. He took so long to respond her belly hurt.

At last, he answered simply, "that's acceptable."

"Thank you." Unwilling to risk saying anything that might change his mind, she held her tongue until they reached her home. "Please excuse me a moment."

Evie entered the cabin, leaned the rifle against the wall beside the door and moved to a shelf by the fireplace. Doubt crept in. She paused a second. They'd always kept their money in the large clay jar. Inside should be some of the money Talbert had paid for Spice and she hoped Ben had left her some coins from the bag she'd seen that morning. One hand crushed her husband's hat as she reached out with the other, removed the lid.

Empty. She tried to ignore reason but the stark truth sank in slowly. His hat fell from her nerveless fingers.

Ben had left her with nothing.

Anger and frustration rose up and muted the worry. Evie wanted to scream or kick something hard yet did neither. The effort to restrain emotion caused her to tremble. It wouldn't do for Mr. Talbert to see her throw a fit through the open door.

Pride stiffened her spine. Shoulders back, chin up, Evie stepped back out into the harsh light of day. She looked over at the animal that grazed only yards from the barn. Her eyes closed a second. She owned little of value other than Daisy.

"Would you consider taking the cow?"

"The cow?"

His incredulous tone caused anxiety to well up. Rigid with tension, Evie broke out in a cold sweat. She forced words out past stiff lips, shame ashes in her mouth. "I'm sorry. She's about all I have. I could throw in a couple chickens."

"No," he studied her awhile. "The cow will be fine."

Mouth dry she gave him a quick nod then marched over to the

barn. She grabbed a halter and a length of rope. The cow stood placid while she readied her to go. Minutes later Evie handed Daisy over to Mr. Talbert as she blinked rapidly to hold back tears.

"I'm very sorry about your son, Mr. Talbert, about everything."

"I believe you are. Your husband on the other hand…" he swung up into his saddle, "well ma'am, out here we consider a man only as good as his word."

Evie winced at the verbal jab but remained polite. "Thank you for accepting the trade."

"There seemed little other choice."

Heat crept up her neck.

"I could stay until the sheriff comes back, if you need."

Composure held by a thread, her smile stiff, forced, "That won't be necessary."

"Are you certain ma'am?"

"I'll be fine, thank you."

"Very well," his tone clipped, his brown eyes filled not with the irritation she'd expected but pity, which felt worse. "Good day, Mrs. Rolfe."

Tense, she watched William Talbert ride away at a slow pace set to accommodate Daisy. Although Evie sensed he'd honor their deal, she didn't breathe a sigh of relief until he disappeared from view. In time, she hoped his anger would fade and they could mend fences someday.

Hours passed. Evie mucked out stalls, tended the chickens, washed dishes and swept the floor. Unable to be still, she then trudged down to the creek and retrieved the sun-dried laundry. She folded clothes, put them away, hung the basket and repaired her clothesline. Even with every conceivable chore completed, she couldn't relax. She paced outside the window in front of the cabin as the day cooled.

It's been so long. Her hands twisted in the fabric of her cloak. Evie looked out to the shadowed lengths of forest. A gentle breeze toyed with loose strands of her hair. The peaceful late afternoon was driving her crazy.

Her angst deepened with each moment that passed. A pair of coyotes emerged from the trees to her left and captured her attention and interest. Frozen, poised to run, they watched her. All at once, she heard the rumble of wheels rolling over the earth. Startled, Evie blinked and the animals melted away.

Her gaze swept to the road, scared and hopeful. She hardly dared to breathe. Minutes crawled by. At last, a team of mules lumbered into view an old farm wagon pulled behind them. Wheels tossed up a light cloud of dust as the sheriff rode around from behind the wagon, straight up to her.

"Did you find him?"

"Yes ma'am." He dismounted, stood in front of her.

An arrow of fear shot through her heart at something in his tone. "Is he...? is he...?" She couldn't get the question out past numb lips.

"He's hurt pretty bad. I sent a man for the doctor."

His somber expression spoke volumes. Tension twisted her gut. Fear rose up, stole her speech. Evie could only nod she understood as the wagon pulled up near them. The driver climbed down. He and Sheriff Green walked her to the back.

Evie leaned against the rough wood frame as the men lowered the tailgate. She drew in a long deep breath for courage then looked in at Ben, bloodied and beaten. His face was almost unrecognizable. Tears almost blinded her. Twice, her mouth opened and shut without uttering a sound.

How much can a man lose without dying?

All sound faded to the edge of her awareness. Evie stretched forward to hold a hand above his mouth. Breath feathered her palm and a fraction of her apprehension eased. Her gaze unfocused, she straightened.

"If you'll step back ma'am, we'll bring him inside."

For a second Evie stared at the sheriff uncomprehending then his words filtered through. She moved, "thank you."

Adrenalin pumped through her veins. Evie darted into the

cabin, ripped quilts off the bed as the men entered. They laid
Ben down on his back on the mattress. She thrust a pail at the
Talbert hand, John, and asked him to fetch some water from the
creek. With hands that shook, she lit the lamp. She set it on the
dresser, looked down at her husband.

Ashen skin made a stark contrast with blackened eyes. His
nose was easily twice its normal size and new smudges marked
his jaw, chin and left cheek. Evie reached down, touched his arm
and whispered his name. He didn't respond.

A single tear ran unheeded down her face as she started to
tend her husband. Evie pulled off his worn boots. The sheriff
helped her strip off his pants. The long, muscular legs sported a
few bruises on his thighs but otherwise seemed unharmed. She
moved on to his once green flannel shirt.

Stained with dirt and wet with blood, the fabric clung to his
shoulder. She gently peeled it away and uncovered more than a
battered body, discovering the source of the blood. Heart in her
throat she stared at the ugly wound. Her fingers, one by one,
loosened the flannel. The ruined shirt fell to the floor. Death
was a real possibility.

"Ben?" Evie touched his uninjured shoulder, soft. He reacted
with a low moan. She tried again in a more forceful tone. "Please,
Ben, wake up. Open your eyes."

His eyelids fluttered a few seconds then stilled. Evie picked up
a blanket and covered him to the waist. She dug out some towels,
scissors and an old sheet then tossed most of the supplies onto
the table, impatient. Fear raced along her nerves as she returned
to sit on the edge of the bed. She put a folded towel over the
weeping hole in his shoulder.

"He was attacked?"

"Yes ma'am."

John returned, set the pail on the floor beside her. Evie got
up, filled a pot with water to heat. While the men built a fire,
she cut a few long strips from faded cotton, her usually nimble

fingers clumsy.

"Who?"

"Ma'am?"

"Who did it?" With a handful of just made bandages, some washcloths and a bowl, Evie returned to her husband's side.

"I don't know."

Her gaze drifted over Ben. The rise and fall of his chest offered small comfort. Evie reached over, brushed back matted hair and found a good-sized lump near his right temple. Tears stung her eyes. She half filled the bowl with water, started to wash the blood off his face.

Anger snapped along strained nerves. Evie shot a glance over at the sheriff. "What do you know?"

"Your husband is a lucky man."

"Lucky?" Her gaze became a glare.

"One of your neighbors saw his mare, riderless; if he hadn't I doubt we'd have found Ben in time."

"Neighbor? Mr. Talbert?"

He shook his head, "Thomas Sullivan."

"Was he the one who hurt Ben?"

"No ma'am." Sheriff Green straightened from his crouched position. He hung the pot she'd filled over flames that danced along sticks.

"But he knew where Ben was?"

"Tom showed us where he'd seen the horse."

"Had seen? He didn't go after her?"

"Well, ma'am, I'm afraid Tom spotted her at some distance and didn't feel inclined to investigate."

The shame burnt her cheeks. "He didn't care about a loose, saddled horse because he recognized Sugar."

"He knew it was your husband's mount." Sheriff Green cleared his throat. "Anyway, Ben was near there, at the bottom of a small ravine."

"How did you know to look there?"

"Just like chasing down a wounded animal, we followed the blood trail."

Evie turned to stare at John with wide eyes, horrified at the images those words invoked. "You what?"

"I think you've helped enough, go on home now."

John had the grace to mumble an apology as she watched him take his leave. A hand touched her upper arm. "You all right?"

Evie started, looked up at the sheriff, "I'm fine."

"You look—"

"Tired? Scared out of my mind?" Her voice, thin, strained despite her desire to sound calm, "I'll survive." Evie got up, walked outside, tossed fouled water out of her bowl. "When will the doctor get here?"

"Soon I'm sure."

All of a sudden, Ben groaned. Evie spun at the sound and hurried to her husband's side. His eyes open, he stared up at her. Pain etched deep lines on his face.

Her fingers lightly touched his, "Ben."

His lips moved in a sad attempt at a smile. "Hey. Pretty. Lady." He drew in a breath between each word as his gaze swept the room. "Where am I?"

Chapter Three

"You're home."

Ben looked up at her. His eyebrows drew together, "Home?"

"Yes."

"I," His eyelids fell shut. "Don't..."

"Ben? Ben?"

Only silence answered. Evie stared down at her husband for a moment longer. He didn't move or make a sound. Her shoulders drooped. Concern knotted her stomach as she moved over to the fireplace and filled her bowl from the kettle.

Without a word, she strode back to Ben's side. Evie lifted the blood soaked towel from his shoulder then dropped it on the floor. Nerves stretched taut, she dipped a fresh cloth in the hot water and started to clean around the wound.

"Mrs. Rolfe." The sheriff paused, Evie glanced up. The tall man pulled up a chair near her and sat down. With a cautious expression and a gentle, careful tone, he asked. "Do you know who'd want to hurt your husband?"

Evie looked back down at Ben. Her eyes burned but she refused to cry. She scrubbed off the last bits of dried blood and dirt, "Ah..." Her task finished, she laid a fresh towel over torn flesh. "Other than Mr. Talbert, I..."

"You think Mr. Talbert is responsible?"

"I don't know, but the other night some of his men—"

A welcome sound drifted through the walls, sending a wave of relief over her. Evie held up a hand and shook her head when the sheriff started to say something. She thrust the bowl on the dresser and almost ran to open the door.

In front of the cabin, a buggy rolled up. A slight built man dressed in all brown from trousers to string tie stepped out of the vehicle. With short light brown hair, plain features and wire-rimmed spectacles, the medical bag in his hand was the only thing of note about the man.

"Mrs. Rolfe, this is Dr. Black," The sheriff walked up, offered an introduction as she motioned the other man inside.

"We've met," she addressed Sheriff Green then turned her attention back to the doctor, clasped his hand. "Thank you for coming." She gestured to Ben. "He's bleeding badly."

"Let me take a look."

Dr. Black moved directly to the bedside, set his bag on the dresser. With quiet efficiency, he examined Ben. A guttural moan escaped his lips. Evie walked over to the foot of the bed as her husband opened his eyes and lightly touched his leg.

"The doctor's here."

Ben looked up at the man beside him then down at Evie. He tried to move, then stilled when the doctor placed a hand on his chest. His breath labored, perspiration covered his face. Pain twisted his expression into a grimace. She averted her gaze to stare at the blazing fire.

Dr. Black laid a hand on her arm, "I'll need hot water and whiskey if you have some."

After a few seconds she nodded, then with a swish of her skirts, stepped away. She reached up on the shelf and pulled down the large flour tin. Cheeks aflame, Evie avoided the men's curious gazes as she dug out the bottle she'd hidden. That it was half-full startled her a moment then, with a sigh, she put the container back. Ben had obviously found it.

Her mouth twisted into a travesty of a smile, she handed the liquor to the doctor. She moved to the hearth, lifted the heavy, steaming pot from over the fire then set it down on a folded cloth in the middle of the table. After that, she added soap, some bowls then hovered, watching the doctor spread out his own supplies.

"Your husband is in good hands."

"I know." Although grateful for the reassurance, her voice came out hollow.

"You know Dr. Black?"

Evie nodded. Her gaze never left the doctor as he helped her husband swallow some whiskey. He turned from his patient, washed his hands then started on Ben's shoulder. She watched him clean out the wound without a noticeable flinch but her eyes widened as he threaded a needle. When the sharp metal pierced her husband's flesh, she felt the blood drain from her face.

Saliva gathered in her mouth. Poise crumbled. She swayed but couldn't look away. Evie heard the sheriff speaking to her as if from a distance.

"Ma'am... Ma'am maybe you should step outside?"

Her mind fuzzy it took a moment before Evie understood what he'd said and her gaze swung to him. She stared at the tall man a few seconds, blinked then stumbled outside. Crisp, cool air feathered her face.

"You were telling me about some men?"

Evie started. The sheriff had followed. She turned, found him right behind her. "I was?" Movement caught her eye. On her left, a few yards away, was a horse, picketed. "Oh, yeah, yesterday late afternoon," she heard a groan, paused, flicked a glance back at the cabin. Worried, on edge, she couldn't stand still, shifting her weight from one foot to the other, "Some men showed up, mad about Eddie Talbert getting hurt."

"Do you know who they are?"

"Other than they must work for the Talberts'?" Evie shook her head. "I'd never seen them before."

"Would you or your husband recognize them?"

"Ben wasn't here and I doubt I could. They were riding all around, yelling, and firing shots. I was scared." The doctor appeared in the doorway and gestured for her to come. Evie took a step toward home then stopped, looked back at the sheriff, "but Mr. Talbert would know. He told me he fired those men."

"Interesting," He inclined his head. "I believe I'll head out now ma'am. I'll be back out soon to speak to your husband."

As the lawman loosed his horse, Evie walked away without another word and ducked back inside. She scooted around Dr. Black and moved to Ben's side. He was resting, eyes closed. She leaned down, brushed a damp lock of hair off his sweaty forehead.

"Is he going to be okay?" Her gaze went to the man next to her in the midst of drying his hands.

Dr. Black gave her a kind smile and prompted, "I need some wide strips to bind his ribs." He waited until she moved to the table and started to cut the sheet before he continued. "I've stitched up the knife wound." With swift, sure motions, he took the cloth from her and worked it around Ben. "He'll likely have a nasty headache given the size of that goose egg and these ribs will take a while to heal."

His neutral tone and carefully chosen words didn't escape her notice. Evie put the scissors down, watched him finish the binding with her arms hugged around her waist. "So you think he'll be okay?"

"As long as that shoulder doesn't get infected, yes."

Dread settled in her gut. Her mouth dry, she didn't speak for a moment. She inched closer. "Is that likely?"

"All we can do now is pray." His gaze held compassion.

"I will," Evie moved back to the bedside. Her hand touched Ben's arm for needed contact, "thank you."

"You're welcome." The doctor started to repack his bag.

"What do I owe you?"

"It's late. I'll be back tomorrow to check on him."

"But—"

He patted her hand. "We'll settle up then."

"All right," she didn't have the heart to protest further.

"The best thing for him is sleep." Dr. Black shrugged into a light jacket and donned a narrow brimmed hat. He gestured to the bottle still covered with bits of flour. "If he wakes up in too much pain, give him more."

Evie walked him to the door. The control she'd held so tight threatened to fall apart. Emotion inexplicable, tears gathered. She exhaled a shaky breath. "He could've died."

"But he didn't." Gentle fingers cupped her chin, tilted her face up so Evie looked into his eyes. "The best thing you can do for Ben now is get some rest. You need it."

"I will."

Without another word, the doctor left. Evie sank down in the chair beside the bed. Weary, she laid her head down, rested her cheek on Ben's arm. Her eyes drifted shut. Sometime later a touch on her hair startled her awake.

"Doll."

"Ben?" She lifted her head and opened her eyes to look at him. At first, he didn't respond. His eyes still closed, she thought perhaps he'd fallen back asleep.

"Hurts."

"What hurts?"

"Head. Side. Shoulder. Everything."

Evie pushed up her feet, poured some liquor in a cup. She slid an arm under his shoulders and helped him up enough so that he could drink. He never opened his eyes or spoke again. She settled Ben back down then eased away from him. His breathing deepened, in minutes it was clear he slept.

Unable to go straight back to sleep herself, Evie moved around the room, restless. She threw his stained clothing and towels in a basket then pushed it under the bed. Exhausted, her head throbbed. She started to clear the table and swayed. One hand reached out, pressed against the wood surface and steadied her. After a moment, she trudged back to Ben's side, resigned to sleep again in the chair.

The night seemed endless. Every time her husband made a sound, Evie jerked awake, fear clawing her heart. It took long moments to calm each time. When morning arrived at last, she felt worse than the night before.

Her eyes burned. Muscles stiff and aching, Evie stumbled through chores then returned, collapsed onto her chair. Hours passed. Her hair went uncombed, face unwashed, dress unchanged, she did nothing but sit by Ben who mostly slept until the doctor arrived around noon.

As Dr. Black checked her husband over, he woke for more than a moment.

"What happened?"

Evie leaned close, spoke soft. "You were attacked."

"I was?" Discomfort clear, he responded with effort. His eyes closed. For a second she thought Ben had fallen asleep yet again, and then he spoke. "Who? Why?"

"I was hoping you'd tell us."

"I don't know. Sorry," he took a breath. "So I'm at your home."

"Our home."

"Our home?" His eyes opened. He turned his head to look straight at her, brow furrowed.

A childhood memory of a man who'd fallen from a horse stirred and concern filled her. "Do you know who you are?"

"You called me Ben," He took an audible breath. "But my full name is Benjamin, Benjamin James Rolfe."

"Thank God," Relief cascaded through her.

Swollen lips attempted to form a smile. "So what's your name, sweet lady?"

A shiver went down her spine. His words pierced her bubble of cheer. Unease crept over her. She stared at him for a full moment, "That's not funny."

"Not trying to be."

"It's all right," Dr. Black inserted. Evie started, she'd forgotten his presence. His low tone a clear attempt to soothe, the doctor continued. "Go ahead tell him your name."

"Evie, I'm Evie."

"That's a right pretty name," his words slurred.

"So you said the first time you heard it," She muttered but her words went unheard. He'd fallen asleep again. Evie turned her gaze on the doctor. His somber expression didn't comfort her. "Is it normal to sleep like that?"

The doctor nodded. "His body needs the rest."

"Okay," Evie accepted that easily and moved on to the question that burned inside her. "Why doesn't Ben know me?"

"Well, head injuries can rattle a person for a time."

Worry sharpened her tone. "There was a man where I grew up who forgot everything, everyone, had to learn to dress and eat again like a baby. Is that what's happening to Ben?"

"I've heard of such cases," Dr. Black took her hand, patted it with his other one. "But Ben knows who he is and that's a good sign. Give him time, let him recover."

"Then you think he'll remember me?"

"Likely."

"But he might not?"

"Let's not borrow trouble. Wait a few days, see how he does." He squeezed her hand then released her, stepped back.

Dr. Black turned to the table, snapping his bag shut. Evie walked him outside. He waited by his buggy while she fetched a small bag of dried apples and a crated chicken.

"Would these cover what we owe you?"

"It'll do," he said, and accepted the offering. "I'll be back out to check on Ben tomorrow."

Arms crossed at her waist, Evie watched him set what she'd given behind the black leather seat. He climbed in, snapped the reigns and drove off. Her shoulders slumped. Alone and solely responsible for Ben, she felt weighed down with worry.

Evie went back to the cabin on leaden feet. Once satisfied her husband rested easy she sat down, closed her eyes but minutes later remained wide-awake. Though far past tired, she couldn't settle down. She got up and changed into a clean dress of blue calico, tidied the room, fussed with Ben's blankets then reached down and pulled out the laundry basket.

After she propped the door open, Evie carried the clothes outside. She soon had water boiling in a large pot hung above a fire and tossed in the stained items. The hot, unpleasant job took up a good portion of her afternoon. She yawned often as she hung the last of the laundry up to dry. The sound of a moan floated out of the cabin while Evie kicked dirt on the fire. She hurried inside straight to her husband, "Are you all right?"

"Could I have some water?" he rasped.

"Of course," She filled a mug from the kettle and returned.

His hands shook as he took it from her, which sloshed the lukewarm water over his fingers. Evie put her hands over his to steady them. Ben raised his head, took in a few long sips then pale, shaking, laid back.

"Thank you Evie."

Tense, hopeful, worried, she hesitated a second then took the mug from his slack grip, put it down on the dresser. Her voice calm, level, "You remember me?"

Ben cleared his throat yet his voice emerged husky. "Of course, you're the pretty lady who's taking care of me."

"So you don't know who I am?"

"Other than your name, no," he paused a moment, coughed, then continued in a soft, forced tone. "But I'm guessing I should."

Evie couldn't keep the words inside, "I'm your wife."

"Oh." He closed his eyes, exhaustion obvious, his words slurred. "That's..."

Ben drifted off again. Evie stomped her foot so frustrated she wanted to scream. She needed him to stay awake more than a blessed minute and talk to her. Her fingers tangled with his as she sank down on the rocker. Tears filled her eyes then spilled over, trailed down heated cheeks. She needed him.

The remainder of the day passed in the same manner. When Ben stirred, they would exchange a few meaningless words. Evie gave him more sips of water and late in the evening, she managed to coax some broth into him. By the end of the very long day, little had changed.

The need for sleep at last overcame her shortly after dark and Evie nodded off in her chair. A glancing blow to her upper arm woke her some time later. She opened her eyes. In the low, flickering light from the dying lamp Ben flailed, not wildly but with soft jerks as if in his dreams, he fought.

"Ben," She leaned over, captured an arm and held it to the mattress. Her tone low, pitched to comfort, "Ben, wake up."

Her husband quieted but didn't respond. Still weary, Evie started to relax, and then what she felt sank in. Heat radiated from his skin. Panicked she jumped up, grabbed the pail and dashed down to the creek without pausing to take the lamp. She stubbed her toes, snagged her dress on a thorny brush and almost fell into the running water but the terror that so often paralyzed her in the dark simply didn't register. She filled her bucket and hurried back.

Through the night, Evie soaked rags in the cold water then applied them to his heated forehead. His skin never stayed cool long before it burned again. Every so often Ben would mutter gibberish then thrash about until she soothed him.

Her back ached fiercely by morning light. Evie straightened away from the bed with her hands pressed hard against the base of her spine. She yawned so wide and long her jaw hurt. Noise penetrated her fog of exhaustion. She went to the window and peeked through the curtains. The little black buggy was a most welcome sight. She stumbled over to the door, eager to let the doctor inside.

After a quick exchange of information, Evie let Dr. Black take over Ben's care. On the verge of collapse, she pulled her rocker across the room out of the way. She sat down, leaned her head against the high back, closed her eyes and slept.

The next few days passed in a blur. Evie rested whenever Dr. Black was there. Naps at odds hours became routine. At the end of the week, a touch on her shoulder woke her from one. She blinked up at the tall man for a moment until her wits gathered.

"Sheriff Green," Evie sat up straight, pushed her hair out of her face. "Do you have news?"

"Well Doc just said he believes the fever broke."

She sagged back against the chair, "Thank God."

"I came out to speak to Ben. Clearly he's in no condition for that now but..."

An uneasy feeling knotted her stomach. "What's wrong?"

"Perhaps we should talk privately?"

"All right," Evie glanced over at the man who sat next to the bed and looked almost as tired as she felt. "I need to step outside with the sheriff for a moment."

Dr. Black acknowledged her words with a nod. She stood and led the sheriff outside. Her gaze swept the area as she emerged from the cabin. She took a deep breath, enjoying the fresh air.

Sheriff Green moved in front of her. "Ma'am you're aware your husband has... irritated folks?"

Evie could barely contain an unladylike snort. She arched an eyebrow. Her tone dry as late fall leaves, "yes."

"In the time you've lived here he's made questionable deals, caused trouble in town drinking and brawling, there's more than one accusation of cheating and he's suspected of—"

"Your point?" Her voice taut, lowered to just above a whisper. That his words were true made them no less difficult to hear. "Are you trying to say Ben deserved what happened?"

"No ma'am, I'm warning you some might see it that way."

"Who? The person or people who hurt him? Do you know who did it?"

"The men Talbert fired were overheard celebrating that your husband was hurt and they had his horse."

"So you arrested them?"

"I did when they started a fight and tore up the saloon. But those are the only charges I'm holding them on."

Evie shook her head, confused. "Not for attacking Ben?"

"I've no proof of that."

"But you just said—"

"It's not a crime to be happy a man got beat up."

"But," with a sinking feeling in the pit of her stomach, she tried again to protest. "They—"

"All swear they had nothing to do with it."

"They had his horse," She enunciated each word with force.

"They claim they found it wondering loose, knew the mare belonged to you and were going to return it."

Heat burned across her cheeks. "So you'll do nothing."

"Not much I can do ma'am. I rode out here hoping Ben could tell me something, some detail that might help but—"

"Dr. Black told you Ben might not remember." Her hands twisted together. A band tightened around her chest.

"I hope for your sake he does."

Wearing a calm mask, she met his gaze, "Why?"

"I can't hold those boys long and I've heard ugly rumors."

She stiffened, "Rumors?"

"Those boys are locals, they grew up here."

"And we've only been a here a few years."

The sheriff nodded. "Word about the Talbert boy has gotten around. There's not a whole lot of sympathy for your husband's injuries. In fact there's some anger directed at him still."

"I see." Her stomach rolled.

"Ma'am I'll do my best but I'm only one man." His serious

tone, the concern in his gaze, slammed his message home. The neighbors likely wouldn't help if someone decided to hurt Ben again and the sheriff couldn't protect him.

"I understand." Her hands clasped tight together, "Anything else? I should get back to my husband."

Sheriff Green studied her for a tense moment. "I brought your horse back. She's in the barn."

"Thank you."

"I checked the saddlebags. They were empty. Did Ben have anything of value?"

"Not that I'm aware of."

"Has he brought home any extra money?"

"What are you really asking?"

"It's important I have the facts ma'am. Did he have any—"

"No. There's no money here. You're welcome to look if my word isn't good enough."

"That won't be necessary."

Dr. Black strolled from the cabin. "I need to get going."

"Of course," Evie managed a stiff smile, "thank you."

Without waiting to see either man off, she stepped into the open doorway. Evie paused there. Her fingers gripped the wood frame hard. The sound of hooves and wheels faded as she stood, stared at Ben who slept yet again. Her head bowed. Worn out, she felt alone, abandoned.

A surge of fury suddenly crashed over logic. Her chin lifted and she glared at her husband. Evie stomped across the room, snatched up a pot, set it down hard on the table. A quick glance showed Ben undisturbed. *I'm tired of understanding.*

Lips tight, Evie shook her head. *Being patient.* She put chicken broth and dried vegetables in the pot then hung it over the fire on a hook Ben had fashioned. *Feeling alone in the same room.* Her actions jerky, she pulled a small crock off a shelf then opened the towel wrapped around the half loaf of cornbread.

Her hands shook as she cut off a couple of slices then smeared butter over them. Movements slowed. Tears fell.

Evie looked over at Ben. Hair fell untidy across his forehead, his face a patchwork of charcoal smudges, a few more colorful bruises and pallid skin. *I almost lost you.*

Drained, she made no effort to wipe her cheeks. Slowly she moved her chair back next to the bed. She grabbed her snack, poured a mug of coffee and sat down. Without enthusiasm, she washed her food down with the bitter liquid. When she finished, Evie reached out and touched his chest.

Her fingers lingered, moving in a soft caress. A dark brown mat of hair spread out over his upper body until it disappeared beneath his bound ribs. Evie laid her palm flat on his lower belly a moment then pulled back. Sadness whispered. She'd all but forgotten how it felt to touch him. She stared at the dregs of her coffee, and rocked herself for comfort.

Ben cleared his throat. The young woman didn't respond, just kept rocking. He cleared his throat again, louder. She stilled a second then faced him, her expression a polite mask.

"Good afternoon."

Though pain tugged at him, Ben studied her, curious about the stranger who claimed to be his wife. Rich, deep golden brown hair tumbled from a haphazard braid to fall about a pretty face with even features dominated by eyes an intriguing sky blue. With sun kissed golden skin and a strong yet gently curved body, she was exactly his type of woman.

"Is it? I feel weak as a kitten."

"You've had a rough few days." Her voice had a low husky quality. "Are you hurting?"

His head pounded, his whole body ached and any deep breath brought pure misery. "Oh yeah."

"I can get you some—"

"Not now thank you... Evie... Is that right?"

A flash of emotion disturbed her expression, "yes."

"And... Did you say you're my wife?"

"I did." Her voice flat, almost lifeless disturbed him.

A spasm of pain seized him, commanded attention. Sweat bathed his face. It took little time before it became tolerable but each second that ticked by worsened his mood. Everything felt out of his control.

Patience fled. Ben challenged the woman, skepticism clear in his testy tone. "How is that possible?"

"Standing before a minister and affirming vows before God and witnesses has that effect," Evie snapped.

Her words hung in the air. Anger flashed in her eyes then they went flat. Ben didn't know how to respond. Her certainty troubled him but what the doctor had suggested just couldn't be right. It couldn't be. Irritated, uncomfortable he shifted.

"What are you doing?"

"I want up."

Her lips pursed in disapproval but Evie helped him without protest. Tremors shot through his body, stole his breath as he moved into a seated position. Finally, she had Ben lean forward and stuffed a folded blanket behind him for support. He sagged back against the padding.

"Thank you."

"You're welcome." Stilted words reflected the awkwardness between them. Evie paused, studied him a moment. "Hungry?"

"A little."

In minutes, she brought him some thin soup and water. He devoured the food then handed her back the empty bowl. Though now every breath spread splintering pain, he took a few sips from his cup, one hand pressed against his aching ribs. What little energy he had left started to fade. Even so, he was determined to address her claim.

"Do you have proof?"

Chapter Four

"Yes." Evie glared at Ben, her tone decidedly cool as she got out of the chair. She knelt down, reached underneath the bed and pulled out a small wooden box. From inside she took out a photograph, handed it to him. "Your wedding present to me."

Ben stared at the black and white picture, worn from many handlings. The upper right corner had a long, narrow white line and along the bottom there were spots from water but the image was clear. "We made a handsome couple."

"Satisfied?"

"Confused." A note of impatience spiced his words as he continued to study the smiling people captured on paper. No memory of that day, place or her stirred. "We're married."

"Yes."

"You're my wife."

Her hand came up. Fingers squeezed the bridge of her nose as she sucked in a deep breath. "Yes."

"Sorry, I don't mean to upset you."

"It's okay."

"I doubt that," his tone full of wry amusement.

Her fleeting smile as she stood acknowledged that truth.

Unsure how he felt or what to do, Ben shifted his gaze from her to look around the room. "This cabin isn't familiar to me."

"Ben," Evie paused. Tension radiated from her. "What's the last thing you remember?"

His thoughts sluggish, it took Ben a few minutes before he answered. "Heading to town with Henry. Is that where we met, in Joplin?"

"No." Her heart sank. Her brother met Ben when they worked in a Missouri mine, a year before their wedding. "That happened when Henry brought you home."

He seized on that bit of information. "We'd talked about that." A wrinkle formed between his brows. "We were sick of working underground, wanted to quit, head west. Then...he got news about his family in...Indiana and, I can't remember why but we were going to go there first." He tilted his head to one side. "You know Henry?"

"He's my brother."

His eyebrows drew together. "You're Cookie?"

"That's what he called me." Her lips curved, a ghost smile.

"Called? Did something happen to Henry?"

Evie shrugged a casual motion to cloak emotion. "I don't know, haven't seen him in years."

"Went looking for gold?"

"Yeah, he left the day of our wedding."

"That upset you?"

"I wasn't thrilled," She delivered the understatement in a dry tone. With their grandfather in poor health, she'd wanted Henry to stay at least for a while.

"So instead of going with him as I'd planned, I stayed in Indiana with you?"

Until Grandpa died. Evie winced, her head started to throb and she decided keep it short. "For a time, then we moved west."

"We're in California?"

Evie shook her head. "Cedar Ridge, Idaho."

"That's not bad. You know, I always wanted to live out west

and have adventures like those in dime novels."

"I know."

His expression tightened, he appeared troubled by the notion that she knew him well, "I need to lie down."

"All right."

Concerned by the weakness in his voice, Evie bent over him, helped him change position. She had Ben comfortably settled in a matter of minutes. As she moved away, he captured her wrist in a strong grip that caught her off guard. She stared at him, shocked. Her heart beat at a furious pace.

"How long?"

"Since you were hurt?"

"Have we been married?"

"Oh," Her tone soft, a trace puzzled, "five years."

"Kids?"

She suddenly forgot to breathe but then in a firm but gentle move, Evie pulled free. She plucked the picture from where it had fallen on his blanket, looked at their image for a few seconds then back up at him. "No."

Evie knelt back down by the open box on the floor. With care, she covered the photograph in linen and replaced it. A folded section of yellowed newspaper rested to one side. She shifted so that her body blocked what little view Ben had and reached for it.

"Evie?"

"You should get some sleep," her tone flat, dismissive as she unwrapped the paper, ran fingers over soft yarn.

Her chest ached and tears stung her eyes. Head bent, she blinked them back. Evie studied what she held a long moment then drew in an uneven breath. She refolded the paper, tucked it away. Her hands shook as she closed the box then pushed it back in its place.

"Evie?"

Again, his soft tone made her name a question, one that she ignored. Evie got to her feet and walked over to the fireplace, her mind on the past. She poured some coffee then spooned honey into the steaming liquid. Fatigue crept over her, numbed her thoughts. Wordless she returned to her chair, sat in silence, sipped the hot sweetness until it at last registered that Ben had spoken.

"Yes?"

"Is there something you're not telling me?"

Evie took a long drink. "Many things."

"Such as?"

"It seems," she sighed, "that I have years to explain."

"Evie I—"

"It's been a long day. I'd rather talk tomorrow." Her gaze focused on her lap, shoulders stiff, Evie braced for an argument that never came. Instead, after an extended silent pause, she heard the deeps breaths of sleep

Dusk had called forth shadows by the time a quick glance confirmed her husband indeed slept. Relief seeped through her as she stood up. Evie placed her mug on the dresser and tucked another faded patchwork quilt over him. She banked the fire and then scooted the table in front of the door for a measure of security. With one gentle breath, she blew out the lamp's flame then sat back in the rocker, shivering under a thin blanket.

Time crawled by. Worry gnawed at her thoughts and kept her awake. One hand toyed with the folds of her skirt. After her vision adjusted to the darkness, Evie studied the stranger who was her husband.

Memories of their courtship danced through her mind. Ben had pursued her with a single-minded intensity. A romantic, he'd used every opportunity to kiss her hands, brought her a flower he'd picked daily and wrote her poetry, bad poetry. A smile teased at her lips. The attention had intoxicated her, touched her heart. Her eyes closed. She'd fallen hard and fast.

In the quiet night disturbed only by his strained breathing, the sad state of her life crowded out the pleasant feelings from those memories. The dreams she had then had since been crushed.

Evie wept quietly until exhaustion claimed her and she yielded to the oblivion of sleep.

Morning arrived fast. To Evie it felt as though she'd just closed her eyes when sunlight streamed through the open curtains and warmed her face. Not fully awake, the sensation of being watched awakened annoyance. She grimaced, turned her head to find the source. Her gaze met Ben's steady regard. The weight of his consideration made her squirm, suddenly self-conscious.

Flustered, she tossed her quilt off onto the bed and got up. Her husband beckoned her to come closer before Evie could put distance between them. Concerned, she leaned down. His fingertips lightly brushed tangled strands of hair off her cheek.

"I've been waiting for you to wake up."

One simple touch triggered a cascade of emotion. His gaze held hers captive. Liquid fire raced heat through her veins and her breath became swift, shallow, audible. Seconds ticked by in sweet anticipation.

"You're one pretty lady."

The spell broke as sudden as it spun. Evie straightened and turned away in one motion. She breathed in deep then let it out slow. The connection between them felt as strong as ever but then chemistry had never been the problem. Her back to him, a single tear ran down her cheek unheeded.

"Did I do something wrong?" His voice husky, threaded with a suggestion of desire.

Lips stiff, Evie managed to keep her tone even while she walked across the room. "No."

"Why'd you move away?"

The gently voiced question scraped on raw nerves and Evie didn't answer for a few minutes. She worked to put the room to rights, addressed what she'd neglected the night before.

"What's wrong?"

Her teeth bit on her inner cheek. She held back words Ben

wouldn't understand, couldn't respond to in any satisfactory way since he didn't remember. Evie sat down and laced on boots, kept her gaze fixed on her fingers. "Nothing."

"Hey, please, talk to me."

The bed ropes creaked. At the sound of a soft grunt of pain, Evie glanced up. Ben had rolled onto his side. Propped up on one arm, he focused on her. The expression on his battered face made it clear that her husband wanted an answer.

She finished her task then met his gaze. Her hands curled into fists, fingernails bit into her skin as she contemplated a calm response when pent up resentment clamored for release.

"You... startled me."

"How so?"

"It's been a long time since you've touched me."

"Why?"

"We—" Evie shook her head. The thought of explaining their relationship overwhelmed. She simplified. "We haven't been getting along."

"Why?"

His repeated one word question relayed demand. "It's complicated."

"I'm not going anywhere, take your time."

"I'd rather not," her voice, low, hollow.

The rigid set of his shoulders and a muscle that twitched along his jaw reflected exasperation. "I need to understand what's going on between us."

"I know," Evie blew out a breath, flattened her hands to rub sweaty palms on her skirt then stood. "I'll explain." Her tone wobbled, "just not now."

Control slipping, Evie strode across the room. She moved the table, hurried outside and shut the door behind her. An almost desperate need to be alone drove her.

Running away again?

Her steps faltered. His voice so clear Evie glanced back at the cabin. Solid wood remained between her and Ben. While he'd made that accusation often before, today it was merely an echo in her mind. Shame bled through her. She bit her lip then pressed on.

Every breath became a tiny cloud of frost. Dew dampened the hem of her skirt as she walked to the barn. Inside, hidden from her husband's sight, waves of emotion washed over her as she leaned against a rough wall. Uncertain if she felt sad, angry, relieved or resentful, Evie sensed the tangled mess within her threatening to tear her apart.

Her breath came in hiccups. Both hands came up, covered her face, but Evie didn't cry, just shuddered. Minutes went by before she regained control. She pulled in a deep breath, held it a moment then released it. Her spine straightened, hands lowered, and she at last tackled chores.

To care for a few chickens and a horse didn't take long but it was more than enough time to worry over the hard conversation Ben would likely insist on having. Feet all but dragging, Evie started toward the cabin a short time later, a small basket of eggs on her arm.

A pair of butterflies, gold and brown, danced on the breeze in front of her. Beauty held her gaze a few minutes then flew away when she reach the cabin. The sound of hoof beats gave her an excuse not to open the door. Evie put the basket down then turned to watch a short, large man ride up on a bay horse.

Her eyes narrowed. If this stranger meant harm, Ben could do little but bleed. She lifted her chin, squared her shoulders and moved directly into the man's path.

He pulled up in front of her, "Mrs. Rolfe."

"Yes."

"I'm William Sims."

"Mr. Sims."

"Do you know who I am?"

An arrogant man who doesn't dismount so he can try to intimidate me. Short on sleep and temper, Evie wasn't in the mood for games. "You've given me your name."

"I'm the bank manager."

"Oh," she tried to keep irritation out of her voice. "And to what do I owe the pleasure of your visit?"

"Didn't your husband mention me?"

"I'm afraid not."

His mouth tightened. Mr. Sims studied her a moment then with a loud put upon wheeze, dismounted, "I bought out the loan on this place."

"I see," Evie felt the blood drain from her face. Her mind blanked for a second then she blurted out, "did you have proof?"

"Proof? Are you calling me a liar?"

"No, I'm asking to see legal paperwork, Mr. Sims."

His jaw clenched. "I didn't bring any."

"Well when you do we can discuss—"

"I didn't ride all the way out here to chat." He stepped forward, got in her face, one hand raised, forefinger pointed at her. "I want you and your husband off my property today."

Her heart raced, she abandoned her argument in panic. "But Ben's hurt. We need—"

"Not my problem."

"A few weeks...a wee—"

"No," Dark brown eyes reflected no emotion; empty, cold.

"Please."

Silence ruled for a moment while they stood, staring at each other, then his gaze wandered down the length of her body and time seemed to slow. He reached out and fingered a strand of hair that had come loose from her braid. Her mouth dry, she trembled, barely breathed.

"Perhaps we could work out an arrangement."

Her knees threatened to buckle, "We could pay some rent."

"That isn't what I have in mind."

Fear crawled down her spine.

She inched back.

He followed her.

The urge to turn and run was strong but Evie was too scared to take her eyes off him.

"That's all I have to offer."

His hand brushed her arm. "You've a great deal to offer."

The calm tone made such a bizarre contrast to the menace she read in his gaze, Evie froze. He smiled. Her eyes widened. Before she could move he lunged, seized her. Fingers dug into her shoulders. She jerked free with a panicked cry.

Frantic, Evie stumbled backwards until she hit the cabin wall. He pursued, trapped her against it, with a hand pressed against the logs on either side of her head. Terror slid like ice in her veins.

Click. Click.

The distinctive sound of a shell being jacked in froze the banker. Evie looked in the direction of the sound. Ben stood propped against the doorframe, naked as the day he was born, the rifle in a firm grip aimed at William Sims.

"Get the hell away from my wife."

Mr. Sims backed up, hands in the air, "I meant no harm."

"Ride off."

"We need to discuss—"

"Between his eyes or between his legs, Sweetheart?"

The banker paled. He hustled to his horse, mounted and rode away at a swift pace.

Evie darted to Ben's side, caught him as he started to sag.

"I might need your help getting back to bed."

"What were you thinking?" With one hand, Evie grabbed the rifle, set it inside against the wall while she placed herself under his right arm for support. "You've probably torn your stitches."

"You're worth it."

"Oh, so now you remember me?"

"No."

The stark word felt oddly like rejection. It stung. Her gaze dropped to the toes of her boots. Self-pity weaved through her emotions. Jaw tight, Evie stepped forward. This wasn't the time to feel sorry for herself. She needed to get Ben inside.

Together they staggered into the cabin and across the room to the bed. Evie did her best to help him ease down onto the mattress but couldn't fully support his weight. He fell in the process. She hovered close, worried, until Ben reached up and cupped her cheek.

"I'm sorry I upset you."

"I'm fine," her voice faint, Evie moved out of reach.

Her gaze moved to his shoulder as she pulled the quilt up to his waist. The activity left white linen stained red. She fetched a rag, water and clean cloths then returned to him.

"You don't sound fine."

"I am fine," Evie removed the bloodied bandage then started to wash the area.

"All right." Through gritted teeth, Ben pushed out terse words. "So what happened out there?"

Evie rubbed a hand over her eyes. "It's—"

"Complicated?"

"No, not really, just," Evie paused, took a breath. "Let me finish this first." Her nerves sang with shock. She had a difficult time gathering her thoughts. "The stitches held."

"Good."

Emotions at once sunny and ugly twisted in her. Evie was thankful he'd saved her and yet angry with him too. The banker wouldn't have been in a position to accost her if not for what Ben had done. She kept her explanation simple.

"You sold our place to that man, Mr. Sims. He wants us gone, now. I asked for a little time."

"For me?"

Evie nodded.

"Then he attacked you?"

"Well in exchange he...he wanted..."

"You."

Again, she answered with a silent nod then stood when he

cursed. She went over to the open doorway. Her gaze swept the terrain. Pleased there was no sign of visitors, she picked up her basket and shut the door. Without a word, Evie slipped on her apron and started to make breakfast.

"Why did we sell?"

"*We* didn't." On edge, she snapped.

"I thought you said—"

"You sold it."

A tense moment stretched between them. "You didn't agree?"

"No."

"We argued about it?"

"Yes and no."

"Excuse me?"

"You didn't give me the chance before." She cracked all five eggs into a bowl then, agitated, and whipped them vigorously with a fork. "We had words when you told me."

"Is that what *complicated* our relationship?"

Evie poured frothy liquid into a pan. "It didn't help."

He was quiet for a time. She felt him watching her but didn't look back at him. When Ben finally spoke, his tone seemed reserved.

"What were our plans?"

"I wanted to stay," She stirred up the banked fire, added wood. "You wanted to move."

"That doesn't sound promising."

Tiny, growing flames held her attention for a moment then slowly Evie shook her head. She positioned the pan so that the eggs would cook. Despite the fire's warmth she trembled. With a soft exhale, she spooned coffee into the pot, filled it with water and hung it to heat.

"Maybe we should buy the place back from Sims?"

"Why would you do that?"

"It seems important to you."

"It always was." Bitterness, sharp and painful, seasoned her words. "Anyway even if it were possible, Mr. Sims wouldn't do us any favors."

"Why wouldn't it be possible?"

One hand squeezed the back of her neck. Again, she felt his gaze on her but didn't look up. "You left with all our money and returned with nothing but your clothes."

"Why did I do that? Where was I going?" Ben demanded his tone impatient.

"I don't know. We argued. You left."

"Why'd I leave?"

Her sigh filled the room. "I said things had to change."

"What things?"

His persistence irritated raw nerves. She stopped stirring the eggs and looked over at her husband. "Why don't you rest and we'll talk later?"

"Why not now?" Ben challenged, one eyebrow lifted, his head tilted to one side.

With a towel wrapped around the pan's handle Evie carried it up to the table and filled their plates. "It's difficult."

"Avoiding what's hard doesn't make it go away."

Startled she almost dropped the heavy cast iron pan. Her gaze flew to the man across the room, eyes wide. Those words, spoken with gentle conviction, had once been familiar. A lump formed in her throat. It'd been years since she'd heard him say that sentiment without the taint of sarcasm.

"Evie?"

"Yes," She breathed, her voice barely a whisper.

"You all right?"

Was it possible? Hope flickered. Her fingers tightened on the towel. Had memory loss returned Ben to the man she'd fallen in love with? Evie put the empty pan down on the hearth.

"I'm fine."

"Good."

With plates in hand, Evie crossed to his side. She put them

down on the dresser then helped him to sit up. His hand reached out, caught hers before she could move away.

"Evie," He paused, waited until she looked at him, his expression earnest, "I need to know what's wrong with us."

"It's not pleasant." Her gaze dropped to their hands.

Ben released her. His arms crossed over his chest as she straightened, "I assumed."

"Fine," Evie sat in the rocker, hands clasped tight in her lap, gaze focused on the wall behind Ben. "Your latest grand plan failed." She heard the sour bite in her tone and paused, took a breath. "Sorry that's not fair. You worked hard, had a number of horses and lost them. You didn't deserve what happened. You were furious, bitter. People started accusing you of cheating them; nothing worthy of arrest but…" In spite of the growing warmth of the day, she shivered. "Then you started disappearing for hours, sometimes all night."

"Where did I go? What was I doing?"

"You refused to tell me, said I shouldn't worry about it."

"But you have a good idea what I was up to, don't you?"

"All I know for certain is you spent a lot of time at a saloon in town, gambling and drinking again."

Ben touched her knee, drew her gaze. "You said again."

"What?"

"I was drinking *again*?"

"Yes."

"Gambling again?"

"All of it," her voice strained, weary, "again."

A number of minutes passed before Ben responded. "It seems I haven't been a good husband."

"At times." Before she would've seized that admission and pounded her point home with the strength of her resentment. Now with his memory loss her sense of honor deemed it unfair. "And at others you've been the best. And sometimes I wasn't a good wife." She held his gaze a moment then stood. "Your eggs are getting cold."

Evie handed him a plate with and a fork beside the food. Without pause, she walked back to the fireplace. She poured coffee into a couple mugs, sweetened each with honey, and then returned.

"Here."

Ben balanced his plate on his lap as he accepted her offering, "thanks."

"You're welcome."

Conversation died. Evie took a sip of her coffee then put it on the dresser, picked up her plate. She sat in the rocker and started to eat. Minutes went by with silence broken only by the sound of forks scraping plates.

"Evie?"

Reluctant to resume the discussion, she allowed some time to pass before she looked up at him. "Yes?"

"If it was so bad, why'd you stay?" His expression tense, still, as if carved from stone.

"I loved you."

"Loved. As in you don't anymore."

Her patience frayed. "Loved as in I don't know you anymore."

Chapter Five

"That's not true."

His calm statement set her teeth on edge. "How would you know?"

"From you, you said we've been married five years."

"You don't remember that."

"But you do."

"Yes," her voice emptied of emotion. Appetite fled. She put her fork down. "I do."

"Then you should know me quite well."

Evie shook her head. "You changed."

"The drinking?"

"Among other things."

"But you said that's all happened before."

Agitated, her left leg bounced rapidly. "Your point?"

"It seems to me the problem was that I hadn't changed."

"It was different this time." Back ramrod straight, Evie stood.

"How?"

Evie walked over, set her plate on the table. "You became... bitter sooner, got worse faster."

"Why?"

"I don't know exactly."

"Did you ask me?" He persisted.

Restless she strolled around the room, moved things here and there. "No."

"Why?"

"You were like a rifle half cocked, about ready to go off all the time and I didn't want to argue."

"So you ignored what I was doing?"

Her lips parted then pressed together. She shook her head, searched for words. "We'd fought about it so often in the past that it was already present between us. You knew how I felt."

"But you said I rode off the day I was jumped because we'd argued."

Evie nodded. "I couldn't let things continue."

"So you confronted me."

"I tried to talk to you. It didn't go well."

"Because I told you I'd sold the homestead?"

"In part." Her answer clipped, to the point. "I couldn't take anymore broken promises and my flat refusal to move angered you."

"But by your own argument, this place is gone."

One hand rubbed over eyes gritty, painful and dry. "You don't understand."

"I was a sorry husband, sold our home, lost the money, and am laying here useless while you do all the work."

"Ah...yes," She looked up, stared at him. Benjamin Rolfe was a passionate man given to intense bursts of emotion rather than calm acceptance. The matter of fact response sounded surreal.

"So what don't I understand?"

Evie looked away, stared out the window. With a tremor in her voice, words spilled out. "For years you'd convinced me it was best if we moved on, that fortune would smile on us down the road." She turned back to face her husband. "Once upon a time, I wanted the pretty visions you'd paint, but I don't believe in fairy tales anymore."

"Then I'm not the only one who changed."

The observation stunned her. She hadn't thought of it that way. His troubles were so dramatic that she'd always focused on what he'd done, how he was different. Words came slow as Evie sank down onto her rocker.

"You married a girl with girlish dreams and I grew up. I don't want a mansion on hills laced with gold. I want simple things. A husband I can trust and a home. The same home year after year surround by friends and family." Her voice fell to a strained whisper. "I'm done chasing rainbows."

Their gazes locked as an uncomfortable quiet fell. A long moment passed before Ben disturbed it. He reached out, clasped her hand and drew her close. His breath caressed her ear, sent heat over her skin.

"I'll make it right."

Confusion swept through her. Unable to make sense of how she felt, Evie pulled her hand free, leaned back. Her feelings raw, she wanted to escape, run out into the woods and hide, but she forced herself to stay. She couldn't continue to run away from difficult issues, not if she wanted to resolve them.

"How?" Evie tilted her head to one side.

"You could choose where we go."

Disappointment brought soft sorrow, "I don't want to go anywhere."

"How about somewhere near your family?"

"Other than a brother *somewhere* in the world that I haven't heard from in years, you're all I have."

"Well at last, something we have in common." His attempt to lighten the mood fell flat.

"That's not exactly true, you have family in Oregon, an uncle and some cousins I think."

"Oh I forgot about that." A wry smile came and went in a matter of seconds. Ben hesitated. "We could go there."

A tangled storm of memories and emotions churned inside her. Bitterness found her voice. "Of course we could and no doubt it'll be wonderful. I'm just being silly."

"I didn't say you're silly."

"Do you really believe another move will make everything all better?" Her response growled forth without thought.

"No. You've made it clear that isn't the case. Nevertheless we have to move."

"I know." Her gaze dropped to her lap. The fingers of her free hand smoothed out a winkle in well-loved fabric.

"So why not make the best of it?"

"That sounds like something you would've said when we were first married."

"Is that good?"

"Yes."

"It'll be all right."

"Please stop saying that," Unrest still bubbled close to the surface and made her voice testy. "You can't know that it will."

"I believe it and that's half the battle."

Evie shook her head hardly able to trust her ears. "You used to say that all the time."

"And you didn't like it?"

"Sometimes," Evie managed a brief smile. The person that earned her displeasure was right beside her and yet not. Could she hold him accountable for actions he didn't remember? "It frustrated me."

"Sorry. How about—"

"Could we drop this for now?"

"Mr. Sims will be back, I think sooner than later."

"I know," she rubbed the hard knot of tension between her brows then met his gaze. "A couple hours?"

Ben shifted nearer to the wall and patted the bed beside him. "Lay down beside me. Let's both get some rest."

"I..."

"That chair can't be comfortable and you look done in. Come on, I'm in no condition to try anything."

Worn down by sheer exhaustion, she couldn't resist the lure of comfort. Although it was mid morning, Evie crawled onto the mattress. She stretched out beside him. Her eyes closed. She waited, ridged as a board. Ben didn't move, didn't speak. Her breathing deepened and she relaxed.

Loud knocking on the door ripped her from a deep, dreamless slumber. She sat up as Ben called out. "Who's there?"

"Sheriff Green."

"Be right there." Evie rolled out of bed. She took a few seconds to pat down her hair and smooth the apron down then crossed the room to open the door. "Please come in."

The lawman stepped inside. She closed the door, waved him toward a chair. "Have a seat. Would you like some coffee?"

"No thank you," expression serious, he took off his hat.

"What brings you out Sheriff?"

Her gaze swung to her husband. Evie was surprised to see that he sat on the edge of the bed, hunched, legs off the side, feet on the floor, the quilt preserving his modesty. "Did you come to talk to my husband about those men?"

"What men?" Ben asked.

"His memory returned?"

She looked back at the sheriff, "No."

"What men?" He asked again, insistent.

"Then there's nothing I can do."

"Evie," Ben's tone, loud, firm, commanded attention. She turned and faced him. "What men?"

"The ones who attacked you and are getting off scot free."

"You knew who did this to me and didn't tell me? Why?"

"Well I've been a little—"

"Folks I'm here on another matter, official business." The Sheriff interrupted.

Evie blew out a breath. "You mean, Mr. Sims."

"Yes ma'am. Sims claims he was threatened."

"He was," Ben confirmed without hesitation then bluntly laid out what happened.

The sheriff was quiet a moment. "Were you hurt ma'am?"

She shook her head. "Ben ran him off before he could do anything."

"I'll speak to Mr. Sims at length when I return to town."

"Are you going to arrest my husband?"

"No, this is a private dispute, his word against yours."

Ben scowled but to her surprise said nothing, restraint she'd never witnessed before in her husband. She used to joke he was only quiet asleep. In recent years, that was also true when he was hung over. Was he changing?

"Mr. Sims also had me verify his claim to this homestead. He has the proper paperwork. It's on file at the bank if you wish to see it yourself."

Evie went numb. She glanced at Ben. He shrugged. "That won't be necessary."

"I'm here to serve notice that you need to vacate."

She didn't bother to argue. "We'll need a few days."

"He's insistent on today and has already hired some muscle to ensure you're gone. I plan to ride out with them and keep it peaceful but at best, you have a few hours." The sheriff put his hat back on and quietly took his leave.

In shock, arms wrapped around her waist, Evie closed her eyes and struggled not to cry.

"It'll be okay Sweetheart. We'll start fresh—"

Evie held up a hand. "Don't."

"I—"

"No more empty promises," Her tone hollow, she opened her eyes held his gaze a minute. "I need to start packing."

"Do we have a horse or wagon?"

She sniffed. "Both. Sugar's in the barn. Wagon's behind it."

"So we need to harness up the horse and bring it around?"

"Yes," Her voice beyond tired, sounded defeated.

"I'll help."

She shrugged, too heartsick to protest. Without a word, she dug clothes out of the dresser and helped him put them on. Ben's face was pale and covered with sweat by the time she fastened the last button on his blue and red checked flannel shirt. Once Evie finished tying his boots, she stood, handed him his hat then trudged outside.

Ben reached the barn as she led the mare out. In silence, they hitched up Sugar and had her pull the wagon around to the front of the weathered building. It didn't take long to gather up their tack, tools, the last bag of grain and half bale of hay. Three chickens remained. Since they still owed Dr. Black for treating Ben's infection, she left them, hoping they'd be fair payment.

Next Evie moved the wagon beside the cabin. Back inside their home, Ben insisted he still wanted to help but the sight of his ashen face finally pierced her emotional fog. She made him sit in her rocker.

"I can help," He protested but his voice lacked strength.

Evie didn't waste time being polite. "You're about ready to collapse and if I have to stop and tend you, that doesn't help."

Without waiting for a response, she stalked across the room to take the large basket off the wall. She set it in the middle of the table and started to fill it. Her cast iron pots and pans went in the bottom, the small amount of dishes they had next, a quilt used to layer and cushion around them. Evie then moved on to the dresser.

In minutes, she'd emptied the drawers onto their bed. Her brush, soap and some clothes went into an old carpetbag that had been her mothers. Grief squeezed her chest, and she had to pause, take a deep breath before she could continue. She stuffed two pillowcases with sheets, towels and washcloths then stripped off the bedding, folded it all. Pillows in hand, blankets cradled in her arms, she headed to the wagon.

"Can I help now?"

Heading back inside, Evie paused in the doorway, studied Ben a few seconds. Some color had returned to his face. "All right, let's get the mattress."

Ben got to his feet and followed her across the room. They carried the straw stuffed pallet out and swung it up, into the wagon bed. He walked back into the cabin slow, sat back down heavy.

"Let me catch my breath and I'll help with the dresser."

"No need, all the furniture except for my rocker came with the cabin and can stay."

"Oh," Ben sounded stunned.

"It's easier to travel without much," Evie pulled off the curtains and wrapped the lamp with them. "It's why we brought so little with us."

"Why don't we have more? Haven't we lived here for years?"

Evie grimaced. "We've lost everything a few times and haven't quite recovered. And yes, we've been on this homestead a good while, and Cedar Ridge even longer. We had a farm closer to town at first."

"What happened, did we sell it to get this place?"

"No we lost it."

"Why?"

"Bad decisions."

"How did we buy the homestead then?"

"Somehow you managed to come up with money."

"How?"

"You wouldn't tell me."

"But if I had money then why didn't I save the—"

"Ben." Impatient, Evie sighed, loud. She picked up the basket and headed for the door. "Can we talk about this later?"

"You say that a lot."

Frustration shaded with resentment filled her ears. It struck a chord. She paused, faced him. "I... It's hard to remember every-thing you don't."

"It's hard not to remember."

"And it's hard to discuss some things."

"But you're the only one who can answer my questions."

"After we're done loading up," she stifled a groan then stepped into the doorway. "I'll answer some, I promise."

Evie didn't wait for an answer. She carried her burden out to the wagon then returned. In minutes, she cleared the table, everything off the walls and from underneath the bed. Before she packed the special wooden box, she removed the loaded pistol and put it in her skirt pocket. Only her rocker remained. As Ben carried it outside to put it in the space she'd left open, she went back inside the cabin.

In the center of the room, Evie stood and turned slowly around. Her gaze swept over every inch to ensure that she'd missed nothing. She hadn't. Hours ago, the cabin had been a home. She shivered. Now it felt empty, barren.

A blue jay perched on the wagon seat, chiding her with its song as Evie walked outside. For a second she stared at the annoying bird then looked around for Ben. He wasn't hard to find, he'd wound up the clothesline with the clothes on it. She stalked over, snatched the stuff out of his arms then went back to the wagon, threw it in. The jay, startled, took flight.

"What were you thinking?" Arms crossed over her chest, she swung around to glare at Ben.

His breath audible, he reached her side, leaned against the wagon for support. "I wanted to be useful."

"You shouldn't even be out of bed."

"Agreed."

Geared for a fight, his response left her nonplussed. She stared at him a moment then shook her head. While he caught his breath, she fetched water for Sugar. Evie patted the mare's neck as she looked up at the clear blue sky and noted to her surprise that the afternoon was still young.

"Are we ready to go?"

"There's one more thing to do." Evie returned to Ben's side. "Can you handle a bit of a walk?"

"If I must."

"It's important," she snagged the rifle from the wagon seat then wrapped her free arm around his waist. Slowly they headed down the path to the creek. She took a deep breath. "When we left Indiana we settled for a time in Whitefish, Montana and then moved on to Salmon, here in Idaho."

Ben laughed, surprising her. "Do we have a thing for fish?"

"The town names?" her lips curved into almost a smile. "When you saw Salmon, Idaho on a map, you said it was fate, that we were meant to go there."

"Sounds like me."

"Yes it does, anyway we had a little place on the edge of town. At first you did odd jobs, I sold eggs, we did okay."

"Then what?"

Shade darkened the path. Evie stumbled a few times until her vision adjusted. "We made friends."

"That's good isn't it?"

"It can be." Leaves tickled her skin. She used the rifle to move a branch out of their way. "Daniel Brown was charming, well liked and shared your passion for fishing. You grew close quick. About a month later, you bought a saw mill with him."

"Was that wise?"

"Seemed so at first." They reached the creek. "Meanwhile as the business consumed a lot of your time, I became friends with a neighbor, Martha. She was my age, married and had a baby girl and a little boy. I loved her kids, really started to want one of my own."

"Was that a problem?"

Evie pulled free and knelt, studied various rocks under the clear water flow. "Yes and no," she handed him the rifle. "We never really talked about it before then, just assumed it'd happen one day. Meeting her changed that."

"You wondered why she'd had babies and you hadn't?"

"Yes."

Her fingers plunged in and drew out the prettiest stone she could find, blue and green swirled, polished smooth. She looked up. Ben leaned on the rifle as a makeshift cane. Evie grimaced as she got to her feet but didn't object. She waved to a path to the left and onward they went.

"What's with the rock?"

"We always take one up to the meadow."

"Why?"

"Let me finish what I started, it all ties in."

"All right, please continue."

"Martha's grandmother swore all I needed to do was drink goat's milk but you were suspicious of her motives."

"Oh? Did I hate goats?"

"No. Martha owned the only goats in Salmon."

"So I thought the old lady just wanted to sell us milk?"

"Yes but we decided it wouldn't hurt to humor her. You got fresh milk for me every morning before you went to work." Evie drew in a deep breath. "Then..."

"It didn't work and the scam started a fight with our neighbors."

"Not the goat's milk."

Ben stopped walking. "The saw mill?"

"Daniel vanished one day along with all the mill's funds."

"And that's why we moved?"

"Not immediately, but you took the loss hard."

"Is that a polite way of saying I started drinking?"

"Yes," she started up the trail again.

Sparrows followed hopping from branch to branch along the trees that lined the path. "If I was drowning all my sorrows how'd I get the bright idea to move?"

"Because." They walked out into a clearing set midway between the cabin and creek but higher. Sun bathed a swath of purple irises. "Ester was right."

"What?"

Evie pointed across the sea of flowers. Nestled near the tree line was a small wooden cross surrounded by a square mound of rocks. "The milk worked."

"What are you talking about?"

Her gaze riveted on the grave, she ignored his question, walked over and sat down beside the cross.

"What is this?"

"This is," Evie laid her rock on the mound, the last one she'd ever place while tears leaked down her cheeks, "our son."

"But you said we had no children," his tone stunned.

Her throat constricted, made speech difficult. "We don't."

A lark sang from somewhere out of sight even as silence stretched between them, heavy, weighted with emotion. Several seconds passed. Evie waited, allowed him time to absorb the information.

"What happened?" His whisper, low, tightly controlled.

"He was born too soon," her voice choked with sorrow recent and raw. "So very small."

"Was that because of the move? Did I—?"

"No. You stopped so often for me to rest that it took us days longer to reach Cedar Ridge. We'd moved out here, into the cabin a week before he was born. Moving had nothing to do with it."

Ben turned from her, looked out at the empty stretches of land that surrounded them. "Then I couldn't get you help in time, could I?"

"Not everything is because of you." She pulled in a shaky breath. "I knew what it meant when I started having pains that day. You raced to the neighbors for help, found the doctor there and brought him right home. But it didn't matter. It wouldn't have mattered if the doctor had been here from the start. There was nothing he could do."

"Why?"

"Once labor starts, it can't be stopped"

"No I meant why did it happen?"

"Dr. Black said it just does sometimes."

Ben lowered down, sat next to her. "What did we name him?"

"James Michael. James after my father and—"

"Michael for my brother."

"Yes."

"And the rocks?" His arm circled around her, warm, solid support.

Evie leaned her head against his shoulder. "We brought flowers at first but they died so fast. You gave me a pretty rock one day to cheer me up. I took it up here, left it with James. Since then we always brought one for him. Silly huh?"

"No."

"So I—"

The thud of horse hooves disturbed her. She was really starting to hate that sound. What she'd been about to say was forgotten instantly and Evie got to her feet. She looked off toward the cabin with one hand up to shade her eyes. "That's probably Mr. Sims and his men."

Anxious she strode off at a quick pace. Evie went several yards before she noticed Ben hadn't kept up. She darted back to him. "Come on, I don't trust him not to go through our things and break stuff."

"This is as fast as I can move. Go ahead, be careful and make sure the sheriff's with them. Stuff is replaceable," he cupped her chin with one hand, "you are not."

"I will." She promised. Pleased by his concern and touched by the tears he made no effort to hide, Evie paused, tempted to stay at his side but the sound of voices broke the moment. She turned around and took off for the cabin.

Out of the tree line, past the sheriff and Mr. Sims, Evie rushed straight to the wagon. A man stood beside it, his hands on her chair and her temper erupted. "Get your hands off it."

"Mrs. Rolfe," Mr. Sims said, "How nice to see you again."

Evie didn't waste her time replying. Her attention focused on the stranger who'd started to lift the rocker. "I said stop. Get away from my wagon."

"The way I read these papers," the banker waved them in the air. "The rocker is mine."

Reason didn't matter. She couldn't take more losses. Evie pulled the revolver out of her pocket and aimed it straight at Mr. Sims. "Tell him to unhand my rocker and step away."

"Now Mrs. Rolfe—"

"I believe I was quite clear." She pulled back the hammer.

The banker paled. "Sheriff, do something."

"Mrs. Rolfe, put the pistol away, we'll discuss this."

"There's nothing to talk about," Her voice hard. "That wagon holds all I've left and I'm not giving up anything."

"Surely you wouldn't risk jail over a chair," his tone full of condensation.

"I'm a dead shot," her stance wide, steady. "Surely you wouldn't risk dying over one?"

Chapter Six

"Are you threatening to kill him?"

"No," her gaze never wavered from her target. "I'm asking how badly he wants to steal my chair."

After a long tense moment, Mr. Sims tersely ordered the man away. Evie eased the hammer down and lowered her weapon. She moved up next to the wagon, careful to keep an eye on the men.

"Are you going to let her get away with that Sheriff?"

"Nobody's hurt, the Rolfes' appear packed and ready to go, I'd prefer to move this along."

"Not quite, where's the husband?" Mr. Sims' mouth puckered as if he'd bitten a sour green apple.

His sulky tone raised her hackles. Her hand tightened on the pistol. Evie didn't trust the man, not at all. "He's coming."

"I don't have all day."

Her eyes narrowed, she glared at the banker. "I appreciate your concern for my dear husband."

"I don't give a flying—"

"Sorry I'm late." Ben ambled up behind Mr. Sims, the rifle carried properly now, visibly startling the older man. He gave a casual greeting to the men as he walked past those gathered near the cabin straight to Evie.

"You okay?"

"Yes." This close she could see his sweat dampened hairline. The rifle shook in his grip. The last few hours had taken a toll on her husband. "Are you?"

"Exhausted, hurting, still standing. For now."

"Time to leave?" Evie slid the gun back into her pocket.

Ben leaned against the wagon. "Yeah."

"Sheriff," Evie looked over at the lawman. "We left three chickens. Could you see they get to Dr. Black? We owe him."

"I'll take care of it."

"Thank you. If there's nothing else we'll leave now."

"I think that would be best."

Mr. Sims called out as Ben gave Evie a hand up, "You're not welcome at my bank Rolfe, close your account today then do us all a favor and leave town."

Evie blinked rapidly. *What account?* Her composure barely held as she stared down at her husband.

"I'll take care of that." Ben passed her the rifle, she scooted over and he joined her on the seat. With a slap of the reigns, they moved forward.

"How do we get to town?"

"Just follow the road for now." The rutted ground rocked her as she untied her apron, folded it, put it behind her.

"How far is it?"

Late afternoon sun beat down on them. Evie squinted. She pulled a man's old beaten up hat out from under the seat and set it on her head so the crooked brim shaded her eyes. "An hour or so."

"Nice hat," Threads of amusement wove through the weariness in his voice but Ben kept a straight face.

"Thanks," her tone dry. "It's an old one of yours I found in the barn. My bonnet is somewhere in back."

They rounded the curve in the road that put the cabin and therefore the men out of view. Tall grass, meadow and forest surrounded them. Evie felt her tension start to ease.

"Do you want to stop and dig it out?"

"No this works, leqt's get to town." She reached over the seat back and put the rifle down behind them.

At a slow steady pace, they jolted along. "Can you drive?"

"Can or will I?"

"Both."

"Yes," Evie held out her hands, "and yes."

Ben gave over the reins and with a muffled yawn rested against her. "Was it the loss of our son?"

"What?" Startled Evie almost drove off the road.

"The drinking."

Her fingers tightened on leather. She sighed, a soft, lonely sound. "It's not that simple."

"We have an hour."

"You should rest."

"My ribs are on fire, my shoulder throbs and my head is killing me. I doubt I'll get any real rest until we get to town."

"I can stop and you could go in the back, lay on the mattress."

"No," His voice low yet emphatic. "I don't trust Sims. He could have someone waiting to jump us."

A rider appeared in the distance in front of them on the road at that moment. Her heart pounded. She transferred the reigns to one hand and put the other in her pocket, gripped the pistol. As he moved along side, Evie felt Ben tense and sit up. The grizzled old man acknowledged them with a nod then rode past. She sagged in relief, loosened her grip on the gun.

"You didn't answer my question."

Ben offered the observation then leaned back against her, didn't prod further. His breath hitched whenever they rolled over a rough patch. After a while, guilt nagged at her.

"You didn't start drinking outright when we lost James… but when other stuff went wrong, I think you were still a little raw."

About a mile passed before he spoke. "Did he live at all?"

"No." Her sorrow whispered into the wind.

"Did I hold him?"

A memory both painful and precious. "Yes."

They didn't speak again for a long time. Gradually the landscape changed. Great expensive fields now stretched out in every direction. To the left, cows munched on grass. On the other side, a lone tree stood among rows of ploughed dirt. A breath verging on a sob escaped her.

"Are you all right?"

"No." A bead of sweat ran down her temple. "But there is nothing to do about it."

"Sad about moving on?"

"You have no idea."

"I'm sorry."

Evie shook her head.

"I—"

"Don't. Don't talk about it."

"All right," Ben straightened away from her, stretched gingerly. "Are we almost there?"

"Getting close. If you can handle it, we should go to the bank and settle that first. I hope there's enough for some supplies."

"You don't know how much we have?"

Evie glanced at him. "I didn't know we had an account."

"Oh," his confusion clear.

"It was probably something you didn't think I shouldn't worry about."

"Sounds like it bothers you."

"You could say that."

"I just did."

"Don't try to be funny."

"What put a burr under your saddle?"

Evie was incredulous. "Years of your life are missing, Benjamin. Tell me, does it make you feel protected to be left in the dark? Do you not have to worry about anything anymore?"

Without hesitation, he replied. "Of course not."

"Well I hope you remember that."

Buildings appeared in the distance, sprawled across the horizon. The steady hum of a large number of people increased in volume with each step Sugar took. Soon it started to jangle her nerves. Cedar Ridge seemed larger than she remembered.

Evie drove down Main Street to the bank in the heart of town and parked in front of it. She stuffed the hat back under the seat, smoothed her hair and went inside with Ben. In a few short minutes, they'd concluded their business. The money gained was modest, welcome but still troubling. It was the payment for their homestead. Where then had he gotten that bag of coins?

Ben stumbled as they walked back outside. Evie helped her husband the last few steps to the wagon, made him climb up first before she joined him. "We'd better check into the hotel. You need to rest."

Eyes closed, face pale, Ben simply nodded. She put them in motion. In minutes, they reached the Patton Hotel. He got down while she stood by, watchful. She handed him the rifle then dug the carpetbag out of the back. As Evie walked down the boarded sidewalk to join him, she noticed that her husband was looking not at her but across the street.

The Bucking Pony. She barely managed to hold a polite mask though her lips curved slightly downward with the effort. "Ready?"

"I was just thinking a shot of whiskey might take the edge off."

"One *shot* was never your style." Evie turned on her heel and walked into the hotel.

"Hey," Ben caught her arm just inside the entrance. "I wasn't going over there. You've made it plain how you feel."

Calm, Evie met his gaze. "I'd like to find a room for us now."

"You want to talk about this?"

"Talk about what? As you said you know how I feel."

"Was it always like this?"

"What do you mean?"

"Running after you, begging you to talk whenever I did something that irritated you?"

Evie flinched.

If you're going to punish me for some offense, at least have the decency to tell me what I've done. The past echoed the present.

Despite his memory loss, he'd already become familiar with her stiff expression, one that shouted 'I don't want to talk about that now.' "We'll have to work on that then."

Without another word, Ben headed over to the desk, leaving his wife to follow.

After they registered, the clerk arranged for their horse and wagon to be taken to the stables. They followed the directions to their room. With faded floral wallpaper, one chair, a table beside a thinly made bed and a frayed rug on the scarred wood floor, the surroundings appeared as depressing as she felt.

Evie drew in a fortifying breath then marched over to the chair. She dropped her bag on the cracked leather seat as Ben leaned the rifle against the wall. From across the room she could see how he shook. He hung his hat on the bedpost then collapsed onto the bed, not even bothering to undress.

"Do you want me to get you something to eat?"

Ben shook his head. "Too tired to care."

"Me too."

"Why don't you come to bed with me then, get some sleep?"

Evie paused, studied him a moment before she agreed. She changed for bed for the first time in many days. From her bag, she pulled out a flannel nightgown, white with tiny faded pink roses. Strangely shy, she turned her back to Ben and made quick work of removing her clothes. She tugged the gown over her head, smoothed it down so that the hem hung at her ankles then sat on the bed beside her husband.

For a long moment, Evie stared at the boots she had yet to take off. She should remove them. It'd be the proper thing to do but she couldn't muster the energy. In the end, she left them on. She lay down on her side and then pulled the blanket up over her shoulder. As Ben shifted close, and brought his warmth up against her, sleep found her in seconds for the first time in a long time.

Light streamed through a gap in the curtains, illuminated the room. Evie yawned, stretched. After a minute, she shifted onto her back and looked at Ben. Serious green eyes met and held her gaze.

"Morning."

"Morning," she echoed.

"How are you?"

"Better than yesterday," He offered her a fleeting grin, charming her. "And you?"

"I'm doing okay."

The sounds of an argument in the next room drifted through the wall. He reached out, tapped the end of her nose. "I guess we might as well get up."

Evie agreed but didn't move, enjoying the moment.

"We need to figure out where to go."

Her good mood fled. "I'm not leaving here."

"Evie all our things are in the wagon. Our place is gone."

"We'll get another." She flung back the covers and sat up.

"Not here."

"I am not leaving." Evie stood. Her boots hit the wood plank floor, a punch of sound in the mostly quiet morning.

Ben reached out, touched her hand. Surprised, she flinched and he withdrew. "Let's get some breakfast and discuss it."

"Food would be good," She walked away, put some space between them.

"Evie whether you like it—" A hard rap on the door demanded attention. "Just a minute," He called out then continued. "Or not, we—" The knocking returned with a loud vengeance. "Never mind, I'll see what that's about while you get dressed."

"I won't be long."

Ben nodded, jammed his hat over sleep-tousled hair, moved to the door then paused, his hand on the knob. "I'll wait in the hall."

Before she could do more than blink, he slipped out. She stared after him and regret swelled within her that things weren't different between them. Deep down Evie knew she wasn't being reasonable. She stood still, torn between dressing and the desire to call Ben back into the room. It took the sound of raised voices in the hallway to spur action.

Worried, she jerked off her nightgown and dressed with haste. She crammed the flannel into her bag then crossed the room to pick up the rifle. With their stuff in hand, she opened the door.

"She's dressing," Ben stood firm, arms crossed.

The manager pulled a watch from his pocket and snapped it open. He looked up, expression hard. "Five minutes."

His jaw clenched as Ben watched him walk away. The urge to go after the manager and slam his fist into the man's smirking face held great appeal. Maturity held him still, barely.

Guilt hammered him. Ben rested his back against the wall across from their room. The casual stance allowed him to see anyone's approach. The fine citizens of this town wouldn't surprise him again.

Ben straightened when Evie stepped out of their room, wrinkled, hair a little wild, but pretty in a way that captivated him immediately, "Can I carry something?"

"Sure," she handed him the rifle. "What's going on?"

"You didn't hear?" He stalled.

One eyebrow arched, her only response.

"The manager asked that we have to leave." He didn't bother to soften the truth.

"Why? Did he think we were the ones arguing?"

Ben shook his head. "Our business isn't welcome here."

"Mr. Sims' influence?" Evie held her composure in place with difficulty.

"I believe so."

"Well then far be it for me to stay where I'm not wanted."

In silence, they walked down the hall, straight to the desk and checked out while the manager watched. Her face hot, Evie was thankful to walk out the door. Outside, sadness welled up until tears spiked her lashes. She'd wanted to become part of this community and now that hope turned to ash.

"Hungry?"

His casual tone blunted her self-pity. Though food didn't interest her, Evie knew he needed nourishment so for his sake, she agreed.

"Good," Ben motioned to her left. "I noticed a new place to eat on our way here."

One hand lifted to her hair. "I'm a mess. I don't think—"

"You're beautiful."

His tone brokered no argument even as his words bathed her heart with warmth. Her mouth opened then shut but she didn't make a sound. Ben put a hand on the small of her back and gently started her forward.

As they moved along, an older man with an unkempt beard accompanied by a well-brushed mutt passed them. The dog's tongue hung out of his open mouth, sharp teeth, blinding white. His canine smile lightened her mood a notch.

A few steps further on, a large family spilled out in front of them. The children dashed away, their laughter floated on the breeze. Ben caught the door they'd opened and the aroma of buttermilk biscuits teased the air. Her stomach growled.

A waitress sat them at a corner table. "Our special this morning is fried ham and scrambled eggs with biscuits."

"Sounds good to me, Evie?" Ben removed his hat, placed it on the bag that she'd put on the floor between their feet.

"Yes please and coffee?"

"With honey?"

Touched that he noticed that small detail, her lips curved in a brief smile. Evie nodded in agreement as he propped the rifle against the wall beside her. The other woman hurried off to return with steaming cups and sweetener a moment later.

Evie thanked her, hands already in motion to doctor her drink. Sips of the rich, hot brew soothed her throat until the waitress returned later with their breakfast. Thick slices of pink meat accompanied by golden fluffy eggs and two biscuits, fresh from the oven and still hot, stirred her appetite. She set her cup down.

"I understand you want to stay here but with Mr. Sims—"

"It isn't just him against us." She disclosed in a faint whisper, her gaze on focused her plate.

"Oh?"

"I'm not sure I want to discuss it in public."

"Frankly Sweetheart, you haven't wanted to discuss much in private either and you brought it up."

Her hands shook as she sliced a biscuit in half and smeared butter on both sides. "You've made some enemies."

"Then it's a good thing I'm leaving."

I? Despite all their problems, the thought of being without Ben struck her heart a blow. She averted her eyes, gazed out the window to hide a wave of panic. A man strolled by with a baby in his arms, waving tiny fists in the air. She wondered if the young father knew how lucky he was.

"You want to leave me?"

"No, of course not, you're my wife."

Relief loosened the knot in her stomach. Her gaze shifted back to Ben. "Does that mean you'd stay if I don't want to go?"

"I don't think that's an option."

"Because you know best." Her mood shifted like sand in a swift stream. She stabbed a slice of meat with excess force.

"Because the people here don't want us to stay." His calm, patient tone shamed her.

"Some don't." She cut her ham into tiny bits.

"I'd say most. Take a look around the room."

Evie did as he bid. From almost every table people stared at her with expressions of either overt hostility or rampant curiosity. A few people even moved their chairs, pointedly, so their backs were to her.

Frustration and anger battled for a voice. Yet Evie kept her tone even with effort when she looked back at him. "I haven't done anything wrong."

"I don't believe you did," Somber eyes met her gaze. "But you're married to me. And I apparently have. They've made up their minds and a man like Mr. Sims will use that to his advantage."

Like salt on raw flesh, his words burned. He was right. It wasn't fair but she knew he was right. Arguing for what might have been was pointless.

Sheer determination brought her fork up to her lips. She managed only a few bites then pushed her plate away unable to swallow more.

"Can we talk about where you'd like to go?"

"Doesn't matter," Her voice hollow, gaze focused on the table, she shook her head.

The waitress stopped by and poured fresh coffee. Evie reached for her cup, grateful for something to do. He captured her free hand.

"You mentioned my family in Oregon. How about there?"

Evie stared at her husband, startled. Before he'd lost his memory, Ben had never consulted her. He'd always announced where they'd go then convince her it was the best, their only choice. Her hand brushed her skirt. Again, she wondered at the change in him.

"Oregon?" Evie pulled her hand free.

"Does that sound good? Unless of course you know something I don't about my cousins."

"All I know is that they live near Fir Mountain."

Her foot started to tap, beat a rapid rhythm on the wooden floor as she considered their options. She liked the idea of living near family. Her yearning to belong continued to beat strong but years after moving to Cedar Ridge people still treated her with suspicion. Evie had hoped to overcome that and make some friends but she hadn't made one. Instead, when she came to town, other women whispered not so quietly that she was an outlaw's wife.

"So what do you think?"

Chatter rose and fell around them. The waitress brushed by carrying a heavy tray. Evie brought her cup close but didn't lift it up for a sip. Instead, she stared down at the black liquid as she turned the cup around and around.

Slowly, calm settled over her. She'd wanted another chance, prayed for one. Her spine straightened and she folded her hands in her lap. She raised her gaze to meet Ben's and took a leap of faith.

"It's a long way to go. We'll definitely need supplies."

His wide smile stole her breath. "We'll grab enough to make it someplace we're welcome then restock, get directions."

"Sounds good." Nervous, she tucked hair behind her ear.

"It might be best to cover some miles before nightfall."

Evie nodded.

"I'll go settle our bill." Ben reached down for his hat then stood. His hand cupped her jaw. "You won't regret this, I promise."

Her skin tingled from his touch while her gaze tracked him across the room. Emotions wove together in a pattern that she felt strongly, yet couldn't understand. "I hope not."

By the time, Ben returned, she stood, bag in hand, ready to go. Then they walked to the general store, purchased an assortment of canned foods and a lantern. Each carried a full box as they headed to the stables a few streets south. There Ben shifted things around to his satisfaction in the wagon while Evie stepped outside for a breath of fresh air.

Evie leaned against a rough brick wall, sheltered in the shadows, hands in her pockets and started to relax just as heavy steps crunched the gravel underfoot. The hairs on the back of her neck rose instantly. She inched the pistol out but concealed it among the folds of her skirt. Mouth dry, she turned to face the danger she was certain she felt, lifted her weapon with a remarkably steady grip, her finger ready on the trigger.

Two men approached. They didn't look the slightest bit intimidated by the gun. "Where's your husband lady?"

"Stop right there." Sweat dampened her forehead.

They continued without pause. "We want our money back."

The soft boot step from behind shook her like thunder. A ball of nausea formed in her belly. They had her surrounded.

"What seems to be the problem gentlemen?"

Relief flooded her at the sound of his voice and she swayed on her feet. Ben stepped around from behind her and stopped just ahead but to the left, where he wouldn't block her shot.

The men stopped. "We want our money, Rolfe."

"I don't have any to give you."

"Liar, you took the pot. You have all our money."

Gambling. Evie grimaced. Maybe that explained all the coins she'd seen.

"That's the risk you take when you sit at the table."

"You had to have cheated." The stranger's voice sent chills down her spine. "Give us our money back now or we'll take it out of your pretty wife's hide."

"Enough," The strength of Ben's anger almost a physical force, Evie shivered despite the sunshine. "Clear out now."

"We're not—"

Ben aimed the rifle. "You have to the count of three."

"You wouldn't dare—"

"One," *click.*

"It's broad—"

Click. "Two."

Dirt exploded into the air right beside the strangers from Ben's warning shot. The men turned tail and ran. Her husband shifted to face her. His dark green eyes glittered with strong emotion.

Her hand shook so bad, it took three tries to slide the gun back into her pocket.

"You all right?"

"A little shaky."

"Understandable." His gentle tone soothed as he wrapped his free arm around her. He dropped a kiss on the top of her head. "I believe it's time to leave. Come on, we're burning daylight."

Evie dug in her heels. "Wait. Who were they? How are you involved with them?"

"I wish I could give you answers," Ben looked her square in the eye. "But I don't remember those men or know what they're talking about, but my gut tells me they are bad news. And they strike me as the type to go cry foul to their friends so let's get the hell out of here before they come back with help."

"Oh." That terrifying possibility made her mind go blank.

"Ready to go?" His breath feathered her ear.

Unsure what to say or feel, Evie allowed Ben to guide her to the wagon and climbed up. He handed up the rifle then joined her on the seat. Evie clutched the weapon in a finger-cramping grip as they drove forward; worried another unforeseen threat would jump out at them.

A short time later, they left Cedar Ridge without another incident and the road for miles ahead of them appeared all but deserted. On either side, a sea of overgrown grass waved in the wind, a much needed, peaceful sight. Evie looked back. As civilization faded from view, tension drained and she slumped.

"You can lean against me if you'd like."

Hysterical laughter threatened to escape and Evie's right leg bounced rapidly. She clenched and unclenched her sweat damp hands, biting the inside of her cheek, hard. Pain and the unpleasant taste of blood bought her some control.

"I'm fine," she said as she smoothed her bunched skirt. She glanced at Ben, slouched in obvious ease beside her and then scanned the horizon. The mare plodded along, the easy pace quickly made her want to scream. "Shouldn't we go faster?"

"I don't think we're being followed and this pace is best for Sugar. Why, did you see something?"

A gentle spring breeze carried away her soft sigh. A pair of crows sounded off from their perch in a dead oak tree. The dusty, rutted road remained empty. No reason for panic. She took a deep breath then let it out slow.

"No, no I didn't."

Sugar's hooves clomped against the packed earth, filled the air with a steady beat. Wispy white clouds dotted the blue sky but the sun shone bright. Evie dug the old hat out of her bag and put it on. It kept falling over her eyes until she ripped it off, grumbling.

"Do you need help?" Ben's deep lazy voice pleased her ear, which agitated her even more.

"No, thank you."

"It'd be my pleasure."

"Thank you," Evie stated again, her tone crisp. The well-worn head cover now crushed in her tight-fisted grip. "But no."

The wagon rocked over an uneven section of road. Ben slid across the seat, bumped her. His head turned, lips a whisper apart, their breath mingled. Awareness pulsed between them.

Chapter Seven

Heart pounding, Evie couldn't speak. Her upper body leaned closer. Nerves crackled along points of contact. She felt his slightest movement, anticipated his kiss.

Without warning, the wagon rocked and their heads bumped together. Her eyes watered and she saw stars. Ben shifted away. "Sorry."

Evie bowed her head and looked away. Silence descended and became more uncomfortable as each second passed. A minute felt like an hour. Her fingers curled in tight fists, nails dug into soft skin.

This is ridiculous. Say something, anything.

"Evie." His voice unexpected, she started and a squeak escaped her. Ben didn't seem to notice and continued, "look ahead, the road starts to follow a river."

Trees lined the roadside some yards in front of them. The breeze, cooled over water, wafted over her. Evie inhaled, moist air filling her lungs. Branches bursting with leaves soon cast a shade over them.

"That's the Foxtail." The sound of rushing water over stones and shore begin to soothe her. "It's beautiful isn't it?"

"Yes it is." Ben turned his head, grinned.

For a long moment, Evie held his gaze and the awkwardness fell away. A spark of warmth came into being in her heart then slowly spread. Finally, she smiled back.

By unspoken agreement for the next few hours, they chatted about nothing of consequence. They discussed the weather, the scenery and Ben's love of fishing at length. Miles later she started to yawn. Despite her best intention, his words began to wash over her. Her chin dropped to her chest. Eyes closed, she drifted off.

The wagon groaned to a halt sometime later, and woke her. The bright sun caused spots to dance before her eyes. Evie blinked and her vision gradually cleared. Only then did she notice her position. Nestled against his warm muscular body, Ben's arm encircled her shoulders. Sheltered, protected, she savored the moment.

"Afternoon," His arm lifted, as he released her.

Reluctantly she straightened up. "Hi."

"Did you have a good sleep?"

"Yes," Evie squinted against the invasive sun. She found her hat in her lap and jammed it back on. The sheltering brim brought welcome ease. "Sorry about—"

"Don't be. I enjoyed being my pretty lady's pillow."

Is he flirting? "Well...I... Why did we stop?"

"Sugar needed a rest and I need to stretch." Ben stood, put action to his words then turned to climb down.

"Oh, I...I mean your arm..." He moved out of sight. "Oh forget it." She muttered.

Evie stretched, arched her back as she brought her hands up to rub across her face. With effort, she got to her feet and looked around. They were beside a large pond in the center of a small clearing. She didn't pay attention to Ben until he'd rounded the wagon, reached up and gripped her waist. The sudden touch startled her and she jerked.

Her hat tumbled off as she fell, slammed against Ben. She sucked in a strangled gasp. His arms wrapped around her, tugged her to him, safe even as the force of her impact staggered him backwards. His breath a warm breeze over her hair, Ben found his balance. He held Evie in a loose embrace, steadied her.

"You okay?"

"I..." Dazed, she stared at her fingers splayed across his chest. The simple yet intimate touch mesmerized her. A moment passed before she eased away from him. "I'm fine, thank you for catching me."

"My pleasure."

Evie knelt down, grabbed the hat then smoothed her skirt in place. A cool breeze off the pond hit her and made a basic need a pressing concern. She excused herself.

Minutes later, leaves caught in her hair, scratched from several prickly plants, Evie returned but Ben had vanished. She called out to her husband but he didn't answer. She looked around the clearing and when it appeared empty, panic gripped her, a seductive haunt that she struggled to resist.

As Evie walked around the mare, a distinct rumble caught her attention. Her lips curved into a smile. Relieved and amused, she followed the sound to its source.

Ben reclined in the shade of a tall ash on the other side of the wagon. His shoulders rested against the trunk, his legs stretched out before him. The hat tilted over his face muffled his soft snores. A folded quilt and the lunch basket rested beside his left knee.

Her stomach growled and with eager steps, Evie went to his side. She picked up the blanket and shook it out, faded colors spread over shadowed ground. Hunger became insistent when she opened the wicker container and looked inside. She sank to her knees and unpacked the contents: cold fried chicken, butter and sourdough bread, several hard-boiled eggs, a couple of pickles and a canteen of water.

"Hey there," Ben pushed his hat back to rest properly on his head. "Looks like a picnic."

"Indeed," Evie smiled at him. "Come join me."

"Happy to oblige ma'am." He scooted over, sat beside her and picked up a drumstick.

Ben polished it off in no time then shifted, tried to get comfortable. The wagon ride was torture. His ribs ached, a persistent pain that drained him though he did his best to hide it. He didn't want Evie to notice. She had enough worries.

His gaze wandered around the clearing. A family of ducks floated on the pond. Ben pointed them out to his wife, enjoyed her unmasked delight. They watched the birds, followed their progress until they swam into some reeds. He couldn't think of something else to talk about that wouldn't risk breaking the fragile peace between them. He reached for an egg, ate it in two bites then downed half the contents of the canteen.

Pale blue eyes captured his attention. *What would turn that cool color warm?* He offered her the canteen. "Thirsty?"

"Thank you," Evie took a long drink.

Ben cleared his throat and with some reluctance decided it was time to move on from polite chitchat about the weather. "I was wondering—"

Sunlight abruptly dimmed and the breeze, once cool, now started to deliver a bite. Ben glanced up as angry gray clouds rolled across the sky, threatening rain. "Never mind, we need to get moving."

"You've had enough to eat?"

"I can chew on this later," Ben broke off a chunk from the loaf of bread, stuffed it in his shirt pocket as he stood, gestured to the gloomy heavens, "we need to cover our stuff before it rains."

A scattering of raindrops fell as he took the basket from Evie then helped her up. She picked up the quilt, balled it in her arms and they rushed to the wagon. Ben dropped their things into the bed while his wife pointed out where she'd packed the canvas and rope.

Before they secured their belongings, Ben made certain Evie had her cloak buttoned around her. He then fastened his jacket snug, flipped his collar up and jammed his hat down tight. As a team, they worked the canvas over the bed. Just as the droplets evolved into steady drizzle, they had it tightly bound over the bed.

Ben walked around the wagon one last time, double-checking his knots while his wife waited by the right front wheel. As he neared Evie, she tilted her head back to look at him. Unexpectedly, her beauty struck him dumb. The blue trimmed hood framed her oval face, accentuated her eyes. His gaze lowered, lingered on crimson lips. It took Ben a heartbeat too long to realize she'd spoken. He looked up at her narrowed eyes and tried to sound casual.

"What was that?"

"Are we ready to go?" With a hint of exasperation in her tone, color stained her cheeks and further charmed him.

"Sure thing, Doll."

Flustered, Evie turned and climbed up onto the seat. She shifted on the wet leather, worked to smooth her cloak so it'd cover the full length of her skirt. Her nimble fingers became unusually clumsy when Ben sat down beside her. He confused her.

Water dripped off her hood and onto her hands, now folded tight together on her lap. She grimaced and pulled her arms up her sleeves for warmth and protection. In the confines of her cloak, Evie hugged herself.

"All set?"

"Yes," She kept her answer short, soft.

Ben set the mare in motion. His action drew her gaze to his hands, strong yet relaxed, on the reigns. She'd lived with this man for years. She'd felt his passion, believed his pretty whispers in the dark.

The wind slammed hostile against her face and Evie bowed her head, pressure building behind her eyes.

"There might be a bump or two, hold on."

"All right," She swayed as they pulled onto the road. The bone jolting rhythm smoothed a little thereafter.

Reigns in one hand, Ben dug out the bread and held it under her nose. "Would you like some?"

"No, thank you."

"Sure?"

Evie fought the urge to roll her eyes, "Yes I am sure."

"Are you comfortable?"

"I'm fine."

"As long as we follow the river, I'll be able to fish." He paused to take a bite then continued. "Do you like fish?"

"I do. In fact I used to go fishing with you."

"Really?"

"Really, but you put the worms on my hook."

"What?" He shot her an incredulous look. "True fishermen bait their own hook."

Evie smiled and shrugged.

"We'll have to go fishing sometime soon then, have some fun together." He paused, paid no heed to the rain, took another bite. "You warm enough?"

"Yes."

"I can get you a blanket." He finished off the last of the bread, brushed off the crumbs.

"I'm fine.

"It'd be no trouble."

"No, thank you."

"You sure?"

"Yes." Torn between irritation and amusement, Evie tried to be firm. "And I'd like the quilts to stay under the canvas. We'll need them dry tonight."

"Well if you change your mind let me know."

"I will."

Just then, the sound of voices sparked unease. Evie twisted, looked behind them. No one followed. Her eyes closed for a second in relief.

More curious than worried now, she faced forward again and glanced around.

Two kids sat on a spotted horse in a nearby field. They halted their conversation, called out and waved as Ben and Evie drove by. Their animated expressions, framed by dripping hair, recalled afternoons long past when she and her brother had ran wild, explored the countryside, heedless of the weather. They'd always come home filthy.

Evie smiled as she waved back. *I miss you Henry.* Tears threatened, but she refused to give her sadness full reign. They drove on, passed field after field, all empty.

A good hour passed before sound again burst into their wet, wordless, journey. Chickens clucked. Piglets squealed. A cow called for her calf as they rounded a bend in the road, passed within yards of a big weathered barn.

The noise emphasized the quiet between them so Evie attempted small talk again. "I think the rain has slowed."

"It seems so."

"The day started out beautiful."

"Yes it did." His tone, polite, even but weary.

Evie took sharper notice of her husband. He seemed more slumped and his face had paled. Foreboding knotted her belly. He shouldn't be out in this weather. In fact, he should be in bed.

"Ben I—"

A buggy driven by a young couple approached from the front, travelling at a fast clip. The girl had her arms wrapped around one of his. As they swerved off the road and went around the wagon, Evie saw them up close. Their obvious infatuation made her chest ache.

After they continued, she picked up where she'd left off. "I think we should stop, let you rest again."

"If we stop I think I'll be done for the day."

"That's fine."

"I wanted to get you to a town."

"Admirable, but I'll be fine camping out."

"You sure?"

"It'll be a little wet but shouldn't be too bad." Evie stated even though the damp cloth of her cloak circled her neck in an icy band. "So you'll stop?"

"As soon as I find us a good spot," Ben looked over at her, his eyes dark with pain, which served only to solidify her concern even more.

"Good."

The rain ceased but the clouds persisted, denying them much light or warmth. As the day darkened further, the air snapped with tension before a storm. A dense growth of trees enveloped them and the shadows made the road seem a narrow, winding trail.

Chilled to the point of misery, sore from the jarring motion of the wagon and almost sick with worry, Evie was more than ready to stop. She wanted to check him for fever and make certain his stitches held. Selfishly she also wanted some dry clothes, the warmth of a fire and her feet on solid, *motionless* earth.

As if he read her mind, Ben pulled off the road and came to a dead stop. Branches creaked with the rising wind. Her lips parted then snapped shut as Ben swung down over the side before she could speak.

Evie shoved her arms back through her sleeves and stood. Needles pricked her skin as her right foot woke from slumber and her sodden tangled hair fell over her eyes. She brushed it back with an impatient hand then froze.

The deepening darkness was isolating. Clouds doomed the promise of moonlight while the brewing storm hovered like a threat and her heart pounded. An owl hooted and she nearly jumped out of her skin. Her gaze searched the shadows.

"Ben?" She meant to yell, but his name only squeaked out.

Muffled footsteps drew her attention. Evie spotted a shadowy figure in front of the mare before it vanished from her sight. "Evie."

Her hand slapped against her chest at the sound of Ben's voice below her, beside the wagon. Lips compressed, she glared at him. Anger flared, burned away her fears and set her in motion. She moved down fast, he reached out, tried to assist her. Once her feet were on the ground she twisted loose.

Hands fisted, Evie faced Ben. "Don't ever do that again."

"Do what?"

"Leave like that," she crossed her arms over her chest.

"I got down and walked around for a moment. I wasn't hiding."

"You could've said so."

"I just did."

"Exactly," She pounced on his words as if they were an admission of guilt. "You should've told me beforehand."

Sore and exhausted Ben raised a hand to the back of his neck and rubbed the tense muscles. "I'm sorry I upset you."

His gentle voice deflated her overblown anger and she looked away. Her arms fell to hang at her sides. She drew in a long breath and let it out slow. "No I'm the one who's sorry."

"Is something wrong?"

Exhaustion tugged at her. "Lately," she wrapped her arms around her mid section. "just about everything."

An awkward moment passed as they stood, gazes locked. After a while, Ben cleared his throat. "Can I do anything to help?"

"Don't leave me alone."

"Okay." He drew out that one word, his tone clearly puzzled.

Evie sighed. It was easy to forget that with his memory loss Ben didn't know why she was so jumpy. "I'm afraid of the dark."

"Oh, would you like me to light the lantern?"

"That'd be great. Thank you." Evie paused, lifted one hand up to rub over her face. "Do we have any water left?"

"Some. I'll dig out the canteen too and be right back."

"No, wait, it's all right I'm not that thirsty."

"I'm only going into the back of the wagon." Evie stared at

him. Tension radiated off her. "Water or no, we need the lantern. It'll be full dark soon." Eyes wide, she shook her head. "Come with me then."

Before she could argue, he moved off. Nervous Evie stayed on his heels, so close that a moment later when Ben stopped, she bumped against him hard. Their bodies brushed as he turned.

"S- sorry."

Ben brushed off her mumbled apology as he leaned in closer and desire slowly started to overcome the fear she felt in the pit of her stomach. Blood raced through her veins. His hands came up and grasped her shoulders. Mouth dry, she licked her lips. He bent down and pressed a soft kiss on her forehead.

Disappointment flowed through her as he turned away. He untied a few knots, loosened a section of canvas and lowered the tailgate. "I have to climb in. I'll be right back. Remember there's nothing to be afraid of."

"Yes Ben."

"You're safe here."

"Yes Ben."

"I'm wasting my breath aren't I?"

A wry grin made a brief appearance, "yes Ben."

With a shake of his head, he heaved himself up. Evie drew in a deep breath, exhaled slowly. In the few minutes he was out of sight, the world seemed to darken rapidly. She could hear him rustling around in the bed, knew he was near and that helped, but barely. Only when he stood next to her once more did she feel a little better.

Evie accepted the canteen with a whisper of thanks. She took some eager sips as Ben knelt down. Her anxiety lowered another notch when he lit the lantern which cast a soft bubble of light out around them. She offered him the last of their water.

"Go ahead and finish it. I'll get a drink from the river when I take Sugar down."

"Is it still close?"

"Through the trees over there," Ben gestured to his right while she quenched her thirst. "Can't you hear it?"

"No."

"Well it's there, trust me."

"Do I have a choice?" Her words, delivered in a light tone nevertheless held a note of challenge.

"No," Ben smiled as he offered her the lantern. "Could you hold this while I unhitch her?"

"Of course," she took the light and watched while he made short work of the chore. "What can I do to help?"

"You could guide us through the trees to the river."

Go first? She stared past Ben to the shadows beyond him.

"Evie?" She couldn't move, couldn't speak. "Evie?" Fear froze her. She heard him muffle a sigh. "Listen, don't worry about it. You can stay here or follow me."

The sound of him leading Sugar away snapped her out of her panic. Her husband should still be in bed recovering from his injuries, the least she could do was help. She stepped in front of Ben, forced him to stop. "I can do it."

Immediately, Evie turned around then set out at a brisk pace. Branches cracked against her outstretched hand as she pushed through trees. Moss wet her palm. Spider web strands broke across her face. Mud and wet leaves clumped to her boots, weighted her steps. *Please God let this be over soon.*

A dark winged shape flew past her. Her fingers tightened on the lantern handle and Evie hastened forward. Seconds later, she staggered out onto the riverbank then stopped dead. Ben led the mare past her to the water. *One, two, three.* She counted each breath in and out until her nerves calmed.

As her heart rate slowed to normal, Evie felt a need she couldn't ignore. She left the light on the ground and nervously eased back a few steps. A twig snapped. She stopped. Just beyond the light's glow, she did what she had to do and scurried to her husband.

"You okay?"

Beside Ben, Evie knelt down by the river, "I'm fine."

"Would you mind filling these?"

"Not at all," Evie took the canteens from him, watched as he swayed then leaned against Sugar for support.

"Maybe you should sit down, rest for a moment?"

"I'll wait until we both can."

"Right now I never want to sit again."

His chuckle floated through the night air. "The wagon seat is a little hard."

"Really," Evie shot a glance over her shoulder as held a container in the river, her voice dripped sarcasm. "I hadn't noticed."

"Well pay closer attention tomorrow."

Evie stood, turned to face him as she capped off the last canteen. Ben's face was a polite mask but those devilish green eyes danced with amusement. "It'll be my main concern."

Her dry tone drew a burst of laughter from him. "Ready?"

"Yes," Evie walked by Ben, retrieved the lantern and they headed to the wagon. This time, she made the trip through the trees without undue distress, her mind preoccupied elsewhere.

While Ben secured the mare, she put the light and canteens down then pulled a box out of the wagon. Cold crept into her bones and she shivered. Together they cleared a small area close by and ringed it with stones. He mounded some moss and twigs within the rocks and lit them.

Fire. She hovered as he blew on the tiny flame. A breathy moan of anticipation escaped her numb lips. "I'll gather some wood."

"Okay," He scooped up a handful of the bits of wood, bark, and pinecones that littered the ground, added fuel to the blaze.

Evie collected an armful of fallen branches, dropped them in a pile next to Ben. She stretched eager hands out to the flickering flames. Heat licked her chilled skin. The pleasant sensation consumed her.

"Would you like me to cook?"

"I beg your pardon?" She turned to warm her backside.

Ben pulled a can out of the box. He set it down beside him then asked again in a patient tone. "Do you want me to make us dinner?"

"Very funny," She tossed more wood on the fire. "You can't cook."

"Of course I can."

Evie went still. "Either you're lying now or you lied to me before because you've never once cooked a single meal our entire married life."

Chapter Eight

"Why didn't you offer to cook before?"

A wry grin spread across his face. "I was laid up."

"I meant before that."

"I don't remember," Ben made a muffled noise that sounded suspiciously like a chuckle.

Evie stepped away, moved to the wagon. "This isn't funny."

"Nor is it a tragedy."

"Because it isn't important to you?" She reached over the open tailgate into the bed, felt around blindly until she found the old laundry basket then tugged it out.

"Because it seems minor."

With care, she dug through layers of items to find a pan, plates and forks then shoved the basket back. "Not to me."

"This bothers you that bad?"

"Yes," the one word delivered soft yet emphatic.

His voice matched hers in tone, quiet, serious. "Why?"

"That's," hands full, she returned to his side, "what I want to know."

Ben sighed. "Why would I lie about something so trivial? For what purpose?"

"I don't know. but you have and it always starts with little things," her tone impatient. Evie tossed yet more wood on the fire then knelt down next to him. The damp sticks hissed, steamed among the flames.

"What do you mean?"

"It was just one beer," Evie put the stuff she brought on the ground in front of the box and between them. "I just need your money this once," she reached into the box, drew out a can and a cloth wrapped bundle. "Only a friendly game of cards with friends," she looked up, stared him in the eye. "I could go on."

"No, I get it." Ben took the food from her as he paused a moment. "I don't know what to say. I don't remember doing any of that."

"But I do," her whisper pained.

He inhaled audibly. "Look, could it be you simply assumed I couldn't and the truth never came up."

"In five years?"

"That seems odd, but I can't see what I'd gain by lying about it." Ben took the wrap off the bundle, drew his knife and sliced several thick strips of bacon into the pan.

Sap crackled in the fire. She took some time, considered his words. "True."

"Evie," Ben hesitated, he rewrapped the uncut meat then looked up, expression solemn. "I can't change what I've done but I can promise you this. From now on, I will never lie to you again."

"I..." His sincerity punctured her defensiveness and hit the tender part of her heart, left her torn. Uncertain what to say she pulled out a small loaf of bread and set it on a plate.

Ben used his knife to open the can. "Believe me?"

"I want to."

"I guess that's a start." His voice wavered. He swayed on his heels, sat back heavy. His breath came out in a rush.

Evie scrambled after him. "Ben?"

"I'm sorry," His eyes closed. "After all that fuss I don't believe I'll be able to cook you dinner."

"That's okay. I'll—"

"I just need a couple minutes. I'll be fine."

"You need to lie down."

"It's a little damp and rocky."

"Cute. Don't move. I'll be right back."

"Not going anywhere." His words slurred which worried her.

Evie quickly piled more fuel on the fire to keep him warm then marched over to the wagon. It took several minutes for her to get the pallet out and drag it over beside Ben.

His eyes opened. "It's going to get wet."

"I don't care," she dismissed his half-hearted concern as she helped him roll onto it then darted back to the wagon, fetched a quilt, knelt down and tucked it around him.

"Thank you."

"You're quite welcome. Now try to sleep."

Ben yawned. "I could get—"

"No," her fingers sought his, squeezed then let go, covered his hand with the blanket, "just sleep please, trust me, I can manage."

"But what if you—"

"I'll be fine."

"You sure?"

"I'm certain."

"Stay close. Shout if you need me."

"I will," Evie agreed though she did not intend to do so.

"I need a little shut eye."

"Yes you do."

The fire popped. She picked up the pan and stood. Leaves squished beneath her boots as she walked around the fire until she found a couple rocks in the fire ring to set the cast iron down on. Hands held out to the heat, soft snores brought her gaze to her husband. The lantern cast clear light over Ben.

The lump near his temple was gone. His bruises had faded to green tinged yellow splotches, an ugly reminder of what had been. She didn't know when to unfasten the bindings, how soon his stitches would need removing or why he was healing so well yet his memories hadn't returned. Restless she snatched up the lantern and walked away to gather more wood.

Tears burned her eyes as she worked. His latest promise of honesty hadn't eased her mind. Broken trust haunted their marriage like a troubled ghost. She glanced over her shoulder at his now shadowed form. Although Evie loved him and wanted to believe this time was different, doubts whispered in her ear. She wondered if she were a fool for even offering her faith one more time, merely even contemplating it.

The tantalizing aroma of sizzling pork filled the air as she dumped her armful of sticks beside the fire. She brushed bits of moss and dirt off her clothing while noting the bacon needed flipping. Evie hurried to the wagon for the spatula. Sadly, the minute it took to find the utensil was a minute too long.

Still bent over the wicker basket, an unpleasant odor hit her. Evie glanced toward the pan. Her eyes widened as she stared in stunned horror. It blazed. She ran over and jerked it away from the heat. Hot iron seared skin. She immediately dropped it. The heavy pan fell with a thud, splattered grease onto damp earth. She beat out the last flickers of flame with the spatula.

"Is everything all right?" Her husband's deep, sleep laden voice drifted from the other side of the fire.

Tears of frustration and pain leaked down her cheeks. The spatula fell unheeded to the ground. She managed a tight but even tone, "everything's fine. Go back to sleep."

Evie grabbed a canteen and the cool water eased her stinging palm until she'd emptied it. With a sigh, she capped it off then put it back with the others. Her pain had lessened but the ache remained. She knelt down to the puddle she'd made sluicing her hand and smeared thick, cool mud over it.

Self-pity snaked through her as Evie glanced back at the charred meat. She was hungry, and tired and hurt and it wasn't fair. With her unhurt hand, she rubbed her face dry and tried to think of how to salvage the meal. She did not want to start from scratch.

Her gaze flicked to Ben. He appeared to have gone back to sleep. She felt a measure of relief. Evie didn't want him to see the mess. She wanted to make it better first. She looked around for inspiration and the can he'd opened caught her eye.

With part of her cloak wrapped around her hand, she lifted the pan onto the rocks but placed it further away from the flames. Evie used the spatula to scrape the nastiest bits into the fire then moved over to grab the can. She stumbled over an unseen root and knocked it over. In disbelief, she stared at the stream of beans in the dirt until the wind blew several strands of hair in her eyes. She brushed them away realizing too late that she'd used her mud-caked palm.

At least Ben isn't awake to see this.

To her dismay, the man sat up as if her thought summoned him. "Dinner ready?"

Evie snatched up the can. The weight assured her most of the contents remained. Relieved, she nudged earth over what had spilled then walked over with deliberate calmness to dump beans over the meat.

"The beans need a little more time."

"Oh, maybe I'll rest my eyes for a couple minutes then."

Happy to distract him, "I think that's a good idea."

The moment he reclined, she looked down and winced. In her haste, she'd forgotten to drain off the remaining grease. Pools of the unappetizing liquid gathered on the surface. Blowing out an aggravated breath, she scooped out as much as possible.

In the end, it appeared her efforts paid off. As the beans started to bubble, the meal actually looked tasty. She leaned over the pan and sniffed. A hearty smell replaced the stink of scorched bacon.

She wiped her forehead against her arm. Her lips had parted to call Ben when the hairs on the back of her neck stood. Someone was behind her.

A band of pressure squeezed her chest. It'd take precious seconds to get the pistol out now that her cloak layered over her skirt. Her mind screamed for help but her voice remained mute. She could barely breathe.

Her grip tightened on the spatula. Unable to stand the suspense, she slowly turned to face the danger. A squirrel met her eyes, its cheeks bulging.

Fear transformed to rage. "You dirty little varmint."

Incensed, Evie brandished the cooking utensil like a weapon and charged the small animal. It streaked away, vanished into the night. Anger still pulsed through her as she stomped back.

"Varmint?"

Ben sat up, wide-awake. His presence only increased her agitation. She gestured to the plate. "A bloody squirrel gnawed on our bread."

"Varmint?" His voice shook with laughter.

"Are you listening to me?"

"Yes ma'am, a *varmint* ate some of our bread."

"Sourdough is my favorite," Her hands on her hips, her foot tapped, Evie glared at him.

His lips twitched as though he tried not to smile. "I'll remember that."

"This isn't funny."

"No ma'am," his face now a mask of pure innocence that she didn't believe for a second.

"What's so amusing?"

"Nothing."

Her eyes narrowed as she stared at him, let her expression reflect her disbelief.

"I...that word from your lips just seems..."

"Funny?"

"Well yeah a little. Where'd you pick it up?"

Adrenalin still pumped through her and Evie was not amused. Her tone flat, "you read me a lot of Wild West adventures."

"Hey," all traces of humor gone from his voice, Ben spoke with quiet earnest. "I'm sorry. I didn't mean to upset you."

The simple apology should've soothed her. It really wasn't a big deal. Yet her wayward emotions wouldn't settle down and Evie didn't know how she felt. Troubled, she took out a knife, sawed off the ruined section of bread and then cut two thick slices.

"It's okay. I'm easily upset these days."

"I am sorry." Ben insisted.

Her stomach growled. She dished up their plates, handed him his then settled on the pallet next to him. Distracted, her hunger fierce, Evie didn't think about what had happened. She took a big bite then almost spit it back out.

Scorched bacon flavored the beans. The taste of ashes coated her tongue and her stomach threatened to revolt. Her cheeks hot, she choked the mouthful down.

"I'm so sorry."

"About what?"

"I burnt dinner."

"It's not bad."

Her jaw dropped as he continued to eat. "Please stop, it's horrid." Heat blazed across her face. "I hoped I fixed it and you wouldn't be able to notice."

Ben mopped up the last of his meal with his bread. "Why?"

"I messed up, it's embarrassing."

"Everyone makes mistakes, don't worry about it." He eyed her plate. "Are you finished?"

His matter of fact acceptance stunned her nearly as much as his desire for more. For a moment, Evie could only stare at the man. The notion that anyone would willingly eat the nasty stuff she'd made dumbfounded her but he appeared sincere. She handed Ben her plate then took a long drink from a canteen, rinsed the vile taste out of her mouth, while he polished off her portion.

Her embarrassment faded as it became clear Ben meant his kind words. She nibbled on bread while he scraped the last of the food out of the pan. He raised the plate toward her, a silent offering. Evie wrinkled her nose and shook her head.

While he ate, her gaze focused on the flickering flames, their dance hypnotic. Her mind drifted. She yawned. Her eyes shut, just for a second.

"I think it's time for bed." Ben loomed over her.

With another yawn, she pushed up to her feet. "I need to clean up first."

"There's not much to do." He handed her the quilt. "If you want to change I'll rinse our dishes at the river."

Startled at his offer, her husband had taken the lantern and dinner dishes off into the night before she could form a response. Evie stared after him a long moment. In good times or bad, Ben never worried about whether something was woman's work or not, he did what needed done. *Why lie about cooking then, it makes no sense.*

She pushed the unanswerable question out of her mind and stood. The thought of warm, dry clothes irresistible, she went to the wagon and got her bag. Although her soft flannel nightgown tempted her, given how close they were to the road, she decided against it. The cool night air covered her skin in goose bumps as she quickly changed.

Alone, even mere steps from the fire, the dark night troubled her. She tucked the pistol into the bag then wrapped the quilt over her Sunday dress for warmth. In the hope that they'd dry by morning, she hung her damp cloak and clothing on the wheel of the wagon.

Uneasy, Evie needed something to do. She grabbed a small hatchet from the wagon and headed to a pine tree close enough to the fire's light that she felt somewhat safe. In minutes, she'd chopped off a number of the lower branches. She gathered them into her arms, carried them over to the wagon and spread a layer of boughs on the ground underneath. As she returned to the fire to warm herself, Ben strode back into camp.

Together they repacked their provisions. While he moved their mattress from fireside to under the wagon, she pulled the rest of their bedding out. Evie made them a bed as he loosely tied down the canvas. On her hands and knees, she crawled under and eased in-between the layers of quilts. She bunched her pillow into a semi comfortable form then rolled on her side, watching Ben walk around their campsite.

Lantern in hand, he strode past her to the front of the wagon and retrieved the rifle. He handed it to her then went to check on Sugar. Evie set the weapon on the ground above her head just as he banked the fire. The soft glow from the coals did little to push back the night's gloom when he extinguished the lantern.

Out of the darkness, Ben crawled in, under the covers, next to her. He rolled on his side, faced her. She could see only form and shadow. Fingers touched her cheek. Her heart beat, loud and furious in her chest.

"Sleep well."

A moment passed before she could speak. "You too."

Ben rolled onto his back and after a second, she followed suit. The boughs beneath the pallet cushioned the unforgiving earth mostly but Evie couldn't relax. Despite the covers, she felt cold, her muscles ached and the darkness troubled her even with her husband close. Anxious and tired, she wished things weren't so complicated between them.

Leaves rustled soft with the breeze. She shifted the slightest bit closer to Ben, craved his warmth, wanted him to hold her, be comforted, but didn't know if she should ask. At one time, he would've cradled her against him as a matter of habit but not now, not for a long time.

Things needed to change. Evie clasped her hands together tight, took a deep breath and gathered courage. She turned to Ben, laid a hand on his arm. His ability to fall asleep in the blink of an eye often caused friction between them, especially after an unresolved fight. She'd never understood how he could rest while she tossed and turned. After a minute, she rolled away, on her side, back to him and huddled in the blankets, only her face uncovered. Exhaustion gradually overcame her.

Her clothing tangled and drenched in sweat, Evie jerked out of the dream to sit upright. She twisted and grabbed the rifle to her heaving chest. The substance of the nightmare fled, left an overwhelming sense of fear. In the early morning light, she looked for her husband, needed him. Ice slithered between her shoulder blades. Ben was gone.

Evie stared at his side of the rumpled bed in disbelief. She blinked, rubbed her eyes then looked again. Nothing had changed. Her chest hurt as she crawled out from under the wagon to search.

Tension eased when her gaze swept the campsite. One of the food boxes rested on the ground. Flames licked at twigs in the fire ring. When Evie noted the mare's absence, her breathing slowed to normal. She brushed her hair off her face. *He's just watering Sugar.*

Lazy white clouds spotted the sky. Dew blanketed the world in dampness. Evie leaned against the wagon, started to relax then a twig snapped to her right. She turned, expected to see Ben and was pleasantly surprised. The fawn's liquid brown eyes stared at her. She smiled as the tiny deer stumbled back into the trees.

Movements unhurried, Evie reached back under the wagon and pulled out her bag. She left the rifle propped against a wheel and walked over to the fire. She pressed a hand to her lower back as she stretched. With a grimace, she sat down on the small rough wood box, an uncomfortable seat but better than the wet ground. She got out her brush and first tamed her neglected, wild mane then weaved it into a tidy French braid.

Ben strode back into camp leading the mare as she slipped the brush back into the bag. "Good morning."

"Morning." He started to hitch up Sugar. "Sleep well?"

"Yes, thank you and you?" She stood up, left her bag there and walked over near him.

Ben favored her with a shy smile. "I did too."

"That's good." Evie knelt down, pulled the quilts out from under the wagon, folded them and repacked them. She next picked her dew-dampened clothing off the wheel, hung the items over her arm. "Would you like bacon again for breakfast?"

Ben shook his head as he dragged the pallet out from under the wagon. "How about something simple? I'd like to get going soon."

"In a hurry?" She poured some water from a canteen into her hands then splashed her face.

"I'd like to reach Challis by nightfall. Mr. Durkin, the stableman, told me we'd reach it in two days."

"Okay." Evie stepped over to her bag, stuffed her extra clothing into it then fastened her cloak in place.

With a stick, she stirred up the coals, coaxed them into flame and added more fuel. Evie filled the coffee pot and set it to heat then pulled out the last of the bread. She cut it up, smeared the slices with some honey.

A short time later, they ate and drank in silence and when they finished, Ben emptied the coffee pot over the last flickers of fire, creating a cloud of steam. "That was good, thank you."

"Hard to burn what you don't cook." Evie studied the dying embers while he picked up the box, carried to the wagon.

"Stop worrying about last night. It was fine."

"It was nasty."

"Evie."

"Yes?" She glanced around to see if they had missed anything.

"I think you worry too much."

His tone, his words weren't remarkable but sounded pure Ben. She smiled. "You're starting to remember."

"Afraid not." Shadows darkened his green eyes.

Evie brushed crumbs off her cloak, "Nothing to be sorry for, you can't help it."

"I disappointed you."

"I just want you to feel better." Bag in hand she went to his side.

"I am."

They stood, gazes locked for a moment until a cloud moved over the sun. Without another word, Ben turned to knot the rope and Evie moved to the front of the wagon.

The steady clomp of hooves broke the quiet as the sun reappeared. She watched the riders appear in the distance, her bag, the pistol inside, held tight.

"Don't worry." Ben strode up behind her, rested his hands on her shoulders.

It'd be some time before the sound of riders didn't send anxiety racing through her veins. "I'm fine."

On the road several yards away, four men slowed, called out then passed on by them. Evie tossed her bag up onto the seat and accepted a boost up from her husband. A soft gust of air teased the edge of her cloak as Ben climbed up beside her. He shrugged off his coat, gathered up the reigns and started them forward. The old wagon cricked and groaned as if in protest.

A couple of hours passed in relative quiet, broken only by a few weather observations and an occasional traveler. The sun delivered welcome warmth. The sky cleared, revealed an expanse of light blue. Trees vanished. The road angled away from the river, and became a ribbon between acres of flat, farmed fields.

"Evie."

Without shading timber, heat beat down on them. Sweat trickled down the back of her neck. "Yes?"

"Umm…"

"What is it?" She removed her cloak, folded it then tucked it under the seat by her bag.

"This is nice and all."

"What's wrong?"

His cheeks turned ruddy. "Yesterday was mostly pleasant…"

"What are you talking about?"

"Us."

"I don't understand."

"How long are we going to talk of nothing but the weather?"

Chapter Nine

Evie looked out over freshly ploughed fields. "All right, why don't you tell me about Oregon?"

"I've heard it's beautiful but that's not what I—"

"What do your cousins do there?" She bent over, opened her bag, pulled out the old hat.

"They run a ranch, mostly cattle but a couple of the brothers started a small herd of horses. Now I—"

"A large family right?" Longing echoed in her voice. She fastened the bag shut, straightened and put the hat on.

"Yeah five sons and a daughter, but Evie I—" Ben glanced over at her and paused. "Couldn't find your bonnet?"

"Forgot to look."

"I can stop, let you look?" He pulled out a cherry red bandana and dabbed his face.

"If you wouldn't mind."

"Not at all."

Ben pocketed his hankie and pulled off the road. They got down and he loosened the rope, folded back the canvas. Over the lowered tailgate, Evie climbed into the bed. In a few minutes, she found her wide brimmed straw bonnet with a broad blue ribbon around the crown and exchanged the old hat for it. After she jumped down, he fastened the tailgate but left the bed uncovered with the pallet propped so it would dry in the sun.

"What's he doing?" As they started to the front of the wagon together, Ben pointed to her right.

Evie turned to look. Her eyes narrowed when she spotted a man running toward them, he started shouting but was too far away for her to understand the words. "I don't know."

As the last word left her lips, she heard the rapid thuds of hooves hitting earth behind them. They both turned and saw a large bull charging them. With a gasp, Evie started to run, caught the hem of her skirt and fell face first. Ben grabbed her arm, yanked her up and lunged forward. At the front of the wagon, he about threw her up onto the seat then followed her up.

Ben put Sugar in motion with a yell and a hard snap of the reigns. They tore out of the field and onto the road. Evie looked over her shoulder. For several yards, the bull gave chase. She watched until finally it gave up.

"That was unexpected."

She drew in a shaky breath. "Yeah."

After a few more minutes, their breathing calmed. Evie glanced up, noticed the sun was almost directly overhead. "Do we dare stop for lunch?"

"We'll just be careful where we park. Are you hungry now?"

"Getting there," Her stomach growled. Her face heated.

"Well then, I'd better start looking for a cow free spot."

Evie smiled, "I'd appreciate that."

A comfortable quiet settled between them. Bright sunshine bathed her in warmth, made her drowsy. She stifled a yawn. Her eyelids started to sag.

"Why didn't I take my uncle's offer?"

Startled, she blinked, suddenly wide-awake, "Offer?"

"He offered me a place on his ranch."

Her sigh soft, floated away on the spring breeze. "You wanted to make it all on your own."

"I did?"

"That's what you said."

"That doesn't make sense," He shook his head.

"Why?"

"Taking that offer was part of the plan I made with Henry."

"I know."

"What changed?"

Her teeth gnawed her bottom lip. "Life."

"Evie please," his voice strained, he glanced at her, the look in his eyes intense. "One night I went out with my good friend and when I woke next I'm here with you five years later, up a creek without a paddle."

"I'm sorry."

"Don't be sorry," The road curved so that it followed the river again. Ben didn't say another word until after he pulled off near the slow flowing water. "Explain."

"What would you like to know?"

"Everything." He held her gaze for a long moment, impressed upon her his seriousness then without waiting for a response, turned, got down.

As Ben helped her down, wind blew over the water, caressed her skin, cool, refreshing. He stepped away, pulled off his hat and used it to gather twigs. For a moment, she watched him move around and struggled with what to say.

"I don't know where to start."

Ben squatted near her and worked to build a fire. "At the beginning, like how did I get from Missouri to you?"

"I sent Henry a letter, our grandfather wasn't doing well, asked him to come." Her gaze wondered from her husband's bent head to the lone tree near the riverbank. "He brought you home with him."

A couple of fish jumped near the shaded bank. Ben stood and faced the river, silent as he watched the rings smooth from the surface. "How'd we first meet?"

"Church dance," Evie moved over the wagon, which drew his attention. She lowered the tailgate, tugged out a box. "Some of Grandpa's friends came to visit and he shooed me out of the house. You and Henry arrived after I'd gone. My brother sent you to get me." She pulled out a number of things, bread, butter, a pan, can and knife. "Instead you danced with me."

"Love at first sight?"

As she filled the pan with beans, Ben found a nice flat rock, put it next to the flames for her. When Evie joined him at the fire, he noticed an unpleasant odor. He scanned the area around them while she knelt, placed cast iron on stone. The cause eluded him until his wife stood.

Flecks of dried matter dotted the side of her face. Ben grimaced. Why hadn't he noticed that before? His eyes watered when Evie stepped closer. Lord help him, she smelled.

"Close." She smiled but it faded quickly. "You showered me with attention. I couldn't think straight."

"Charmed you, did I?"

How do I tell her? Now that he had her talking, Ben didn't want to stop the flow of information. He wiped sweaty palms on his pants. His glance swept down, stopped on the dark stains on the side of her skirt. A sinking feeling in his gut warned him that he needed to handle this gently. His wife had been a tad prickly.

"Yes you did."

"Um...I...ah...think you may have some stuff on your skirt."

"Likely dirt," Evie didn't even look, "from when I fell."

While he tried to think of another approach, Ben carried on with their conversation. "What about Henry? Did he approve?"

"He loved that you'd be family. You guys had grand plans."

"So what happened, why'd he leave?" The smell seemed to grow by the minute. "Hold that thought." Ben went to the wagon and grabbed soap and a cloth. "Be right back." A few quick strides brought him to the riverbank. He washed his hands and face then slowly trudged back to his wife. "That felt good." He smiled, hopeful she'd take the hint but Evie simply nodded. "Continue."

"After a while, Grandpa seemed better and Henry's feet started to itch. We argued. He thought Grandpa was fine, a tough old man. I disagreed."

"Did that cause problems between you and me?" Ben pulled in a deep breath, exhaled slow and seriously considered holding his tongue.

Evie frowned as she stirred the bubbling beans. "You tried not to take sides but felt torn between us."

"And you won."

"We compromised. You and I were to stay with Grandpa a few more months while Henry went to California. He was supposed to let us know where he settled so we could join him."

"Sounds reasonable, what went wrong?" Ben put space between them by going to the wagon to get a towel and a couple mugs.

"Grandpa died."

The absence of emotion in her voice stirred him as deeply as if she'd cried. Ben left the mugs on the tailgate, went to her side and took her hand. "I'm sorry. He was the only family you and Henry had left wasn't he?"

"Yes he was but," She squeezed his hand then eased free, as she always did. It bothered Ben but he didn't object. "It was a long time ago."

He bent over, wrapped the towel around the pan's handle and carried it to the wagon. "So why aren't we with Henry?"

"We never heard from him." Evie brushed against him as she reached into the box for plates and forks.

Without making it obvious, Ben inched to one side, amazed she didn't appear bothered by the smell. "Was that it? Why didn't we go to California anyway, look for him?"

Evie took out a canteen, moved to one side and she washed her hands. "I don't know exactly. For months we talked about what we'd do when we got his letter then one day I noticed we didn't anymore."

"We gave up."

"I inherited Grandpa's farm. You tried to make that work."

"And I failed?"

"There'd been a drought for a couple years." She lifted one shoulder in a half shrug. "We couldn't hold on. We packed a few special things into this wagon, sold everything we could and headed out to the land of opportunity."

"Montana?"

"Montana," Evie took the towel, headed back to the fire.

"And then why Idaho?"

"We tried running a boarding house. It didn't go well. You wanted a fresh start."

"Evie..." Words refused to come.

"Yes Ben."

"I..." His gaze dropped to the ground. "I think—"

"You think what?" She reached down for the coffee pot.

After a heartbeat, he blurted out. "You need to wash."

"What?"

"Well you..."

"I what?"

"You smell."

The pot fell from her slack grip onto the fire. Hot liquid splattered, extinguished the flames. Ben grabbed Evie, yanked her out of harm's way.

"Are you all right?"

Mouth agape, she broke free, glared at him. "No."

"Were you burned?" His gaze swept the length of her.

"No."

"Then you're not hurt?"

"Physically no," embarrassment fanned the anger that bled through the tight weave of her restraint as she stomped over to the wagon. Evie grabbed her bag, a towel and the soap. "I'm fine but it seems I need a bath. Enjoy your beans."

"I didn't mean...I think you just need to change, maybe a quick wash. When we get to Challis, you can have a proper bath there."

"I'll bathe *proper* right now. So I don't offend you with my stench."

Ben put his hand on her shoulder. "Now Evie, I didn't mean it like you're taking it. You need to calm down."

"Don't tell me what I need to do." Her hands fisted. Hot emotion strained for release, her whole body shook. One hand pushed against his chest hard, forced him away with strength.

Ben stumbled back. "Evie I—"

"Don't say another word."

"Listen I'm—"

"You're what, sorry?" Evie lifted her chin. Her bitter tone, sharp and raw, sliced the air. "You're always sorry and it doesn't change a damn thing."

"What in the—"

"I'm going down to the river. Do not follow me."

"Hey."

Evie ignored her husband, slapped his hand away as he reached out to her and stomped down to the water's edge. She dropped her things on the grass, flopped down and worked off her boots. *How dare he?* She rolled off her stockings, flung them to one side then stood. *Rude, insulting man.* With rough, angry motions, she peeled off her dress and let it fall to the ground.

Cool air flowed through her thin undergarments and over bare skin. Goosebumps soon dotted her flesh. Chilled, Evie nevertheless stepped into the river. The freezing contact stole her breath and quickly started to cool her temper.

Mud squished between her toes and the clear water turned mucky as she snatched the bonnet off her head. With a sharp exhale, she tossed it up beside her bag then grabbed the soap. Evie eased deeper, inch by inch, until she stood wet to mid thigh. Her teeth chattered as she swiftly washed.

Before she could think twice about it, Evie submerged then came up gasping. She sloshed back to land numb to the point of pain. The gusting wind triggered violent shivers. As soon as she reached the rocky bank, she dropped the soap and snatched up the towel.

After Evie dried off, wrung out her clinging small clothes as best she could without removing them, she still shook non-stop. The harsh call of a raven drew her gaze as she dug in the bag for her other clothes. She stared at the bird perched on a branch of the only tree they'd seen for miles. Fresh embarrassment dawned on her suddenly and she froze. Nothing shielded her from curious eyes.

Her gaze scanned the surrounding area without moving a muscle. Aside from the bird now flying over a nearby field, she found no sign of life. Relief lasted seconds then died. Someone could show up any minute. Evie grabbed the dress she'd shed moments before and with haste pulled it on.

A horrid smell filled her nostrils. Evie looked at her hands. Nasty brown mud streaked both palms. She looked for the source, found the ugly stain on her clothes. *That's what he was trying to tell me.*

Tears flooded her eyes. Shame burned through her as she picked the soap back up, returned to the water. *He must think I'm crazy.* Evie scrubbed her skirt, skin, and hair, everything, until certain she was clean. Drained, she sloshed onto the bank.

"Are you okay?" Ben shouted from where she'd left him.

Soap fell from pale fingers. "I'm fine."

"Hungry? I saved you some of the beans?"

"I don't want any thank you."

"Okay, I'll make you a sandwich."

"All right," With the damp towel clutched against her chest, she swept up her things. "I'll be right there. Thank you."

As Evie walked back, slowed by her bare feet, she tried to think of ways to apologize for her behavior. The breeze swung a clump of dripping hair over her eyes. Hands full, she flipped it back with a shake of her head. Distracted, she tripped and almost fell.

"You all right?" Ben called, his tone laced with worry.

"I'm fine."

"Feel better?"

"A little."

Ben had built the fire back up while she was gone. She put her things down and held her hands out, grateful beyond words for the warmth. Though her cheeks burned with embarrassment, Evie resisted the urge to look at the ground. Her gaze met Ben's square.

"I'm sorry I lost my temper."

"It's okay."

"No it's not. There's no excuse. I don't know what came over me but I won't let it happen again."

"Okay," his smile, broad and sincere, reached his eyes and warmed her heart.

With her head tilted to one side, she twisted her hair and wrung out water. She picked up the towel, dried the mass as best she could. Strands fell over her face. Evie pushed them off with a self-deprecating chuckle.

"Now I smell fishy."

"Ah..." She speared him with a look. "Maybe, a little."

"Maybe a lot."

"Okay, well are you hungry?"

"Starving, but first," A gust of wind blew through her wet clothing and stole her breath. Seconds passed before she could continue, "I need your help to change."

His mind blanked, eyebrows furrowed, "Change?"

"I need to change my clothes. I'm soaked to the skin."

"Oh," A mental picture of Evie stripped, her skin white, soft, damp, unfolded in his mind. He blinked and it faded. "I see," Ben grimaced at his choice of words. He cleared his throat. "Um, why don't you..."

His voice tailed off as he looked about and her dilemma became clear. Flat fields for miles and the tree, poised on the riverbank, offered no protection. Its lowest branch jutted out higher than her head, its trunk would block only one line of sight. "Oh, I *understand*, could you wait—"

"Look at me." Evie broke in, impatient, face pale, lips tinged blue, her dress clinging to every curve. "I'm freezing."

Guilt swamped him. "I'm sorry."

"Please don't be, my foolishness got me in this mess, just help me figure out a way to deal with this without losing the last of my dignity."

"Of course," Ben glanced around again and the quilt he'd pulled out for them to sit on caught his eye. "If you stand by the wagon I could hold a blanket up around you."

"Sounds good," Evie gathered her stuff and hurried off.

Stunned by her quick, easy acceptance, Ben remained for several seconds then grabbed the quilt off the tailgate. He shook it out while Evie knelt, rummaged through her bag. She stood and draped dry clothing over the wagon wheel. He took a corner in each hand, spread his arms out wide and against the wagon on either side of his wife while his chin held the middle to his chest so that the quilt created a half circle shelter around her.

Only inches apart, Evie turned to face him, her gaze direct and unflinching. His heart pounded. "Close your eyes."

"I am your husband." He managed to state calmly even as heat swept up his neck to scorch his face.

"Right now we're practically strangers."

"But we—"

"Ben please."

"All right."

His eyes shut tight, Ben averted his face as much as he could and still hold up her cover. In the self-imposed darkness, his other senses became acute. Whenever she brushed against the quilt, her movement whispered over his flesh like a caress. The sounds of

126

her fumbling with buttons, peeling wet cloth from her skin and her muffled groan of relief when what had to be her soaked dress plopped onto the ground, all roared in his ears.

Sweat soaked the back of his shirt. *Damn, she was naked.* His imagination flooded with possibilities. Evie bumped against his chest.

"Sorry."

"No harm done." His voice came out strangled as fabric rustled and his imagination ran amok. "You almost done?"

"Just about. I'm putting on my stockings."

Over her beautiful calves no doubt. "Good."

"Are you okay Ben?"

"Ah, yeah, just, ah…" *Think about something else.* "My arms are getting tired."

"Oh, I'm sorry. I'll be finished soon promise."

Fishing. Horses. Mucking out stalls.

"I can't wait to get to town, have a real bath."

His breath caught.

"All done."

Ben opened his eyes, met her gaze for a split second then looked away. He dropped the quilt, turned and walked away, his speed greater with each step. "I'll go put out the fire." *Or jump in the river before I do something stupid.*

Startled by his odd behavior, Evie studied her husband while he kicked dirt over smoldering sticks. She doubted his efforts had caused his flushed face. A tiny flutter of confidence beat within her. He found her attractive. A smile spread across her face. It wasn't love but it was a start.

Ben walked up next to Evie, disrupted her thoughts. He repacked the box, pushed it back into the bed. Curious, she moved close and put a hand on his arm. Tension emanated from him. Her smile broadened.

"Is there a problem?"

"No."

Ben looked down at where she touched him then back up at her, clearly uneasy. "Are you ready to go?"

"Almost." She handed him her bag then moved away to wrap her wet clothing in the quilt. "Are you in a hurry?"

"I want to reach town before dark." His tone terse, Ben took the bundle from her, tossed it into the wagon.

She sat down, started to pull on her boots. "Okay."

"Ready?" Ben prodded.

One boot on, unfastened, and one still off, she looked up, a sassy response on the tip of her tongue. The fine lines of strain around his eyes dissolved it. Evie quickly finished her task and stood. "Yes."

Without another word, Ben helped her up. A moment later, they headed out. A mile passed in relative quiet. Two fluffy white clouds meandered across the sky. Evie studied her nails, tried to think of something to say.

"I thought—"

"I forgot," His elbow jabbed her in the ribs as Ben dug in his shirt pocket to pull out a squished, sad sandwich, "to give you this."

"Ah, thank you." Evie smiled and accepted his offering, a chunk of salt pork riddled with congealed fat between uneven slices of dried out bread. "It was sweet of you to make this for me."

"You're welcome. See, I told you I'm good with food, just wait until I cook for you."

With evidence of his skill in her hands, the thought of Ben preparing a meal made her stomach protest. Globs of butter squeezed out, smeared her fingers. Evie wanted to toss it to the ground but didn't want to hurt his feelings. "Um, I'm really not hungry now."

"Are you sure?"

Nausea crawled up her throat. "Yes."

"Would you mind if I ate it?"

"No, of course not," Evie handed him the sandwich back then looked straight ahead.

They bumped along, silent until Ben finished, "Evie?"

"Yes?" Her tone distracted as she spotted the structures of a large town in the distance. A hot bath followed by a night in a real bed sounded like paradise.

"We're married. I think we should act like it."

Emotion swelled. Her heart pounded. "We are."

"I meant we should... share a bed."

"We do."

"Not as husband and wife."

"Oh, I see."

"I don't think you do."

Excited, nervous, Evie whispered, "you want your rights."

"I want us not to be strangers so I can be your husband," He paused, the look in his eyes intense, "in every way."

Chapter Ten

Her mouth went dry. A moment passed before Evie could speak. "You're different now."

"Is that bad?"

"No but..."

"I don't want to live like this forever."

"What do you mean?" Her stomach rolled. "Are you saying you'd leave me?"

"Every time we touch, you pull away as soon as possible."

"And you think the answer is to insist on intimacy?" Her voice soft, strained, she looked down the road. Several of the townspeople were visible now. The sound of voices and activity hummed in her ears.

"I think our marriage needs," his tone calm yet firm sent a shiver down her spine, "some level of physical affection."

Uncomfortable, she shifted on the seat. "What do you want, specifically?"

"You."

Evie sucked in an audible breath. His one word response rocked her to the core. Wide-eyed, she turned to meet his level gaze. Knowledge simmered between them.

"I want to touch you in ways a husband should."

"In bed?"

"Someday, soon I hope, but given our current circumstances, I thought we'd start small. I'd like to hold your hand, kiss you and hold you close at night."

Hope spread like warm honey through her being. Countless replies tumbled in her mind. Evie clasped her trembling hands together in her lap and gave simple consent. "Okay."

"Okay." He smiled at her a moment then faced forward as they entered the town, Challis.

Nerves taut, she waited for Ben to do or say something but some minutes passed without action. They passed by a number of outlying buildings with silence between them. Her fingers laced and unlaced. Dust clogged the air. Her gaze darted from the people now visible in every direction, to her husband whose calm expression left her uncertain.

Partway down the street, past a small white washed church, they pulled up in front of a hotel. Without a word, Ben helped her down. He reached up, pulled the rifle out from under the seat then stilled, studied her a moment. Her heart started to beat faster. He indicated the wagon with a jerk of his head and stepped away toward the tail end. After a brief hesitation, she followed.

Ben pulled her bag and the quilt with her wet clothing out of the bed. Eager for something to do, Evie took the bundle of laundry. She chewed on her inner cheek and shifted her weight from one foot to the other while he refastened the canvas that covered their belongings. Task completed, one large hand palmed her carpetbag together with the rifle while his free arm curved around her waist.

"Come on, let's get checked in."

Evie tensed. Although hyperaware of every inch of physical contact, she didn't protest. In fact, she didn't utter a sound the entire time that it took Ben to register them, arrange for a bath and care for Sugar. She allowed him to keep her close until they were alone in their room then stepped away, sank down onto the only chair.

"That wasn't so bad was it?" Ben put the bag on the bed and

propped the rifle against the wall by the window.

"No…" Tension reduced her voice to barely a whisper as she lowered the quilt bundle to rest on the floor by her feet. Her gaze fixated on the bed. "But I—"

A brisk knock sounded on the door. "Hold that thought, I think that's your bath."

Ben crossed the room and let in a brawny man who muscled in a large, metal tub. The man exited while a maid carried in bucket after bucket of steaming water to fill it. In the end, the woman placed soap and towels on the washstand, accepted a tip from Ben then left.

"I'll give you some privacy. Take your time, I'll grab us something to eat." Ben placed his hand on the doorknob, started to twist then stopped, looked back at her. "What were you going to say earlier?"

"Ah…I forget."

"All right, lock the door behind me."

"I will," Evie assured him and put action to her words.

For a moment, she leaned against the solid wood but the hot bath proved to be an irresistible lure. She stepped over to the tub, stripped out of clammy clothing. Evie snatched up the soap and stepped in. Warmth seeped through her. She submerged up to her shoulders. A moan of pure pleasure passed through her lips, echoed in the room.

For a time, Evie just relaxed. Her eyes drifted shut. She wallowed in the bath like a small child. Sometime later heavy footsteps outside the door sounded, broke her peace. Her eyes flew open. She sat up straight, stared at the door and held her breath.

The steps continued past. Her breath released and, with a sense of urgency, she started to scrub. Once washed from head to toe, she tackled her soaked, stained clothes. A long while later, tired but content, she hung her things about the room, on every available surface to dry.

In her comfortable flannel nightgown and light robe, skin

tingling, Evie sat on the bed. She brushed her squeaky-clean hair in the soft radiance of sunlight that filtered through thin, beige curtains. The familiar task, the rhythmic strokes, soothed her.

"It's me," Ben called out, and rapped on the door.

Evie let him in. She smiled at the sight of cloth-covered plates in his hands. "That smells good."

"Yes ma'am, chicken and dumplings and some milk from the restaurant across the street."

"Thank you." She accepted a plate then sat on the bed, pulled off the cloth and inhaled the delicious aroma.

"You're welcome."

Ben set his plate on the chair and pulled a jug, a couple of metal cups and spoons out of a bag that hung from a cord over his shoulder. He poured them each a drink then handed her a cup along with a spoon. "What would you like to do after we eat?"

Her mounded spoon halfway to her mouth, Evie froze. "What do you mean?"

"It's a mite early for bed unless—"

"I'm not ready for bed."

His tone calm, one eyebrow arched, "looks like you're dressed for it."

"It's all I have that's dry." She put her spoon down.

"I could fetch you something from the wagon."

Slowly she shook her head. "This is all I have."

"Are you telling me," his expression stone cold, voice serious as one hand waved at the damp items around the room, "these are all of your clothes?"

Her gaze dropped to her plate. Evie nodded then picked up her spoon. Until something dried enough to wear, and without a fire that meant several hours at least, she couldn't leave. Her stomach growled. She took a bite, started to chew slow.

"I don't like this."

Evie swallowed hard. Eyes widened at his low, angry tone, she looked up at Ben. "The chicken?"

"The food's fine." He dismissed the notion and as if to prove the point scooped up the last of his meal, ate it before he spoke again. "But you not having clothes isn't."

"I have clothes."

"Precious few it seems." Ben downed his milk and stood.

"I have enough."

"None you can wear outside this room today."

"They'll dry."

"Not like this they won't."

Mouth agape, Evie watched her husband stomp around the room and snatch up every wet garment. "What are you doing?"

"I'm going to find a proper place to hang these."

"No, don't. I – "

Ben left without another word. For a moment, Evie stared at the closed door in stunned silence. She ate out of habit, without thinking. Pride was an unaffordable luxury. If he found somewhere they could set in the sun and breeze, it'd be worth the embarrassment of strangers seeing her things.

As soon as she finished her meal, Evie stood and crossed the room. She'd just stacked her empty plate and cup on top of his when Ben opened the door, a self-satisfied smile on his face. "All settled."

"That was quick."

"Mary, the girl who brought your water, takes in laundry."

"Oh, good."

"Now that's taken care of, I'll go return the dishes and see about having the tub removed." Ben grabbed the plates and ducked out.

Evie tramped down frustration at his quick exit and took the opportunity to weave her hair into a single thick braid. As she tied it off, a brisk knock heralded the arrival of hotel staff. With quiet efficiency, they completed their job and left. The door had shut for only a minute when a soft meeting of knuckles against wood sounded.

His hat in hand and hair rumpled as if fingers had mussed it,

Ben entered the room. Strands of wet hair against his neck drew her attention. Awareness tingled. So close they almost touched, she inhaled a faint scent of soap. He'd taken the time to wash.

"Here," He thrust a brown paper wrapped bundle into her hands.

"What's this?"

One eyebrow arched. "Open it and find out."

"Okay," Hands tore open the paper, revealed crisp brown calico. "I don't understand."

Red tinged his ears. "You don't like it?"

"Like it," she echoed as if in a daze, "I…" She shook out the dress and soft white fabric fell to the floor. Evie knelt down, picked up the chemise and drawers. "You shouldn't have."

"You needed them."

Evie stood and tensed. His set jaw and hard, stubborn gaze birthed a sinking feeling in her gut. Ben's obstinate pride had been at the center of countless arguments.

"But we don't—"

"Have much?" His tone firm but unexpectedly soft. "I know, but you needed them."

Worry that the cost of their room, bath and meals had already dwindled their funds filled her. "I could've made do."

"You could have." His ready agreement confused her.

"But if we're going to—"

"I almost got you a different dress. It was brown too but with flowers the color of your eyes." He reached out, smoothed a tendril of hair off her cheek. "But I know how important a home is to you and that we'll need every cent for that. It's not as pretty but didn't cost much and I thought it'd do."

In the past he'd offered more flowery words, made grander gestures but somehow often missed the point of what she actually wanted, needed. A slow burn started in her heart. Evie fell a little more in love with her husband.

Her smile soft, shy. "It'll do just fine. Thank you."

"Why don't I step into the hall, you change and I'll take you for a walk about town?"

"Are you feeling up for that?" Concern laced her voice. He seemed a shade paler than earlier.

"Finer than a frog's hair."

Her head tilted to one side. "Which is what you always say when you don't really feel well."

"There's a serious downside to this memory loss thing."

"You couldn't fool me with that before either."

"What would you have me say?"

"The truth," Evie lifted her chin, challenged him.

"Even when it's not pretty."

"Especially then."

Ben sighed. "I'm sore. Pain reminds me not to breath deep and I'm more tired than a man has a right to be."

"We could stay here, let you rest."

"I want to take my wife out."

"But—"

"A short walk?" He smiled, dimples deep.

Only slightly impressed with his charm, her left eyebrow arched. "If you promise to see a doctor before we leave town."

"Do I look that bad?"

"No, but I worry."

"Well I can't have that." Ben put his hat on, tugged at the brim. "You have my word."

Bemused she watched him walk out, whistling. Evie slipped into her new clothes, pulled on her boots and bonnet then joined her husband. He took her hand in his and he led her outside in the sunshine. They wandered the streets for a pleasant few hours, enjoyed each other's company. Unlike the 'avoid at all costs anything serious' exchanges on the trail, they chatted as they had during their courting days.

As the afternoon darkened to evening, the light breeze carried the scent of rain although not a cloud appeared in the sky. True to his word, Ben sought out a doctor. The older man, in a brisk, no nonsense manner, assured them all was as expected much to her relief. After that, they ate dinner at the restaurant but tired, they didn't linger. Evie's nervousness returned as the day ended and they returned to the hotel.

"Shall I light the lamp?" Ben asked as shut the door.

"That'd be nice."

The strike of the match roared in the quiet, dark room. The soft glow of the light calmed her slightly. "Shall I wait in the hall again?"

"No."

"I'm dead on my feet," Ben moved past her, sat on the bed.

The dull thud of boots dropped on the hard wood floor made her start. With hands that shook, she undressed. As she tossed her nightgown over her head, Evie listened to the soft sounds of his clothing discarded. The rustle of blankets followed. Her mouth dry she folded her new things with care.

"Would you mind opening the window a crack?"

A glance through her lashes found Ben reclining against the pillows, bare broad shoulders above the covers. Evie moved to the far wall, pulled the curtains aside and did as he asked. On her way to bed, she blew out the lamp. In the dark, she sensed, rather than saw, him pull back the blankets and crawled in beside him. Rigid as a board she waited for him to make a move.

Long moments passed. A half moon cast beams through the window, gentle light illuminating the darkness. Hoof beats, creaking wagon wheels and murmured voices came in with gusts of wind. She shifted, sought a comfortable position.

"Good night."

Evie nearly jumped out of her skin at the sound of his voice. "Good night Ben."

A sigh stifled, she stared at the ceiling. Evie counted a hundred and fifty seven cracks above her before she turned on her side, faced Ben. He remained on his back, hands behind his head, face shadowed.

"What's wrong?"

"Nothing really, I'm tired but can't sleep."

"Me too." His head turned on the pillow. He studied her a few seconds then reached out and pulled her close.

A shiver went down her spine. She swallowed the knot in her throat. As she had done so for many nights in years past, Evie rolled so she faced away, backside snuggled up against Ben. His breath tickled her ear. His hand splayed over her stomach. His warmth both disturbed and comforted.

"Better?"

"A little," tears thickened her voice as melancholy took hold. Muffled conversation drifted from the next room through the wall in front of her.

"You want to talk about what's bothering you?"

Her fingers toyed with a loose thread. "No."

"I'm sorry."

The wealth of sadness in his simple statement commanded Evie's attention. She turned to face him again. "What are you sorry about?"

"Everything," His arm remained over her waist but his hand now rubbed gentle circles on her back.

Shock rendered her mute for several seconds. "You aren't responsible for everything."

"I'm responsible for us, for what went so wrong."

"No," she lifted a hand, cupped his cheek. "We're responsible for what's wrong and we'll fix it, together."

"I hope you're right."

"Of course I am. Have you ever known me to be wrong?"

Her transparent attempt to lighten the mood made Ben shake his head. "My dear wife, my memory of you is measured in weeks."

"And in that time?" Undeterred she persisted.

"I can't think of any specific instances."

"Exactly."

He snorted. "You are unbelievable."

"I'm glad you noticed." Humor flavored her voice.

"Seriously, you are."

Her mood shifted without warning. Her tone dulled. "I wish you believed that before."

Silence enfolded them like an old wool blanket, suffocating and uncomfortable. Minutes ticked by, slowly.

"I can't change what's already happened," his tone somber.

You'd carry a grudge to the grave.

Is 'I'm sorry' never good enough?

Echoes of the past haunted her and embarrassment heated her face. Whenever they made progress toward healing their strained relationship, she seemed to ruin it.

"Ben I—"

"We need to sleep. Let's talk in the morning."

"But," then she noticed the deep lines of exhaustion on his face. "Sure that's a good idea."

Evie watched him close his eyes, waited until he started to breathe deeply then rolled onto her back but stayed in the circle of his arms. Her gaze shifted, to stare through a section of window into the night. A cloud floated over the night sky, and eclipsed the moon. Regret nagged her as the room darkened. A long time passed before she could join Ben in sleep.

Around dawn, Ben jolted awake. He sat up with a muffled curse, scanned the room for what rudely disturbed him. A hard kick to his calf gave him the answer. His wife twisted and turned in her sleep as if she fought an invisible foe.

"Evie." He laid a hand on her shoulder, hoped to calm her.

The instant his hand touched her she punched him. Knocked off balance by the unexpected strike, Ben fell back, out of the bed. He groaned, picked himself up and returned to her side.

Though he tried to evade her flailing fists, she landed blow after blow. Ben shook her shoulder hard. "Evie, wake up."

"No." Her voice rang with determined anger.

In self-defense, he grabbed one wrist and pinned it above her head. Her legs kicked free of the covers. He swung onto the bed, threw one leg over her thighs and pinned them. Ben then captured her other wrist and held it with the first in a firm one-hand grip. His body pressed down on her, sought control against her opposition.

With his free hand, Ben stroked her cheek. His face inches above hers, he rambled nonsense in a low soothing tone until she stilled. Her eyes opened. Evie stared at him, her expression confused and haggard. The flush her struggles brought to her cheeks leeched away.

"You okay?"

Caught up in his concern, he didn't think to release her or move away. Ben ran a hand lightly over her hair, a gesture of comfort. Worry deepened at her lack of response. He whispered assurances unable to look away from her brilliant blue eyes.

All at once, the intimate nature of their position brought charged awareness. Her body, curved in all the right places, fit against Ben as if created just for him. His world narrowed until it held only the two of them. His free hand propped him up as he released her wrists to cup the side of her face.

Fascinated by its shape, Ben focused on her mouth. His body stiffened with arousal. He lowered his face, slowly savoring antici-pation. His lips felt her breath a second before his brain registered the agitation in her voice and he stilled.

"What are you doing?"

"Ah, you were having a nightmare—"

"And you crawled on top of me to snap me out of it?"

"Well kind of, yeah."

Her expression skeptical, she blinked several times, stared at him. "Did it occur to you to try saying wake up, you're having a nightmare?"

"I tried that. It didn't work."

"Then you should've tried again."

Ben tried to defend himself as he eased off her to stand beside the bed. "I did."

"Obviously not loud enough," her tone sharp with suspicion, sarcasm dripped with each word. "Is this how you act married?"

"No," his tone sharp, emphatic.

Evie sat up. "So you merely seized the opportunity."

"I wasn't trying to rush you or take advantage." Ben held her gaze a moment then reached down for his pants, started to dress. "I was trying to help."

His voice, steady and a shade cool, finally pierced her haze of anger. The dream and her fear within it still felt real. She took in a deep breath. As Evie sought calm, she noticed that the skin around his left eye appeared puffy and red. She pointed to the area.

"Did I do that?"

"Yes ma'am." Ben shrugged into his shirt.

"I'm sorry."

"I've had worse." He finished buttoning up his shirt then sat on the bed, pulled on his boots. "Don't worry about it."

"Still, I am sorry."

Ben looked her straight in the eye. "For hitting me or making accusations after?"

"Both," Her whisper soft, husky.

"Okay," he leaned in close. "And I'm sorry I upset you."

"I overreacted, I was disturbed by the dream."

"You want to talk about it?"

"Not really."

"All right."

"Ben," Evie licked her lips, anticipation raced through her veins. "Are you going to kiss me?"

"Definitely," His tone dead serious left no doubt.

Chapter Eleven

Rendered speechless, Evie stared at her husband, eyes wide, heart a flutter as her lips parted slightly.

"But not now," his expression appeared strained but his gaze held hers, calm and steady. "I don't think either of us can sleep again. We may as well get moving." Ben stood and put on his hat. "I'll go get your clothes and fetch the wagon."

By the time, Evie snapped out of her daze, he'd left. She got up, crossed over to the window, pushed aside the curtain and leaned her forehead against cool glass. Her gaze found Ben as he exited the hotel onto the street two floors below a couple of minutes later. Tears welled up, spilled onto her cheeks when he strode out of view. Sunshine poured through the window, which delivered light but little warmth.

Evie shivered while she dressed and wished she hadn't left her cloak in the wagon. She tied on her boots then made the bed. In a hurry to be ready before Ben returned, she shook her hair loose, ran her brush through it and braided it again.

"Ready?" Ben walked in without knocking, which in an odd way comforted her. A normal husband acted with familiarity.

"Almost," Evie stuffed her brush into the bag then handed it to him. "I need a few minutes. "

"Okay. Bill's settled. I'll wait for you downstairs." He grabbed

142

the rifle and left again.

Evie followed at a slower pace. In the hall, she paused, watched Ben walk away until he moved out of sight. Her feet dragged as she headed after him a short time later. With such a jarring, emotional start, she didn't hold hope the day would get better. She stepped into the room and Ben turned to greet her.

The warmth of her husband's smile struck her dumb. He reached out, took her hands in his. When he spoke, his low voice rang with sincerity. "You look lovely."

"Thank you," Evie returned his smile full measure.

"Can we put aside what happened upstairs?"

"I'd like that."

"Good." He squeezed her fingers as they walked across the room and out onto the busy sidewalk. "Hungry?"

Despite the number of clouds that crowded the blue above, Evie felt her day brighten. "Yes, yes I am."

Hand in hand, they walked to the restaurant where, for over an hour, Ben charmed her. He held out her chair, fed her choice bits off his plate and entertained her with stories she'd heard a hundred times before yet held her in thrall nonetheless. All too soon for Evie, the meal was over and it was time to go.

Ben gave the boy he'd asked to watch the wagon a coin. For a second he watched the young one scamper off then he turned to face Evie. His lips curved in a suggestion of a smile, forest green eyes mesmerizing her. When his hands came up to span her waist, she gasped. Her hands rose to cover his.

Warmth radiated from where they touched. Ben moved closer. Her skirt brushed against his legs. His face was close enough to touch. Their breath mingled. Her eyes started to shut.

"Ready?"

"Yes," an exhale, a whisper, she answered.

Before she could form a coherent thought, Ben stepped back, twisted her about then lifted. Evie struggled to put her feet and hands in the correct places as she climbed onto the seat. A moment later, her breath hitched as he slid up beside her. She stole a sideways glance at him under her lashes, nervous. He stretched, arched over the low back of the seat, arms above his head.

The power implied by his action triggered memories that her imagination built on and delivered potent imagery. Her pulse raced. Transfixed, several seconds passed before she averted her gaze to look overhead. The sun had disappeared and a dismal gray painted the sky. Evie clasped her hands together in her lap and tried not to shiver.

"You cold?" Ben straightened, touched her arm.

His attention brought heat to her cheeks. Flustered, she rubbed damp palms over her skirt. "A little."

"Want your cloak?" He looked over his shoulder. "I think I can reach it."

"That'd be nice."

Evie deliberately didn't look at him as he got the garment and tossed it in her lap. "Thank you."

"You are quite welcome." He snapped the reigns, which set them in motion and drew her gaze to his muscled arms.

A beat of excitement pulsed through her when she thought of the sheer strength he'd used to boost her up. Scattered drops of rain fell, which prompted her to pull on her cloak. In that innocent motion, her thigh brushed his. Doubt snaked in even as the whisper of a touch quickened her breath. The strength of their physical bond had distracted her in the past, made it all too easy to ignore problems.

Troubled, her emotions felt jumbled and Evie fell silent as they headed out of town. Tall, slender oaks grew in clumps on either side of them. Cattle grazed among the trees for the first miles then farms and their livestock became rare. The road roughened and Ben slowed their pace, tried to avoid the deepest ruts.

"Was it the nightmare?"

"What?" Startled, Evie shot him a puzzled look.

Ben continued to focus forward. "It seems to me that after being married for five years," he cleared his throat. "It shouldn't have upset you for me to be on top of you."

Evie pulled in a deep breath and let it out.

"So was it the nightmare or me?"

"Both." Random droplets became a persistent drizzle. She pulled her hood up, covered her head.

"Will you tell me about it?"

Wind gusted, blew hair in her eyes. "The night before you were hurt, you were gone." She tucked wayward strands behind her ear. "Some of the neighbors' ranch hands harassed me." Memories flitted through her mind. "I ran in the cabin and eventually they rode off, never touched me. In the nightmare though, one of them broke in the door then..."

"You woke with me on you."

"And I just..." Evie shook her head, "sorry."

"No I'm the one who's sorry."

"You didn't cause the nightmare."

"Didn't I?" Eyes dark with emotion, Ben looked at her, expression fierce. "Why wasn't I there that night?" Evie bit her lip, wouldn't answer. "I was out drinking wasn't I?"

"I'm not sure where you were." Her gaze dropped to her lap. "But I found you in the barn the next morning, passed out, smelling of whiskey."

"And those men, they were harassing you because of me, something I'd done, weren't they?"

"Yes."

"That won't happen again."

"Okay." His harsh whisper tugged at her heart but didn't banish doubt or heal her hurt.

"You've no reason to believe I'll be different do you?"

Evie didn't know what to say and so said nothing. She felt his gaze for a long moment before he looked away. Waves of emotion flowed off him but Ben didn't break the silence between them. In fact, her husband didn't speak again until a river halted them in their tracks around midday.

The road led directly into the water then reappeared across from them after a few wagon lengths. In either direction, the river stretched out as far as the eye could see without a bridge or ferry. Already miserable, her spirits sank further.

"The crossing will be rough."

Evie watched a tree limb float past them, "Should we wait?"

"The rain isn't letting up," his tone grave, Ben waited for her to face him. "Best we go now, it'll only get worse."

Her lips pressed tight together, Evie nodded. He gave her shoulder a brief squeeze then eased them forward. Water churned around the wheels and in minutes splashed the mare's belly.

Thunder clapped. Their small, light wagon barely resisted the current's pull as they inched onward. Rain fell harder and soon drenched them. Her gaze swung to Ben, sought hope but found little comfort. His clenched jaw and rigid upper body shouted tension.

Without warning, the wagon shook hard. She glanced forward and saw Sugar had stumbled. They rocked dangerously as the mare struggled. Water whipped into froth around them. She grabbed Ben, her nails dug deep into his sleeve.

"We'll be fine," his voice gentle as he firmly removed her hand. "Stay calm."

To her surprise and immense relief, he was right. Sugar regained her footing and they moved forward. Some tense moments later, they made it across. The muddy road sucked at the wheels, stalled them a few feet from their goal. Before Ben could object, Evie swung down to see if she could find some brush to help their traction. All it took was one slip, and suddenly the current swept her away.

"Evie get back up here." With a white knuckled grip on the reigns, Ben shouted. Thunder offered another roar. "Evie?"

Seconds stretched into a full minute. Water dripped off the brim of his hat into his eyes. The wagon rocked as Sugar pulled forward in starts and stops. His gaze searched frantically, unsuccessfully for his wife until he twisted to look where he wanted to least. His heart stopped. In a tangle of branches down river, yards from shore, he saw bright blue.

Immediately he dropped the reigns and jumped down. Ben ripped off his jacket as he ran along the bank. His hat blew off, his breath rasped and his still healing ribs screamed protests he ignored. He charged over rain-slicked earth until she was almost within reach then jumped in.

The icy water stole his breath. Choppy waves slapped his face. Ben grabbed one of the slick branches that trapped Evie and used it as an anchor. The current's constant pull sapped at his strength. Hand over hand, he advanced to his wife. Fingers numb, Ben reached her more through desperation than skill.

"Please God…" With one arm still wrapped around the branch, he pulled her against him, held her head above the water. Eyes closed and expression pale, slack, Evie didn't respond.

With a sharp crack the branch he clung to broke, the water started to pull him away from his wife. Splinters pierced his skin as he clawed at other pieces of wood until he gained a new hold. Frantic, Ben groped underwater, blindly, until he found what exactly trapped Evie.

Wet, slimy branches wedged together, formed a deadly net, which held one leg fast. Wind whipped rain beat his skin as he tore at the sticks, cursed and pleaded with God. When at last he freed her, the current swept them down river. His muscles quivered as Ben fought to hold onto his wife.

His mind and body numb, he acted on instinct. Pain shot through his shoulder during the long process of towing Evie to shore, the cost of keeping her dead weight afloat. It took what felt like forever to reach land. For every yard forward they were carried several downstream but in the end, Ben got them to the shallows.

Weary, he struggled to stand. Thick muck imprisoned his foot when Ben tried to take a step. Frustration, worry and fear sent curses flying past his lips. He pulled up too hard and fell back, almost lost his hold on her when his shoulder slammed against an underwater stump.

Pain snapped everything into sharp focus. They had to get out of the water. Ben got to his feet and lifted Evie in his arms. Rain and wind continued unabated as he stumbled forward on pure stubborn will. His ribs on fire, he was barely able to breathe. He moved in a ragged diagonal path toward a clump of trees some distance from the water.

The water level dropped to mid-calf level. Movement became easier even as gusts of cold air sent daggers of frost through his clothing. Ben couldn't feel his fingers, his feet felt like blocks of ice.

Determined, Ben trudged on. It seemed like an eternity before they were out and away from the river. He collapsed to his knees. Beyond exhaustion, he first sat then lay down on the ground, flat on his back, with Evie on top of him from the waist down. His arms held her close even as his eyes shut.

"Evie," Ben woke with a start, looked up at a clear section of sky. The rain had stopped. In the cloud-strewn heavens, the sun shone directly overhead, which meant only a short time could have passed. "Evie?"

When she didn't respond, he eased out from under her, laid her out beside him. Apprehension shook the hand as he stretched out above her mouth. Seconds passed. His heart crashed against his chest. Ben stared down at her pale features, panic built up swiftly, and then he felt her breath.

"Thank God." He gathered her to him, rocked her in his arms. "Thank God."

Without warning, Evie coughed then spewed a huge amount

of river water over him. Ben froze. After a moment, he gently laid her down on her back. He rubbed his face with hands that shook then let out a long breath. Relieved, the slight rise and fall of her chest captivated him for a time.

Ben reached out and caressed her cheek. "Evie." When that didn't get a response, he shook her shoulder and got a mumble out of his wife. He tried again in a forceful tone. "Come on honey, open your eyes for me."

Her eyelids fluttered but didn't open. His gaze drifted over the length of her, looked for obvious injuries. To his great relief, he spotted nothing but when he looked back at her face, blue tinged lips brought concern. Ben stood but a sound drew his attention before he took a step.

His thoughts sluggish, it took him a moment to link the noise with the sight of Sugar and their wagon a good distance up river. Ben raked fingers through his hair. He didn't know what would be best. To build a fire quickly, he needed supplies. In his current condition, it'd take precious time to carry her or he could leave her here, rush to the wagon and drive back.

A low rumble of thunder interrupted his thoughts, caused him to look up. Angry clouds appeared in the distance, poised to retake the sky. He had to act. With the relative shelter of their branches, the trees several feet away, offered an option.

Sweat dripped into his eyes as Ben picked her up. Every few steps he had to stop and catch his breath. When they reached the destination, he set her down, touched her cheek then without giving himself the opportunity to waver, he strode away, refused to look back, eyes focused on his goal.

Concern that she remained unconscious haunted him, and spurred Ben onward. His long strides covered ground rapidly. Along the way, he spotted his coat and hat and recovered them with little effort. The river roiled against the confines of its banks by the time he reached the wagon. He climbed up and slapped the reigns, drove at speed back to his wife.

Shivers racked Ben by the time he pulled up as close to her as he dared. He jumped down, hurried to the back and lowered the tailgate. With an armful of quilts and her bag snatched out of the bed, he ran to Evie.

At her side, he dumped it all on the ground. Ben spread out a blanket then with fingers made clumsy by cold and fear stripped off her soaked clothing. He wrapped the rest of the blankets snug around her. The entire time she remained unresponsive. Worried, he parted the covers just enough to put his ear on her bare chest.

Breath feathered the top of his head. Her steady heartbeat should've calmed Ben but instead fear clawed his belly. Evie's skin felt so very cold. He got up, rushed back to the wagon to fetch their pallet.

Once Ben settled her on it, off the damp earth, he started a fire. He coaxed fire from a handful of twigs then fed it more tinder until he had a steady blaze. Careful not to smother it, he added some nearby sticks so the flames could devour the dry wood.

Wind whistled through the trees. Without pausing to enjoy the welcomed heat, Ben stood. He gathered some armfuls of fallen branches and set them near the fire where he hoped they'd dry enough to use.

His teeth chattered as he returned to Evie's side but Ben ignored his discomfort. He laid his palm against his wife's cheek. She seemed warmer but he couldn't be certain. His fingers were still numb.

The lure of dry clothes warred with the need to rest. He bowed his head, closed his eyes for a few seconds. Ben sighed then forced himself to move. If he didn't take care of himself, he wouldn't be able to help her much longer.

Evie still appeared out cold, which worried him. His gaze moved on, scanning the landscape. The flat land seemed empty. Once satisfied that no other threat was lurking he started to change.

Ben opened her bag and pulled out his dry clothing. His boots wouldn't come off without a fight then the uncooperative material of his soaked clothing left him hissing in frustration before he got everything off. Finished, he kicked them to one side with gratuitous force. He propped his boots up on a rock near the fire to dry then piled more fuel on the flames.

A raindrop hit his arm. Ben glanced up and saw that storm clouds once again covered the sky.

A groan broke the quiet. Ben turned to look at his wife in time to see her eyes open at last. Relief turned to worry when Evie stared at him as though she'd never seen him before, her expression one of startled confusion.

Pain travelled up her neck to pounding temples. Her heavy eyelids lifted slowly. She groaned. Her vision a blur at first, Evie couldn't comprehend what she'd seen. She squeezed her eyes shut tight then opened them again. Her breath caught. The fire cast gold light over Ben's body, nude save for the bindings over his ribs.

Her conscious whispered to her that she should avert her eyes. Proper women simply didn't stare at naked men even if the man was her husband. And yet Evie couldn't look away. Ben turned to face her and smiled. A wave of scorching heat swept up her neck as he moved toward her.

"Hey stranger," Ben sat down beside Evie, his bare thigh against her arm. She felt him despite the layers of blankets between them. "How are you?"

"Alive."

"That's half the battle."

She grimaced. "What happened?"

"River carried you off," he patted her shoulder. "You got caught in a mess of branches." Ben carefully lifted the quilts off her enough to join Evie in the cocoon of warmth and molded his body to hers before she knew his intent. His arms wrapped around her, a wealth of emotion delivered in his next, soft-spoken words. "I thought you'd drowned."

"You saved me?"

"I got you to shore." His tone matter of fact, Ben reached up, brushed hair off her forehead and dropped a soft kiss there.

"Thank you."

"How do you feel?"

"My head hurts and I'm a little cold. Tired."

"Is there any whiskey left?"

"Why? Are you in pain?" Her voice sharpened with concern.

"Not for me, for you."

"You didn't answer my question."

"I've felt worse."

Evie leveled a strict look at him, didn't say a word.

"It hurts to breath but," he grinned at her, one hand slid down her back then up along her ribs, brushed the side of her breast before it settled on her shoulder blade. "Maybe that's because I've a beautiful woman in my arms."

Her skin tingled where he'd touched. "Flirting with me will get you nowhere." She tried to sound serious, firm but her breathless whisper gave lie to her words. "I've heard all your lines before."

His gaze lowered to her mouth. "Shall we test your theory?"

"Ben I—" A hard shiver rocked her.

He bowed his head so his forehead touched hers. His voice husky, he whispered. "Sorry Sweetheart, I got carried away, that'll have to wait until we get you all warmed up."

"I—"

"Shall I go look for the whiskey or stay here and hold you?"

"You're not wearing any clothes."

"Just noticed that?"

"No I..." Her cheeks felt a blaze. Rational thought fled. "Why?"

"The river was a mite wet."

"And that's ...ah...why you removed mine too?"

"You were freezing. I had to." Ben held her gaze steady as she fussed with the edge of the covers.

"Oh." Seconds passed then Evie continued. "I put the whiskey in the box with the potatoes."

"I'll go get it."

"Thank you."

Ben eased out of their bed. With a firm grip on the quilts, Evie sat up. Her headache worsened. Without a word, her husband retrieved her bag and placed it against the base of the tree behind her. "Just rest, stay warm."

Evie reclined. "Thanks."

"I'll be right back."

Despite the pain behind her eyes, her gaze still followed her husband as he moved away from her, amazed at his apparent lack of self-consciousness. Ben threw more sticks on the fire then stepped over to the wagon. Minutes later, he brought her a bottle and a canteen. She noticed his lips were oddly pale before he stepped away.

"Thank you," Evie watched, amazed as Ben returned to the wagon. She cleared her throat. "What are you doing?"

"Going to start some coffee."

"Aren't you going to get dressed?"

Ben walked past her, pot in hand to the fire. "Taking care of you first."

"I'm fine."

"Did you drink the whiskey?"

"I will."

"Do it now."

"You're going to catch your death."

"Does that worry you?" Ben stepped over, wedged the coffee pot between two fire ring rocks to heat near the flames.

"Yes."

"That wasn't my intention." He stood, took a couple of steps, stopped beside a pile of clothes and started to dress.

Her head killing her, Evie took a healthy swig of the liquor and choked. She grabbed a canteen, tilted it back and gulped down water.

"Though to be honest, I rather enjoyed you watching me."

Evie spewed water for the second time that day. "What?"

"Are you all right?" Ben buttoned on pants that hung low on his hips. She couldn't help but think about the fact he wore nothing underneath.

"Fine," She sputtered, "Just fine."

He shrugged into his flannel, an old brown shirt, faded from years of use. She'd threatened to toss it out numerous times but he'd always resisted. His dimples on full display, he'd claim it was comfortable, just broken in. Her lips curved at the memory, she relaxed just a little.

"So tell me," he rolled his sleeves up to his elbows, "have you always liked to do that?"

Confused, her brows drew together. "What?"

"Watch me parade around naked?"

Chapter Twelve

Her jaw dropped. His slight smirk caught her attention, making it plain Ben expected a certain reaction. Her shock faded and resolve stiffened her spine. It was time to show him he wasn't the only one who knew how to play.

Her lips curved in a self-satisfied grin. "Yes."

Ben stilled. He blinked several times. "Excuse me?"

"Yes," her smile broadened, stretched across her face.

"Are you saying—?"

"That I enjoyed seeing your body, yes. I especially always loved skinny dipping with you."

"We..."

"Were married for five years, we did many things."

"I...I..." Ben shoved his feet into his boots. "I'm going to get more wood."

Evie chuckled under her breath as he swiftly walked away from her. She watched Ben use his coat as a bag and gathered more wood. Minutes later, he brought a load over. Sticks rained down onto the ground but before she could say anything, he moved off.

A short time passed, the sharp crack of a stick breaking floated through the trees. Evie could hear the murmur of Ben's voice, the soft sounds of his footsteps. Another moment then the mare, Sugar, wandered close, munched on grass and her husband returned. Instead of greeting him with lively words, she yawned, the whiskey and her dunking combined made her sleepy.

"Are we camping here?"

"I thought we'd get some rest then push on in the morning."

Evie yawned again. "Sound's good."

"When we reach a town, I want you looked at by a doctor."

"I'm okay."

"You could've died." His voice flat almost emotionless.

"But I didn't." Evie held his gaze, steady, serious. "And I don't need a doctor, I just need sleep."

A muscle ticked in his jaw. "Close your eyes, rest."

His abrupt, authoritative tone struck a nerve. Her lips parted, irritation poised for expression then he stepped near the fire. The deep lines of strain on his face killed her ill temper. She took a breath and waited, in silence, as he tended the flames, held his hands out to the warmth.

"Uh, Ben?"

"What's wrong?"

"Would you mind handing me some clothes?"

"Oh, yeah, sorry." he picked up the bag, handed it to her.

"Thanks," Evie patted his hand. "Now find something to do and let me get dressed before I fall asleep."

Her soft but firm command earned a wry smile and an attempt at good humor. "Okay, but I like you fine as you are."

"I appreciate that, but," Evie waved a hand out in a broad gesture to indicated their surroundings. "I'd hate to wake up naked as a jaybird if strangers rode by our camp."

"I see your point," animation again left his voice as Ben turned his back to her, moved closer to the fire.

Flames crackled, heat drifted on the air as Evie withdrew what she needed from the bag. Though awkward, she managed to slip into dry clothes within the warm cocoon of blankets. The effort depleted the remnants of her energy.

"All done," she rasped out, her stubborn pride clear. Wind

tossed hair around her face. She watched, amazed, as he walked off. "What are you doing?"

"Getting the rifle."

"You want to hunt?" Her voice rose to make sure he heard.

"I want it at hand."

The crisp concern evident in his reply reminded Evie of the miles of unfamiliar countryside around them. Her gaze swept their surroundings. "Okay."

Ben set the weapon down at her feet less than a minute later. He took the time to feed the fire then picked up their wet clothes. As he draped them over various branches, she bowed her head to conceal another yawn and started to get up.

"Stay where you are."

"I can help."

"No, stay there."

Her eyes narrowed at the curt command. "Excuse me?"

"Humor me," Ben's voice softened, "I'm worried about you."

"I'm fine."

"You need rest."

Grumpy now, she scooted back down, turned on her side and drew the covers up over her shoulders. She allowed her heavy eyelids to close. Her body relaxed and in seconds surrendered to sleep.

Dusk loomed by the time she woke. Evie sat up, blinked, groggy. "Ben?"

"Right here, how are you?"

"I need to get up."

"Okay," her husband drew out the word, his tone wary.

Limbs stiff and sore protested motion as she emerged from the blankets. Without sparing him a glance, Evie ignored the shadows that inched over every surface and stumbled away. Not fully awake, she staggered like a drunk toward a thick brush.

"Are you all right?"

Cold, tired, her voice terse, "I've had better days."

"I understand." His whisper floated through the early evening. She heard his exhaustion clear as day.

His pallor worried her.

"Are you hurting?"

"I'm fine," his tone rough, weary though Ben shifted his weight from one foot to the other, restless. "You thirsty?"

"Yeah but…"

Before she could object, he trudged to the river, filled a couple of canteens and returned. When Ben returned, he poured Evie a cup of cool liquid. She took what he offered with a smile then watched amazed as he gulped down a large amount of water.

"Coffee?"

"That'd be wonderful but—"

"You want something to eat with it?"

"Maybe later," Evie put her empty cup down. "I'm not really hungry and I think you should—"

"You need to eat."

An unexpected stream of moonlight chased the darkness away. Frustrated with her husband, Evie looked up as she made a silent prayer for patience. The clouds had cleared. Faint glimmers of distant stars were visible. *No more rain. Thank God.*

"Did you hear what I said?" Irritation colored his tone.

"Sorry," she stepped up next to Ben, touched his arm in a gesture of apology. Evie noticed he'd lit a lantern and spread out some fixings on the tailgate beside it. "How about I fix something for us while you pour coffee?" Without waiting for his answer, she went over and put meat, butter and bread together then rejoined him, sat down on the edge of the bed. Her voice sweet persuasion, "please eat for me."

Once he accepted the food, her attention shifted to her own sandwich. Hunger suddenly became a need, and she sank her teeth into stale bread with enthusiasm. Gusts of cold wind blew through the trees, set off a round of shivers. She longed for her cloak to be dry but a quick glance revealed it hung heavy on a nearby branch, dripping. Ben reached behind her, brought a blanket up to her shoulders and tucked it around her.

She snuggled in the welcome warmth, "thank you."

"You're welcome." He handed her a cup of steaming coffee.

Her first sip birthed a murmur of delight. The hot, bitter brew trailed delightful warmth down to her stomach. Some honey would've improved it but it wasn't worth the effort to get back up and find the sweetener. They sat in companionable silence during the meal.

As soon as Ben finished, he got to his feet, fetched a length of rope and tied it between the two trees closest to the fire opposite them. Evie swallowed a sigh, brushed breadcrumbs off her skirt and joined him. Together they transferred all the wet clothing onto it to speed up the drying process.

"I'm going to water Sugar."

"Ben," Evie shook her head. "Come sit with me. Rest for a minute, she's fine."

"If I sit for long I won't get back up before morning."

Her husband looked as if the weight of the world rested on him. *Stubborn as ever.* She didn't say another word, knew arguing would be futile. While he was busy with the mare, Evie emptied the canteen into the pot and added a couple spoonfuls of coffee. The tantalizing aroma of strong brew soon filled the air.

Long moments later, with Sugar settled for the night, Ben returned to where she once more sat. He wrapped his coat sleeve around the pot's handle then carried it over to Evie and studied her in the flickering firelight. "More coffee?"

"Definitely."

Ben filled their cups, set the pot safely to one side then sat next to her. "Cold?"

"A little."

Ben shrugged out of his coat and draped it around her.

His body heat radiated from the garment and warmed her on

many levels. "Thank you."

"I should've given it to you before. I don't know where my head is."

"You're fine."

Ben shook his head then drank some coffee. After a few swallows, he set his cup down. He tugged his boots back off and put them close to the fire next to where she just noticed he'd put hers. Out of the bag, he drew out thick wool socks and pulled them on with a groan of satisfaction. He glanced down and before she could pull them out of sight, noticed her bare feet. With another shake of his head, he put another pair over her bare skin.

The simple, thoughtful gesture warmed her heart even as her toes felt like ice.

"How are you doing?" He shifted the blankets so they covered her legs as well.

"I'm fine."

"How's your head?" Ben waited to ask until she came back.

"Tolerable."

Side by side, they ate in silence. Evie washed down her last bite with the last of her coffee. After that, Ben refilled her cup repeatedly. They drained the pot over the next several minutes, more out of desire for the heat the hot liquid delivered than real thirst. She laid back, eyes closed, barely noticed when Ben stretched out beside her. For a few seconds, she relaxed then, inevitably, concern started to nag at her and, restless, she had to get up.

Back at the fire, Evie fed dying flames while cold leached up from the dense soil. Shivers rocked her even though she held Ben's coat tight around her. She shifted from one sock covered foot to another and hovered near the tiny blaze.

"We should move our bed under the wagon in case it starts to rain again." Ben's weary voice floated out of the shadows.

Tired to the bone the task seemed enormous. "Must we?"

"It'd be best. I don't think either of us needs soaked again tonight."

When Ben stepped into the edges of the fire light, Evie noticed that he looked as tired as she felt. She grimaced but didn't object further. Together they grabbed the thin pallet, blankets and all and moved it. He immediately crawled into bed.

"Come here, lay down with me."

"In a minute," Evie returned to the fire.

Ben pressed her. "I'm still half frozen and I'd wager you feel the same. Together we'll stay warm as the fire dies down."

"Yes but..." Words escaped her, Evie shook her head, she was being silly. "I'll be right there." She banked the fire.

"Good," his tone weary, his brief smile wan. "Hurry."

"I will." She grabbed her bag, the rifle and strode back to the wagon quickly, the dark made her heart race.

The night seemed alive with murmurs of life as she stood by the tailgate to repack the supply box without care. Evie told herself she was fine repeatedly under her breath. At last, she shoved the box into the bed, closed the tailgate and put out the lantern. As she knelt down, Ben shifted over, made room for her to scoot in beside him.

"Do you have the rifle?"

Inches separated them, darkness an intimate cocoon. Evie felt Ben's proximity. She took off the coat, spread it out on top of the blankets then pulled the weapon beneath the covers, against her side.

"Yes."

"Good." His voice husky, he reached with one arm and drew her close against him. "So where were we? You like skinny dipping?"

Her head pillowed on his shoulder, she smiled. "yes."

His lips grazed her forehead. "I wish I could remember that." His arm tightened around her a second. "Sweet dreams."

"Sweet dreams," she echoed.

Soon his even breathing told Evie he slept but she still couldn't settle down. She breathed deep and steady. When that failed, she counted sheep. Over a hundred woolly creatures jumped through her imagination to no avail. She rolled onto her back, stared up at the wooden boards above her, frustrated.

All of a sudden, Ben started to breathe more deeply. The constant familiar rumble comforted her. The anxiety melted away. *Some things never change.* Her muscles relaxed and within moments, sleep claimed her.

"Evie," his urgent whisper jerked her awake shortly after.

Still mostly asleep, she yawned more than spoke. "What?"

"Shh, quiet, I heard something."

"What?" She asked again but this time in a wide-awake whisper.

Clouds drifted above, covered the moon. She gripped his arm, hard. Her gaze darted around, tried to pierce the shadows.

"I think who might be a better question."

Distinctive clomps drifted through the gloom. Horses were approaching. She eased up into a sitting position, the rifle in her grip.

"Go." In a voice taunt with tension, he ordered, "hide."

Evie scrambled to her feet, grabbed the coat. "But I—"

"Don't argue, just go."

"But what if—"

"Now Evie," Ben flicked a glance at her, his expression fierce as he eased the pistol out of her bag.

Sick with fear and worry, she stumbled away, trusted that her husband wouldn't have sent her out in the dark without good cause. Sticks snapped under hooves. She moved faster. Ben's sense of danger had saved them more than once. Even after her vision adjusted to the pitch black, she tripped and almost fell a number of times. Her choices limited Evie crouched in a dense cluster of trees opposite the wagon and waited.

Seconds crawled by like hours. *Only desperate people ride in the dead of night, desperate for help or...*

The rank odor of stale sweat saturated the air. Two men rode past her, within yards, straight toward the glowing coals of the fire. *Dear God.* Her body tense as a bow, she held her breath.

Evie shrank further back into the shroud of shadows, prayed they concealed her. She buttoned on Ben's jacket. One shaking hand at a time, she wiped damp palms on her skirt then took careful aim. Her finger rested against the trigger, ready to squeeze if necessary.

"It's a little late for visiting, gentlemen." Ben's deep voice rang through the night.

Silent expectation ruled the darkness for a heartbeat.

"We want our money Rolfe." The man on the left responded.

Clouds parted. The moonlight revealed the riders to be the men from Cedar Ridge. Before she decided if that fact relieved or terrified her, a crack sounded somewhere behind her and to her left. She turned. Her gaze caught the movement of a person creeping toward Ben.

Evie brought her weapon to bear and in a low, lethal tone warned. "Stop right there or I'll put a hole in your gut."

The man froze then slowly turned his face and stared in her direction. Evie's skin crawled. Shadows twisted his features into a sinister mask. She tightened her grip on the smooth wood of her rifle stock but didn't waver.

"Walk over and join your friends slow and easy now." Evie ordered. She wanted the men gathered in one place. "Any sudden moves and I'll show you just how good a shot I am."

"Yes ma'am." He replied, his voice tinged with insolence, and then with exaggerated slowness complied.

Evie kept him in her sights every step of the way. Nerves taut with fear, she kept her finger on the trigger, ready to address any threat.

"I've nothing for you." Ben announced when they reached the others. He cocked the pistol, the sound ominous. "It's best you *gentlemen* ride on."

One of the mounted men pulled his cohort up on his horse behind him. "This isn't settled, Rolfe, not by a long shot."

His expression grim in a cast of moonlight, Ben offered no response. A long moment passed in edgy silence then the men rode off, disappeared. Tension palatable, Evie locked gazes with her husband. They waited, listened long after the hoof beats faded into the distance.

Her ears strained for any sound that the men doubled back but heard nothing alarming. Night sounds had resumed. Crickets chirped. Frogs croaked. Still, Evie couldn't calm down. She took a step toward Ben.

"Go hide in another spot."

The barely audible words sent fresh fear skittering down her spine. Her voice hushed, "you think they'll come back?"

"They followed us all this time only to give up without a fight, not even an argument? Way too easy to believe. I doubt they went far and I'm certain they'll be back."

Evie slumped. She lowered the rifle from her shoulder and cradled it, waited. Weariness pushed against her need to take action. Her steps dragged as she moved to a new position some yards to her husband's left.

Evie leaned against a tree, and waited. Over time when nothing happened, her eyes drifted half-shut. The faint call of a coyote, a lonely song from nature, became her lullaby. In the next heartbeat, her peace shattered.

Her eyes opened wide. The thunder of several horses shook the earth beneath her feet. Evie straightened, terrified.

Cold fingers reached out and brushed hair off her face. A scream crawled up her throat then died before it crossed her lips as her eyes narrowed to slits and she shot daggers at Ben. Before she could give him a piece of her mind, a large group of riders rode into their camp guns drawn.

Control hung by a thread. It hurt to breathe. She brought the rifle up once more. Ben took aim beside her.

"I'm Marshal Myers." The man in the lead of at least a dozen others spoke in a voice that rang with authority. "Don't make my men beat the brush for you. Things will go easier if you boys step out now."

"Sheriff." Her jaw dropped as Ben lowered his pistol and complied. "We're glad to see you."

"We?" Marshal Myers pounced on that information. His gaze found her in seconds. Her fingers tightened into a painful grip on the weapon, her only defense. "Ma'am."

"Sweetheart, put the rifle down. I'm certain the sheriff and his men will help us."

A rushing sound filled her ears. Ben's calm voice seemed to come from far away. The weight of numerous stares further unsettled her. Evie swayed. Hysterical laughter threatened to spill from her lips as she lowered the weapon.

"I'd appreciate it if you'd join us." The undercurrent of steel in the sheriff's polite tone made it clear it wasn't a request but a command.

A couple of men dismounted and collected their weapons while Evie walked to Ben's side. His arm curved around her as the lawman dismounted, stepped close then blistered her ears with an explosive curse.

"Sorry about the language ma'am." His tone echoed pure frustration. Marshal Myers holstered his revolver. "We're hunting three cowards who robbed an old widow woman." He ripped off his hat, slapped it against his thigh then slammed it back on his balding head. "Their trail led here. When we spotted your fire, we thought we'd caught them."

"We're not criminals."

"I'm inclined to believe you ma'am. I—"

"But those men were here."

"You know them?" The weathered man's eyes narrowed in suspicion, his hand on the butt of his gun.

Exasperated, she burst out. "I didn't say that."

"Honey," Ben patted her hand. "Let me handle this." His steady gaze held hers until Evie nodded then he turned to meet Marshal

Myers scrutiny. "Three men rode up an hour ago, maybe less. We don't know them but we had a run in with two of them a couple of days ago in Cedar Ridge."

"What happened?"

"They threatened my wife and demanded money, claimed I cheated them at cards."

"Any truth to that?"

"I don't remember ever seeing them before."

"And tonight?"

"They demanded money again. Rode off when I threatened to shoot."

"Which way did they go?"

"North," Ben pointed to illustrate. "But I have a gut feeling they'll come back after us."

"John, you and Robert stay here with me in case those polecats return. Jason, take the rest of the men and track them down." In less than a minute, the posse departed. The older man turned back to them and extended his hand. "Marshal Robert Myers."

"Ben Rolfe and this is my wife, Evie." Her husband clasped the older man's hand.

The sheriff doffed his hat. "Ma'am," he greeted Evie.

Suddenly, shouts and gunshots broke the pre-dawn quiet. At once, the sheriff and his men sprinted to their mounts and raced off. For a moment, they didn't move, listened to the loud disturbance in the distance. Her teeth started to chatter. Ben indicated with a sweep of his arm their rumpled blankets.

"Shall we try getting some sleep?"

"No." Exhausted but wide-awake from the drama, Evie stood next to him, fidgeted, restless. "I don't think I can and besides the sun's coming up. Also we don't know if those dreadful men have been caught or not and I'm sure the sheriff will be back."

"How about we pull the bed out, crawl under the covers and get warm again?"

"Seems silly that we keep moving it here then there," she

grumbled even as she helped him move the thin mattress.

A breeze brushed over her, Evie shivered, chilled. She burrowed under the blankets, his coat still on, and pulled them up to her chin. Ben slid in behind, squeezed her against him.

"You were very brave. I think that man believed you'd have shot him."

"That was my intention." His solid warmth comforted her.

"Of course it was."

Sunrise painted dull gray clouds with a brilliant display of color. The note of disbelief in his voice had her turn over, look straight at him. "You don't believe me?"

"It was dark my dear, how good a shot are you really?"

A corner of her mouth curved up in a half smile but her tone was dead serious. "You taught me."

"That tells me nothing; you could've been a poor student."

"I'm an exceptional student," Evie placed her hands on his chest. "Who excelled at *everything* you've ever taught me."

Chapter Thirteen

His eyes darkened. Ben lifted one hand. Fingers traced the contours of her face. Evie felt the furious beat of his heart beneath her palms. His gaze held hers captive while his light caress moved down the side of her neck, over her shoulder then down her back. He pressed her close, palm flattened over her spine, tight against him.

Evie moved one hand up to the back of his neck, entwined her fingers in his shaggy hair. With slow, deliberate intent, she stretched upward. Her lips hovered just below his a moment then touched. Her kiss feather light was a taste, a tease, but no more. She drew back just enough to share a look. With a low growl of pure need, Ben seized control.

His mouth covered hers, hungry. Passion blazed through her veins. Evie wound both arms around his neck, strained closer and responded in equal measure. The kiss grew wild, raw with need. He broke it off, his breath hard and fast and looked at her. Her embrace tightened as she made an incoherent sound of protest, unwilling to let him go.

"Evie," his voice husky with desire, he eased back. She refused to allow it. Every inch he scooted back, she moved forward. "Stop."

"Why?"

"Are you sure you want this?"

"Yes."

"I'm not talking about kisses. I wanted to take this slow, and court you properly but," strong emotion flickered across his face. "I almost lost you. I need you." His gaze held such power her heart pounded harder. "If we continue now I don't know if I can stop."

Evie released her grip. Her hands came up, framed his face. "I don't want you to."

For long seconds he didn't speak, move or respond in any way. The silence started to crush her. Finally, Ben lifted one hand, took hold of one of hers, and shifted slightly to graze his lips on her palm. His gaze still locked on hers, his mouth then tasted the sensitive skin of her inner wrist. Evie sucked in an audible breath. His lips left a trail of heat as he worked his way up her arm to the crook of her elbow. He nibbled there and desire pulsed through her veins.

"Ben," his name whispered on her exhale.

Green eyes now almost black snared her. He moved his grip, tangled his fingers in the hair at the nape of her neck. "Are you sure?"

The answer burst from her, "Yes."

With aching slowness, her husband brought his lips down to taste hers. She looped her arms around his neck. Ben increased the intensity of the kiss so slowly Evie wanted to cry with frustration. Pressure parted her lips. His tongue darted in, explored, teased. He coaxed, seduced, set her nerves on fire.

One hand roamed the length of her back, caught her hip in a tight grip. His kiss became demanding, wild. Clear, sharp longing overwhelmed her. Her hand moved down, unfastened his top button. Evie breathed in his scent and wanted more. Eager to touch more of him, feel his flesh, her fingers tugged at the next button.

Without warning, he broke off the kiss, pulled back. She reached up and tried to renew contact. "Ben?"

"Stop." A hand on her shoulder held her fast.

Pure need, hot and urgent, demanded satisfaction and blinded her to all but what she wanted. Evie moved against him, "please."

"Listen," His insistent tone pierced her desire's haze.

Evie stilled. Her eyes closed. The sound of approaching horses doused her passion as fast as if he'd thrown her back in the icy waters of the nearby river. A bitter wave of resentment crashed over her and her eyes opened to slits when her husband scrambled out of the blankets to stand beside the bed.

A scowl pulled down the corners of her mouth. Everything unpleasant in the last few weeks had been heralded by thundering hooves. Evie threw back the covers and joined her husband. If this kept up, she'd seriously try to persuade Ben to work with something other than horses. Her frown deepened. Without his memory, what dreams would he chase?

Troubled on more than one level, her gaze sought the cause of her initial displeasure. The sheriff and one of his men were easy to spot, approaching fast. As Evie noted the unobstructed view, her face heated. She cringed at what they might have seen had her husband not heard them. Awkwardness and tension between them, she and Ben stood silent, side-by-side, until the men pulled up.

"Did you get them?"

"Sure did ma'am," The sheriff looked worn but pleased. "My men are taking them to Elk Bend as we speak."

"Thank God," her voice reflected heartfelt relief.

"Indeed," Marshal Myers acknowledged her then directed his man to hand their weapons to Ben. "I wanted to return these."

"Thank you."

"I don't mean to be rude but it's been a long night and we'd like to get home. If you don't need anything, we'll be off."

"Do you happen to know how far we are from Oregon?"

"If you head out soon and keep a good pace you'll probably reach it in a few days. Planning to settle there?"

"Yes we are."

"Safe journey then, I hope this good weather holds."

"Thank you," Ben stretched up a hand to each man in turn then without further ado, the men rode off. Alone again, her husband turned to her, a wry grin on his face. "Any chance we could pick up where we left off?"

Evie resisted the urge to roll her eyes. Sunshine started to ease the morning chill. She stared at him, allowed him to read her expression.

"I'm guessing that's a no."

Her arms crossed over her chest. She tilted her head to one side. Her lips pressed together, her mouth a thin line.

"Instead we could get an early start on the road."

One eyebrow arched but otherwise Evie didn't move.

"Or we could eat?"

Breath exploded from her in a huff. Evie snatched the pistol from him as she shook her head. "I'm tired. I'm going to lie down and sleep. You're welcome to join me but that's all we're doing right now and heaven help me, I'll shoot the first thing that rides in, man or beast, that disturbs my rest."

"Yes ma'am."

Desperate for sleep, she turned, stomped over to their bed and crawled under the covers. Evie placed the gun within easy reach. Her eyes closed. Crisp air tingled her nose while she tried to relax, listened to Ben move around until, at last, he lay down next to her.

"Can I hold you?"

Weary, the comfort he offered was irresistible. Evie moved over, stretched out near him. Ben pulled her closer, tucked her against him so her head rested on his shoulder, his chin on the top of her head, an arm cradled her to his warmth. The sound of water lapping at the nearby bank soothed her. In seconds, she was asleep.

Sometime later, Evie woke. She looked up through the thin canopy of branches above her, clear blue painted the sky. The sun's rays filtered down to warm her face. Her husband's soft snoring made her grin. Careful not to wake him, she inched away from Ben, eased out from under the quilts then smoothed them back over him.

Evie studied her husband a moment after she got up. Though his bruises had faded, the pallor of his skin still worried her. She reached down, her hand gentle, touched his face. Ben had always healed fast. Fingers brushed over a cheek roughened with dark whiskers. She hoped all he needed was rest.

Her gaze swept the area for her shoes and found them a few feet away. Feet cold, she hurried to her target without pause. Evie found her boots mostly dry but clammy. She grimaced but pulled them on.

Hours late, Evie tackled the morning chores. She uncovered coals and coaxed their heat into a steady blaze. Hungry she next got out a pan, sliced bacon into it and set it near the flames to cook. After adding more wood to the fire, she readied the coffee pot then put it near the pan. She sought privacy in the brush then went down to the river to wash up and fill the canteens while breakfast cooked.

Although the sun was almost directly overhead by the time Evie returned, her husband still slept. In silence, unwilling to disturb Ben, she stirred the meat, sliced potatoes and onions into the pan to cook in the grease. The sound of movement to her left startled her as she finished her task. With the knife clenched in her hand, she turned and discovered Sugar.

Guilt swept through her. She should've tended the horse as soon as she got up. Evie hurried to do just that. Afterwards while she warmed her hands over the fire and checked on their food, her gaze wondered over the vast countryside. A flicker of disquiet shot through her. With her husband asleep, she was, in effect, alone.

A few quick strides brought her to his side. The snoring man didn't skip a beat. Nervous, she plucked up the pistol and put it in her skirt pocket. Evie noted the rifle on the ground near Ben as she sat down on the edge of the pallet.

With weapons and husband in reach, she felt secure. She pulled out her brush, worked out the tangles. Nerves steadied, she put it away then went to check on their meal, her fingers on the gun for reassurance. She moved the pan away from the fire, breakfast fully cooked, but before going to wake Ben, she checked their clothing. A few touches discovered they were nearly dry.

Pine needles crunched. Another footfall sounded behind her, loud. Evie reached in her pocket for the pistol as she turned. A hand touched her shoulder and she let out a shriek.

"Ben!"

"Yes?"

"Stop sneaking up on me." She put the firearm away.

"Have you always been this jumpy?"

Evie pulled in a breath, blew it out. "Yes you used to think it was great fun to make me jump or scream."

"Sounds irritating."

"It was," her voice softened as sweet memories came to mind. "But I loved how you'd make up to me afterwards."

Ben smiled then leaned down to press a soft, lingering kiss on her lips. "Was it something like this?"

"Yes, yes it was." She breathed. "Are you hungry?"

"Yes I am."

Evie smiled broadly. "Good, breakfast's ready."

"Not quite what I had in mind but it looks good all the same, I'm starved," Ben fetched them each a cup, spoon and plate. As soon as she dished up, he took a bite. "This is very good, thank you."

"You're welcome."

Ben poured them each some coffee then they sat on the end of the pallet. "It's a pretty day."

"It is."

"Warmer."

"The sun feels good." Her gaze followed a robin, hopping along a branch.

Silence fell for several moments as they ate. She relaxed, satisfied her hunger, soaked up the sunshine. It felt like they were alone in the world, peaceful.

"Evie?"

"Hmmm."

"I was wondering. Did we farm?"

"What?"

"You said I didn't start the drinking and gambling after we lost our baby—"

"James," She interjected softly.

"James," Ben echoed, paused to touch her hand, a silent acknowledgement of their loss. "If losing James didn't make me want rotgut whiskey what did?"

Sadness weaved through Evie. "It doesn't matter."

"It does to me," His voice soft, wistful.

"You can't change the past."

"What past? The one where I'm a miner dreaming of how perfect my life will be when I'm a cowboy out west or the one where I wake up with a bitter, angry stranger, who says my dreams ended in crushing disappointment?"

She flinched. "Why do you want to know now? You didn't seem to want details before."

"Yes I did," Ben disagreed gently. "I asked but you didn't want to talk about it. I thought I'd remember."

"You haven't remembered anything?"

The sorrow in his eyes stunned. He shook his head. "I'm starting to believe I never will."

"I'm sorry."

"Not your fault."

"I'm still sorry, I can't imagine..."

"What it's like to have a big gaping hole in your life."

Evie laid her hand on his forearm.

Silence ruled again for a few minutes.

"I know you can't fill in every minute I've lost but I need you to paint a picture for me and, if you'd be so kind, include a few details of times when I wasn't a good for nothing husband."

"Like skinny dipping?" She tried to lighten the mood but her tone fell flat the weight of unpleasant memories.

"I'd enjoy that, but right now would you tell me what I was doing to support us in Cedar Ridge and what went wrong?"

"Okay." Restless, Evie stood, took his things and put them in the pan. "We had land, a cow and a few chickens." She got soap and a cloth from the wagon then headed to the river with the dishes. Ben followed. "We'd planned to sow a couple of crops; corn and hay. So I guess you could say we farmed but..."

"I messed it up? I didn't like it?"

"You liked it fine but the farm was just survival, shelter, food, and you wanted more." She knelt down, grabbed a handful of gravel and scrubbed the pan.

Ben sat down, washed dishes with her. "To be successful."

"To be rich," she lifted a shoulder in a half shrug. "Show everyone your wealth."

"Sounds like splitting hairs."

"So you've often said."

"You disapprove?"

"Other people's opinions shouldn't matter so much." Cold water made her hands ache while she rinsed the dishes. Evie pushed up to her feet with a soft exhale then continued. "You decided to capture wild horses, tame and train them."

"Was I any good at it?"

"You did okay, sold a couple and had satisfied customers."

"What happened?" They started back to the wagon.

Her teeth sawed on her lower lip while she contemplated the simplest way to explain the messy circumstances. "A neighbor claimed you stole some of the horses off his ranch."

"Did I?" His voice rough, expression stone faced, Ben faced her square when they stopped at the tailgate.

Empathy swelled as she struggled to answer. "The property lines weren't marked. We learned that the canyon where you'd caught most of the horses was on the Blakes' ranch. With the judge being a relative of the rancher's wife, we were lucky he dismissed the theft charges and allowed you to keep two horses."

"How'd I get so *lucky*?"

"By pure chance the sheriff witnessed you catching those particular ones on our land, near where it bordered the Blakes' property. He testified that he believed you'd made an honest mistake." Evie took out a towel dried the dishes then handed them to Ben who repacked the box.

"So I started staying out to all hours drinking."

Her stomach clenched at his hollow tone. Memories flashed through her mind. Tears blurred her vision but Evie refused to let them fall. She moved over to the pallet and started to fold up their bedding unable to stay still.

"Not at first."

Ben joined her and together they made short work of the task. He waited until they had loaded their mattress, and then pressed her for more. "What happened then?"

"You got discouraged easily after we lost James. It was like your emotions were raw all the time." Evie held his gaze a moment then walked over to gather their hanging clothes. Ben took the time to kill the fire. She felt his expectation in the silence. "It was difficult to find buyers after that and easy to find trouble. You started riding off alone and coming home late."

"Drunk?"

Arms full she still managed to wind up the rope. "Yes."

Back at the wagon, she put their things away then secured the tailgate. Her husband walked past, headed to Sugar as Evie shrugged out of his coat. She carried it along with her cloak up to stand near Ben while he hitched up the mare.

As soon as he finished with Sugar, Ben helped his wife up onto the seat. Pensive, he climbed up next to Evie and set them in motion. They bumped over rocky, uneven ground for a number of minutes until they rolled back onto the road. Countryside; wild, dotted with oak and pine, surrounded them.

"It seems I've become what I least wanted to be."

"What's that?"

"A man who chases after every *sure thing* and always fails."

"Like your father."

"I told you about him?"

"Just that you didn't want to be like him. You never said much about him or your family. I assume talking about the fire is painful."

"The fire?"

"The one they died in."

Ben stiffened. "I told you that?"

"Yes."

"That's not right," his hands tightened on the reigns. "My father died in a prison fight while serving time for robbery. Mom just faded away after that. I buried her a year later. There was no fire."

"Your father was an outlaw."

"My father was a petty thief who spent more time in jail then at home."

"So you lied to me?"

"It appears so," his voice strained.

"Did Henry know?"

Ben shook his head. "As far as I remember, no. I'm ashamed of my family. I didn't talk about them and Henry never asked. But you must have."

"Yes, I did. What about your brother? What happened to him?"

"I honestly don't know. Michael's a younger, more charming version of our father. He wanted to be just like Dad and I wanted to be a better man. I haven't seen or heard from him, that I know of, since we buried our mother."

They hit a rough patch in the road. A long series of bone rattling bumps interrupted the conversation. As soon as their path smoothed he glanced over at his wife. Her face had paled.

"You're mad at me?"

The mare moved forward at a brisk, steady pace. A good mile or so passed. Evie took so long to answer he started to wonder if she would.

"I don't know what I feel right now."

Her sad whisper struck a chord within him. "I'm sorry."

"Why?"

"For upsetting you. I seem to do it a lot."

"No," Evie shook her head. "Why'd you lie?"

"Good question." Ben stared down the road ahead. Long minutes went by while he struggled against the blankness in his mind. "My best guess is that I was embarrassed."

Another long awkward pause then, "but you aren't now?"

"Oh I am," his jaw worked, he couldn't look at her. "But I'm not going to lie about it."

"What changed?"

"You've made it plain how important it is for me to be absolutely truthful with you."

Her tone, soft, sorrowful, "you've always known that."

"Evie, I couldn't have known that when I first met you."

"True," she conceded, "but you had five years to tell me the truth."

"I don't know what else to say, other than I'm sorry."

Ben glanced at his wife. Her face averted, she seemed to look off in the distance. Over the course of the afternoon the conversation remained awkward and strained, despite his efforts to put things right. Discouraged, he almost welcomed silence.

As dusk chased daylight away Evie dozed, her head on his shoulder. While looking for a good spot to stop for the night, he noticed a farmhouse set back a short distance from the road on his left. A deep-seated urge to try to make up for the past triggered the thought that his wife might enjoy a night off the cold, hard ground. A few minutes later, Ben pulled up in the farmer's yard and an older couple emerged.

"Evie," her husband coaxed her from slumber. She sat up straight and yawned while Ben continued. "I found us a place to stay tonight."

"Mmhmm," she rubbed her hands over her face.

"I'll help you down in a minute."

"Okay."

The seat squeaked as Ben left. Evie heard him jump down, tracked his footfalls until she judged her husband was next to her then opened her eyes. She gasped. The homeliest man she'd ever seen filled her vision.

Suddenly the man smiled and his face transformed. His eyes, a deep brown, crinkled at the corners, radiated warmth that enveloped her. Although still far from handsome, his kind expression reminded Evie of her late grandfather.

"This is Edwin Way." Her gaze flicked left, noticed Ben waited, arms stretched up for her. "He and his wife kindly offered shelter for the night."

Evie climbed down with Ben's assistance.

"Sorry I startled you ma'am," Edwin offered her his hand.

Her smile shy, she shook his hand. "Call me Evie."

"Good to meet you Evie," in a sweeping gesture he indicated the person on the porch behind him, illuminated by the light the poured through the open front door. The birdlike woman's white hair, braided, fell to her waist. She had pleasant features and her smile was broad and warm. "This is my wife, Ella."

After an exchange of greetings, Ella led her into the house while the men stabled Sugar. At the end of a narrow hall, they entered a cozy bedroom. A sturdy four-poster oak bed with plump pillows dominated the space. To her right sat a large dresser and on the left was a mirrored vanity topped with a basin of water, soap, a washcloth and a towel.

"Thank you," Evie put her bag down on the floor by the bed.

"You're quite welcome," Ella paused. "Have you eaten?"

"No but we'll be fine."

"You must eat with us then, it's no trouble. Freshen up, rest a little and I'll wake you when dinner is ready."

Before she could object, Ella left a lit lamp on the dresser and closed the door behind her. Evie stood a moment, stunned, still half-asleep then stepped to the mirror. Lips pressed into a white line, she strode up to the vanity focused on her tousled appearance. She scrubbed with lavender scented soap then brushed out her hair.

Her gaze swung to the lush bed and pillows. The desire to rest on that softness was a physical ache. Evie hung the cloth she'd used over the edge of the basin and yawned. Her eyes closed for a split second. Her knee knocked against solid wood furniture.

Unladylike words flashed through her mind. Her fingers pinched the bridge of her nose until the worst of the throbbing subsided. Evie blew out the lamp, limped over to the bed and sat on the edge. Her eyes half closed, one hand over another she clawed back the covers and crawled in. Her head sank on the feather pillow. Snuggled in soft warmth, she slept.

The creak of the door opening accompanied by the aroma of fried chicken awakened Evie. She opened her eyes, looked over to see Ben enter the room. Her husband carried a candle, a soft glow in the dark, as he came to her side.

"Did you get some sleep?"

"Yes," Evie sat up. Pleasant surprise filled her. For the first time in a long time, she felt rested. "I did."

"Good." Ben put the candle down on the nightstand then touched her cheek, briefly, as though he couldn't resist the contact. "Dinner is ready."

Her stomach grumbled. "It smells wonderful."

"I'll let you get ready." He crossed to the doorway in a few quick strides. "The kitchen is at the end of the hall."

The door closed as Evie got out of bed. She splashed her face and quickly braided her hair. Ready, she took the candle and stepped out of the room. Her husband's familiar deep voice rumbled through the house, led her to straight to him.

Ella wiped her hands on her apron then carried a plate stacked high with biscuits to the small table in the center of the room when Evie walked in. She greeted the older couple as Ben rose from his chair, seated her beside him. The bounty of food before her made her mouth water.

Crispy chicken sat on a platter with bowls on either side, one with creamy potatoes, and the other with peas. Evie soon realized that for Ella and Edwin, company was rare. Long after she had eaten her fill, the other couple lingered, engaged in pleasant but long conversation. The hour was late when Ben excused himself to check on the mare while Evie helped clean up.

The lamp washed the bedroom in light when she entered. Ben already lay in the bed. Evie blew out the light, changed into her nightgown in the dark. With soft, slow steps, she moved over to the bed, slipped in beside her husband.

"We need to talk about this."

"You need sleep," her tone held reluctance and concern.

"I'm fine," blunt to the point of impatient, Ben assured her. "And ignoring it won't solve anything."

Her sigh filled the room, "I'm not sure talking about it will either." Tension pulsed. "It's an issue of trust."

"You don't trust me?"

"I'd like to."

Ben reached down took one cold hand in his, entwined their fingers, squeezed. "Then do."

"How can I," Evie turned to face him, her voice taut with pain. "When you lie to me?"

Chapter Fourteen

Darkness shrouded them, "I'm not lying to you now."

"But you have."

"We've been over this—" A floorboard creaked. Muffled voices carried through the wall, reminded them that the old couple were in the next room. Ben lowered his voice to a whisper. "I can't change what I did in the past."

Her fingers caressed the quilt cover. Chest tight, her voice hoarsened with raw emotion. "And I'm not certain I can forget it."

"Can you forgive it?"

His question uttered so soft she barely heard it. Her lips parted then closed again. Doubt nagged at her. The back of her throat burned. Words flitted through her mind but Evie didn't know what to tell him.

"I don't know."

"It's difficult to be held responsible for things I've no memory of doing."

Frustration a common thread held and bound them in a web of their own creation. Evie shook her head. She knew it wasn't fair. "I'm sorry."

"Couldn't you just take me as I am now, ignore our past, give me a little trust?" His tone threaded with resentment.

"No," she voiced weary aggravation. "I can't and trust isn't given, it's earned."

"Fine, so how do I earn yours?"

Her anxiety heightened another notch, "I don't know."

"If we're going to stay married we better figure this out."

Her heart slowed. "Are you threatening to leave me?"

"No," his denial came hard, emphatic then he continued in a measured voice. "But I think," Ben startled her by getting out of bed. In quick, rough motions, he removed his clothes then lay down beside her again but only pulled the sheet up to his waist. "That without trust or at least the possibility of trust, there isn't much of a marriage."

His words, at first, barely made an impression, his actions so confounded her. Evie stared at Ben for a long moment before her scattered thoughts reformed. "Why did you do that?"

"Do what? Undress?" Surprise raised his voice.

Evie breathed in and blew out with force. "Yes."

"I was hot."

"You're naked," disconcerted, she tried to sound calm.

"Yes I know."

"We're in the middle of an important conversation."

"Yes," Ben drew out the word. "We are."

"So what are you doing? Are you just going to insist on—?"

"I'm not insisting on anything. I was hot."

"And so you stripped."

"Yes," he bit out, impatient, irritated. "So what?"

"You're naked." Heat crawled up her neck.

"You've already pointed that out."

Her tone strained, "you need to put something on."

"Why?"

"Because…" Like a moth to a flame, he drew her in. His form vague, a dense shadow, but his body heat radiated across the inches that separated them, scorched her, "…you do."

"It's late. I'm tired. My side hurts like the devil. The pain had me sweating so badly my shirt is about soaked. You've seen me naked before. I woke up in that cabin without a stitch of clothes on so why does it bother you now?"

"Because...I just. Before...you..."

A long-suffering breath escaped him. "I don't know what I did or didn't do with you before. I can only be as I am right now which is hot and flat out exhausted."

"But I—"

"Oh for the love of—" Ben turned away. She heard him grab something off the floor then he continued. "If it bothers you so bad I'll—"

"Stop." the absurdity of the situation sank in. She'd seen this man nude countless times and had slept in his arms, skin to skin, "I'm being silly."

"Yes you are," his ready agreement tinged with agitation.

"Stay as you are."

Movement stilled. "Are you sure?"

No. With his chest only inches away, her fingers itched to touch bare flesh. Troubled by that distraction, her voice was soft, uncertain. "Yes."

"Okay then," Clothing hit the floor, Ben reclined, his head on the pillow. Minutes passed. Another long pause marked by tense silence in this awkward exchange. He released an audible breath. "I wasn't trying to make you uncomfortable."

"I know." Her teeth chewed on the inside of her cheek. She felt nervous and ridiculous. The situation, both familiar and strange, seemed frightfully intimate.

"I think for both our sakes, you need to make a decision."

"About?"

"Whether or not you can trust me."

The butterflies in her stomach morphed into hummingbirds. Her temple throbbed. She lifted a hand to rub it. "You know I can't simply decide to do that."

"Why not?"

"As I said, trust is earned."

"But you won't say how I can earn it." His words, delivered in a cool, polite tone, set her teeth on edge.

Vexed, she snapped, "because I don't know."

"This conversation is pointless." The hollow exhaustion in his tone revealed how badly Ben needed to rest.

Worry added another layer of concern. "How about we talk about this tomorrow? It's been a long day."

Silence hung heavy and thick. Long seconds lengthened into minutes. Her husband took so long to speak that Evie started to think he wouldn't answer at all.

"Very long," his leg brushed hers as he stretched. "All right, let's get some sleep."

His easy response and matter-of-fact tone startled her, almost made her want to push for a reaction. Instead, Evie took a deep breath, reminded herself sternly that she'd gotten what she'd asked for then shut her eyes.

"Good night."

"Good night."

Evie turned over, put her back to her husband. She tried to ignore the heat that radiated from him. With worry a common thread, one troubled thought after another chased through her mind. She scrunched the pillow, squirmed until comfortable then closed her eyes. A long time passed but sleep remained elusive.

Covers rustled, the mattress moved, Ben shifted. One long arm came up over her, settled on her waist. She stiffened then relaxed. Her husband pressed against her, gently. His warmth eased the chill in her heart. Safe in his embrace, she soon calmed.

The knocking made no sense. Evie looked around the grassy meadow, but couldn't find a source and so dismissed it. She smiled at her companion then urged her mount to a faster pace, laughed at the man who chased her, dared him to 'catch me if you can'.

A bronzed hand grabbed her reigns. Her heart pounded, her smile broadened. Their horses slowed, stopped under a tall oak tree. A strong arm snaked around her waist. The man pulled her in front of him, into his embrace.

His hand cupped her jaw tilted her face for his kiss. Her gaze travelled over his broad chest, the width of his shoulders and his firm jaw. Excitement danced through her veins as she gazed at his beloved face.

"Evie," her dream shattered as Ella knocked again, called to them from the other side of the door. "Ben, breakfast is ready."

"Thank you, we'll be right there." Her husband answered his voice gruff with sleep.

Reluctantly Evie opened her eyes, mourned the loss. She pushed hair off her face and crawled out of bed. A glance back at Ben caught him just after he'd thrown back the sheet. In the midst of a morning stretch, she froze. Riveted she watched her husband stand and start to dress. When he looked up, found her focused on him, she turned immediately and walked to the vanity.

"Good morning."

Her gaze met his in the mirror. "Morning."

Nervous Evie dug out her brush and tended her hair. While Ben pulled on his clothes, she stayed quiet. Minutes later, he excused himself and left the room. She completed her morning routine in short order. Hair tamed in her standard tidy braid, dress donned, she took a moment to put the room to rights then headed to the dining room.

"Good morning." Ellie flashed a smile at her as she set a plate stacked with pancakes down on the table. "Have a seat."

Evie sat. "Good morning."

"Did you sleep well?" The older woman placed a platter of sausages in front of her.

"Yes ma'am, thank you for breakfast and all your kindness."

"Young lady, I asked you to call me Ella yesterday."

"Yes ma'am, I mean Ella."

Evie caught a glimpse of the other woman's pleased smile as she bustled around the table, poured them each a steaming mug of coffee. She laced her strong brew with honey and cream and then wrapped her hands around the cup, breathed in the scent. After a couple of long sips, she set it down when Ellie sat down beside her. Edwin entertained them with funny stories about raising their children, long since grown, as they ate and time flew by.

After the pleasant meal, the older man went outside with Ben to hitch up Sugar. Evie enjoyed visiting with Ellie as she helped clean up the kitchen. It'd been a long time since she'd had the company of another woman. When they finished she took her leave with sincere reluctance. She gathered her bag from the bedroom then exited the house to seek the privy. Needing a moment to herself after attending her needs, she walked over to two giant oaks some yards distant on the other side of the yard.

In the shade beneath gnarled branches, a band tightened around her chest. Soon they'd be on their way. Sometime this day they'd resume last night's conversation and she still didn't know what to say. Faced away from the house, Evie stood and for several minutes stared out over the flat grassland. A pair of hawks swooped through the sky.

"Ready to go?"

The smack of boots against hard packed dirt warned her of Ben's approach long before he spoke.

"Aren't they beautiful?" She turned to face him, gestured toward the birds in flight. "It must be wonderful to be free."

"You all right?" His concern plain, he ignored her musing.

Evie considered lying then dismissed the idea. Honesty was necessary for their marriage to have a fighting chance. "No."

"What's wrong?"

"Everything," her anger flared without warning. Dull red splotches marred his wife's high cheekbones. A grimace twisted her lush lips. Her gaze met his, eyes bitter, burning orbs, a pale fire in startling contrast to her thick, dark lashes. "I should be at our cabin, not among strangers again." Tears welled in her eyes. Like a child she stomped her foot. "It's not fair."

Sympathy coursed through him as she thrust her hands into the pockets of her cloak, looked at the ground. He reached out, touched under her chin gently and tilted her face up until she met his gaze. Beneath the obvious signs of fury, her otherwise ghost white face revealed a woman under tremendous strain. Ben moved his hand, cupped her jaw.

"No it's not."

The soft-spoken words of accord drew a strangled scream of frustration from Evie. Tears wet her cheeks. The light in her sapphire eyes dimmed. His fingers moved over her face, caressed her skin, offered silent comfort. A pained sigh emerged from her.

"You can't understand." Her misery tangible, Evie made a half hearted effort to step back.

Ben wrapped his arms around her. Evie allowed him to pull her close, embrace her. He tucked her head against his shoulder and pressed a light kiss on her hair. "Maybe not totally, but I get that it's not fair. Nothing about this is fair for you."

Her emotional storm tempered. She leaned in, absorbed his warmth. Her breath slowed, mood mellowed. Guilt pricked Evie as the minutes passed. She tried to pull free.

"I don't know what came over me."

Ben refused to let go, hugged her closer. "You're fine."

"No, no I'm not." Her lips twitched in a sad attempt at a smile. She rubbed her face with one hand. "But thanks anyway."

"You're welcome," He captured her hand with his, brought it to his lips and kissed her knuckles.

The romantic gesture warmed her. "So what do we do?"

"Be together, learn to trust and love each other."

Evie avoided his gaze. The strong steady beat of his heart in her ear, she whispered against his chest, "I'm afraid."

"So am I." His arms tightened around her again then one

large hand rubbed circles on her upper back. "But I have faith we'll be okay."

Though his answer pleased her, doubt remained. How could Ben really believe in a union he didn't remember? "I wish I could say the same."

"Someday you will." His hands moved up to frame her face, tilted it up once again and looked deep into her eyes. "When I earn your trust back."

His intensity filled her senses. Her heart sped. Breath became rapid. Her gaze dropped to his mouth. She couldn't look away. Invisible threads pulled her closer until she felt his breath on her lips.

"Evie," her name came out on a low groan as Ben's fingers slipped into her hair.

Desire overwhelmed caution. She needed his touch, craved passion. She dismissed the whispers of fear and looped her arms around his neck. Her lips brushed his. Ben moaned. Instantly she broke contact. His fingers flexed but otherwise the large, muscled man held himself still. Their breath mingled.

Seconds passed in tense anticipation before she realized Ben wasn't going to take control. He stayed motionless, almost rigid against her. Evie felt the back of his neck dampen with sweat. With the beat of her heart thundering in her ears, she dared another soft, short kiss then begged.

"Please—"

His mouth covered hers, a swift response to her plea. Her sigh of pleasure muffled. Ben coaxed her lips apart, and his tongue delved in. Arched against him, Evie forgot the rest of the world.

"Pardon me."

A gruff voice killed desire. She broke off the kiss, bowed her head. Cheeks aflame, Evie hid her face against Ben's chest and took deep breaths, struggled for calm as her husband lowered his hands to rest on her waist.

"You young folks need anything else?"

"No thank you sir, I believe we'll be on our way."

"That'd probably be best." Edwin's tone quivered as though he suppressed amusement.

"Yes sir."

"Ella packed you a lunch."

"She didn't need to do that."

"It pleases her. We'll be waiting on the porch."

As the old farmer walked away, she eased out of Ben's loose hold, avoided eye contact. Evie took a step away. Her husband caught her hand, stopped her. Startled, her gaze found his.

Ben squeezed her fingers. "It'll be all right."

The warmth reflected in his dark green depths stirred up bitter-sweet longing, a desire to be as carefree as they'd been in her dream. For a couple of seconds, she smiled. Her tangled thoughts simplified. Evie squeezed back.

"I hope so."

Despite his grin, his expressed seemed drained. Her guilt rekin-dled. "Are you okay?"

"I'm fine."

Evie arched an eyebrow. "Why don't I believe you?"

"I don't think I'm a believable guy." He rubbed the stubble that covered his chin and had the audacity to wink.

Hand in hand, they returned to the house. Her face heated as she took in the broad smiles and knowing looks of the farmer and his wife. Evie was grateful the goodbyes were swift and a few minutes later, they were in the wagon headed down the road.

The day passed quickly. With steady traffic, every time one of them attempted to broach any serious issue a vehicle or rider would appear. By dusk Evie felt strained again. Her composure brittle, body tense, she noted turkey vultures circled in the distance, in the direction they were going. The symbolism soured her stomach.

They made camp in a large meadow only a few yards off the road. With sparse trees, the wide-open area again left her with the sensation of being exposed, vulnerable. Edgy, she waited for her husband to bring up what she'd worried all day over but throughout the evening, he kept the conversation light.

The moon shone in the clear, star-studded sky when she slid the last dinner dish back into a box. A faint breeze whispered through the grass, carrying a bite to it and Evie shivered as she walked over to join her husband by the fire, grateful for her cloak.

Ben turned, faced her. His gaze wandered from the top of her uncovered head to the tips of her battered boots then back up to meet her eyes. He held her gaze a long moment then turned back to bank the fire. Anticipation made her pulse race when he finished and took her hand, led her over to their bed under the wagon.

As he sank down, she lingered a minute on her feet. Evie studied the bright stars while a rustling filled her ears. Her heart pounded in her chest. Palms dampened. She wondered if Ben had undressed completely as he had the night before.

Quiet, heavy and expectant, continued for the next few minutes even as the wind picked up strength. Even with the bright moonlight, she could barely make out the trees at the meadows edge. Boughs bent, they swayed in rhythm. Nervous, she removed her cloak, knelt down then crawled in to lie beside her husband. Evie could feel Ben awake beside her. Words tumbled through her mind as she tried to think of what to say.

"That was some kiss at the farm."

With an audible intake of breath, Evie turned from her back to her side, stared at her husband. "Ah yes it was."

"Thinking about it is keeping me awake." His arm snaked out, pulled her close.

Her voice breathless, "don't think about it then."

"I can't help it. It's been on my mind all day."

"Ben."

"Evie," his hand caressed up her back to the nape of her neck. "Would you kiss me like that again?"

"Ben I...No," she couldn't think straight, felt agitated.

His fingers threaded into her braid. "No?"

"No, we need to talk."

"Maybe we've talked enough." His lips grazed her temple.
Her words came softly. "It's so hard to resist you."

"Then don't."

"I don't think it's the right thing to do."

"There's nothing wrong with a woman kissing her husband."

"Um no, not exactly but," a lump formed in her throat and she couldn't continue. She shook her head.

"But you don't you want to?"

Evie cleared her throat. "I do," even in the darkness, she felt the full force of his charming grin. "But..." Her voice trailed off. His nearness intoxicated her. Reason battled with longing, she leaned into him. "I..."

"Evie?"

"No." Her hands curled into fists. Evie pulled back as memories both sweet and sad tormented her. She squeezed her eyes shut but a couple of tears leaked out. "I don't want..."

"What don't you want?"

"It to," Her breath hitched. A tremor rocked her. She sniffed, "happen again."

"What do you mean?" His tone gentle, Ben reached out wiped her cheeks dry.

"Before," Misery shadowed her heart. "When we'd survived another bad stretch, when we'd start getting along, we'd start kissing and..." Her voice rough with emotion, rasped. "Well the intimate part of our marriage has always been the easiest." Evie released a shaky breath then opened her eyes, leveled her gaze at her husband and tried to make Ben understand. "But passion only lasts so long, it burns hot and fast then it's over and we fall apart."

"You're worried I'm moving too fast?" His fingers brushed over the length of her jaw then down the side of her neck.

His caress caused the flow of her thoughts to sputter. A number of seconds passed before she could answer. "Yes."

"Well, pretty lady," his hand slid possessively around the curve of her hip. "How about we take it slow?"

Chapter Fifteen

The statement hung in the air between them. Nerves wobbled her tone. "What do you have in mind?"

"Kisses," his voice soothed as one gently brushed over her hair. "Just your sweet kisses tonight."

"Just kisses?" She echoed.

"Yes," Ben inched closer, cradled her against him.

The wind's whine faded from her consciousness. His warmth intoxicated her. Evie couldn't resist a touch. She placed one hand on his chest, felt bare skin and sucked in a breath.

"Yes."

His fingers trailed the length of her spine and stroked the base. His hand moved slowly over the curve of her hip then Ben reached up, took hold of her hand. Her breath quickened and her heart pounded when he kissed the back of her hand then turned it over. His lips caressed her palm, the inside of her wrist then worked his way up to the crook of her elbow. He stopped there, put her hand on his shoulder.

Evie pressed a soft kiss in the hollow of his throat then looked up, breathed his name. Anticipation pumped through his veins. His mouth hovered above hers. She closed her eyes and he could wait no longer. He swooped down to claim her lips. His kiss soft at first, a lover's greeting, and then slowly Ben demanded more.

Desire heated the blood in his veins as his tongue teased at her bottom lip. He increased pressure and with a muffled groan, her lips parted. Ben deepened the kiss, delving in to taste his wife.

In seconds, his need almost overwhelmed him. He tore his mouth from hers and instead his lips glided over her cheek. Her hands clutched his shoulders as his teeth teased her earlobe. His body, hard, already ached for release.

Breath rough, ragged, Ben molded her curves tight against him then rolled onto his back taking her with him. Evie gave a startled cry then fell silent when his motion ended with her on top of him. For a moment she stared at him frozen, then with slow deliberation his wife leaned down and nuzzled his cheek. Her breasts rubbed against his chest, stoking his passion. Strands of her hair trailed, feather light, over his face as she eased back. He reached up with both hands to stop her.

His hands curved over her jaw brought her mouth down within reach. Lips now forceful with need, his kiss devoured. Her thighs brushed over his hardness repeatedly and his hands moved over her sides then roamed down her back, impatient, driven. A moment later, she unexpectedly broke off contact.

Unfazed, Ben rained hot, wet kisses along her jaw then down the side of her neck. A whimper escaped her. Hungry for more, his mouth captured hers again. She arched against him, tangled her fingers in his hair. Their tongues danced. Desire consumed him almost to the point of being out of control. With his arms wrapped around her, Ben rolled them again to lie on top of her.

His fingers moved to the buttons of her dress. Lost in the moment and sensations that burned along nerves, the consequences of what Ben was doing didn't register at first. When his hand brushed her breast, panic cut through the haze that fogged her mind. Evie turned her face to the side and pushed on his shoulders.

"Please stop."

Ben pulled back. Drained, Evie had no words to express the feelings that stormed within her. For some time, they remained frozen. Their harsh breathing filled her ears. For reasons she didn't understand Evie struggled against the urge to cry.

"Sorry."

"Don't be," Ben rolled off her, then reached out with one arm and cuddled her to his chest. "I'm not."

"But I..." She blew out a frustrated breath. "I'm sorry."

He dropped a kiss on her hair. "Stop it."

"Sorry."

"Evie."

"Yes?" Edgy, she fidgeted. Her thigh brushed him and he winced.

"Maybe we should get some sleep." His strained voice only increased her tension.

Her heart still pounded. Her breath had yet to slow. His suggestion seemed ridiculous. "Sleep? You want to sleep *now*?"

"What I want—" Ben stopped. He sucked in a deep, audible breath. The arm around her shoulders tightened then relaxed as he exhaled.

Confused and a little irritated, she didn't press. "Fine."

"Evie."

"What?"

"Nothing...Good night."

"Good night Ben."

Even as she said the words, Evie didn't really believe her husband would try to sleep. Certain Ben would admit what he'd proposed was impossible, she waited, silent. With each breath, her anxiety sharpened. She couldn't settle down. Every second her need to talk over what happened increased. Her lips parted then clamped shut as an all too familiar noise of heavy breathing filled the air.

Evie stared at her husband in utter disbelief. It took less than a minute for doubt to creep in. His touch had swept her away as usual but Ben didn't appear affected by her. Tears stung her eyes. Their kisses couldn't have meant much to him, not if he could sleep so easily. Wide-awake, she shifted onto her back and looked up at the underside of the wagon. Thoughts tormented her, denying her rest for most of the night.

"Good morning." Evie forced her gritty eyes open to see Ben crouched by her side. "Breakfast is ready."

"I'm not hungry." Her stomach growled before she finished speaking and revealed her false words.

His chuckle did nothing to improve her mood. Evie scowled as she swept back the covers and scooted out of bed. She got to her feet then stomped the few steps to the end of the wagon.

"There's a small stream at the edge of the meadow, more like a trickle really."

Evie ignored his cheerful comment, snatched up her cloak and continued on toward some brush in search of privacy. She returned a few minutes later to find her husband right where she'd left him. Ben gestured to a pot on the tailgate.

"I got you some water to wash with." He sounded markedly pleased.

"Thank you." Out of sorts, her words were terse.

"You're welcome." Ben leaned against the wagon.

His gaze followed her as Evie walked over and retrieved her bag from the bed. She pulled out a sliver of soap then splashed cool water over her face. A quick wash made her skin feel clean and refreshed, improving her mood slightly.

The day had dawned dull, the sky overcast and grey. A damp layer of dew settled on everything. Evie wrapped the soap in a dry scrap of cloth, put it away and pulled out her brush. While she worked on her hair, her gaze wondered everywhere but toward her husband, though she was vividly aware of the man only steps from her.

Soft thuds heralded his movement. In seconds, she felt Ben right behind her. She focused on a stubborn tangle, didn't glance in his direction.

"I'll go get your food."

His light kiss on the nape of her neck shocked her. She froze. Ben had always been one for gestures of affection in public and private – that is until bitterness ate away at the loving man she'd known. A kiss separate from the pursuits of the marriage bed become so rare she no longer expected that kind of spontaneous touch from her husband. She turned, stared after him as he walked over to the fire. Words escaped her while she watched him fill their plates with fry bread and beans.

When Ben started to walk toward her, carrying their meals, Evie at last looked away. She quickly finished her braid and put the brush back, set her bag on the ground. He joined her as she straightened. Slowly, she turned, faced him. Awareness arched between them.

Before she could say a word, Ben spanned her waist with his hands, lifted her onto the wagon. His gaze steady on hers, he lingered. His fingers moved in a gentle caress. Her breath hitched. He smiled and stepped back.

"Thank you," her voice soft as her mood improved when Ben then sat beside her.

"You're welcome."

Evie bit into the bread with trepidation. She remembered the last time he'd made food. It was heavy but quite good.

"Mm, good job on the bread."

"Actually…" She glanced over to see heat spread across his cheeks. "I was trying to make biscuits."

Lips pressed tight together, she choked back laughter. "It tastes good regardless."

"I'm glad you like it and you don't have to worry about the beans. They were out of a can, I just heated them."

Except for the scrape of forks, the meal was silent. Ben cleaned his plate first. He looked around, quiet, waited for her to finish. All of a sudden, he swore under his breath and hopped down.

"What's wrong?" Evie called after him as he headed toward the dying fire.

"I forgot the coffee."

"Oh, do we have time for it now?"

Ben knelt down next to the blackened pot then glanced back at her. "Are you in a hurry?"

"Well, we're wasting daylight."

"I suppose," his tone light-hearted, playful, as he poured hot brew into two mugs. "That depends on what you consider wasteful."

"You're not in a hurry to get moving?" Evie set her plate down on the tailgate.

"Nope," his warm gaze locked on hers, her husband walked up to her. "I'm enjoying a peaceful morning with my wife."

The remnants of her grouchy mood evaporated. Warmth filled her heart. A broad smile spread across her face. Evie beamed her pleasure as she accepted the cup he offered. Ben rummaged through a box until he found a little jar. With a grin, he spooned honey into her coffee.

"Thank you," she leaned over and kissed his cheek when he sat back down beside her.

His arm came up and encircled her shoulders. Evie leaned against him and sipped her sweetened coffee with eyes half closed. It was a precious moment, one to savour. She'd missed the effortless way they'd used to be with each other. This was how it had been before, no need for conversation, no awkward, strained silences.

Before. Evie stiffened. It would be easy to push aside the past, pretend it never happened. She straightened away from Ben. She'd done that in the past and he'd wounded her heart.

"Evie?"

"I'm going to start cleaning up."

Ben slipped off the tailgate then helped her down. "It's probably best we get moving. I just felt a raindrop."

"Worried about crossing another river?"

"Concerned with possibilities," he grinned. "But I'm sure we'll be fine. I'll go put out the fire and hitch up Sugar."

"Okay."

A few drops soon became a persistent drizzle. The rain provided strong motivation. Evie cleaned up and repacked the wagon in a matter of minutes. As soon as he finished with the horse, Ben shoved in the mattress then retied the canvas. A moment or two later they were headed down the road.

"What was bothering you this morning?"

"What?"

"You were a tad grumpy," Ben shot a glance at her. "Do you want to tell me about it?"

"Not really," Evie shook her head. Anxious, she looked straight ahead, anticipating that he'd press the issue.

"All right, what would you like to talk about?"

"I don't know."

"How about you tell me your favorite color?"

Memory flashed in her mind. Her eyes welled with tears. He'd asked her that same question when they first started courting, on a long buggy ride through the country.

"Green."

"The color of spring," Ben laughed. "Well, usually. Right now, it seems to be grey. Mine used to be yellow."

"Sunflowers and sunshine."

"Exactly, how did you know?"

"Wild guess."

"A good one," he looked over at her again, his expression thoughtful. "But I believe I've changed my mind. Now I'd have to say blue."

"Because that's the color of my eyes." A bittersweet pang went through her as the past continued to overlay the present.

"Another guess?"

"You could say that."

Their conversation halted abruptly when, without warning, the steady rain became a deluge and the wind blew stronger. The road grew muddy and increasingly difficult. While Ben concentrated on driving, Evie focused on her husband.

In many ways, Ben was as he'd always been; smart, funny and, at times, downright charming. He didn't remember the failures, disappointments and grief so it made perfect sense that his sour attitude had disappeared. She didn't understand why his driving ambition also vanished. What changed? His need to succeed had always been part of him. Although Evie liked his new laid-back attitude, how could she trust that it was a real, lasting change without knowing what inspired it?

Their pace slowed to a crawl as the road dipped. They eased into a deep puddle and couldn't get out. Time went unnoticed as they worked on the problem but no matter what they tried, the wagon wouldn't budge. In the end, both husband and wife were muddy, wet, miserable and stuck exactly where they started.

Ben untied the end of the canvas and propped it up with a couple of scavenged sticks. Evie crawled into the cramped shelter and moved things to give them as much room as possible. While she did that, he tended Sugar. Her husband unhitched the mare then tied her in a group of trees to give her some shelter. By the time he joined her, she'd made something to eat. Uncomfortable and cramped, they ate while they waited for the storm to pass.

"Something bothering you?"

"Aren't you mad?"

Ben shrugged which was quite a feat for the large man in the small space. "Frustrated."

"But we're stuck."

"I chose to continue when the road got nasty." Evie braced herself. If Ben wasn't mad then she was certain that he'd start berating himself. Instead, he surprised her. "But I can't undo what's been done. Are you mad?"

Startled Evie stared at him. "No."

"Good. Now since we're likely to be here for awhile, any

suggestions on how we pass the time?" He winked at her.

Evie leveled a look at her husband, "Ben."

"Yes dear?" His tone was far too innocent for her to believe.

"We're in the middle of the road." She gestured to the edge of the canvas held up just enough for them to see a few yards behind them. "Someone could ride up."

"I can pull the canvas down."

"No," her cheeks burned. "I'll find our cards."

"We have cards? That's nice. What games do you know?"

"You taught me Poker." She dug the deck out of the basket.

"Thought you didn't approve of that? Wasn't my gambling part of what went wrong between us?"

Evie shuffled, considered his question a few seconds then answered, "Poker's just a game. I objected to how you used it, what it did to us, did to you."

"What do you mean? What didn't you like?"

"You tried to use it as a way to 'get ahead', instead you lost often and a lot. And I don't like gambling with the intention of cheating."

"You think I cheated?" His voice tight, controlled, but he spoke without heat.

Evie started to deal out the cards then paused. In the dim light she looked up into green eyes, studied them a moment while she considered her answer. In the end, she decided that it was best to stick to the truth, though it'd likely be painful to hear. Evading it would serve nothing. She took a deep breath.

"It took months to sell one horse after the others were lost and that was for a fraction of what you'd expected." She put the remaining cards in a stack between them.

Ben picked up the hand she'd dealt him. "And so I became a bitter drunk."

"You lost faith in everyone." Evie struggled to find the right words as she arranged her hand to her liking. "You'd say there was no point in being good when others got to do whatever they wanted to do."

"You took that to mean I stopped *being good*?"

"Usually when we've needed money, you picked up odd jobs, but not after that. You'd be gone for long stretches of time and all I know is that you spent some of those hours at The Bucking Pony. Sometimes I'd find our money jar empty after you left and sometimes you'd come home flush with money but wouldn't say how you'd earned it."

"Why didn't I catch more horses?" Ben put three cards down while she discarded two.

"You said you didn't see the point." She drew replacement cards. "Others reaped rewards doing nothing so why work hard."

Ben laid down a pair of tens but she won the hand with three twos. "So you believe I earned money gambling and don't approve of profiting from that?"

"I think if fools sit down at a table and willingly lay their money on the luck of the draw it's their business."

"Then you only disagree with me in particular winning at cards?"

"I object to cheating."

"If I was a cheat," disdain dripped from his voice and his gaze focused on the cards he shuffled, his expression grim. "I must not have been a good one. We've little more than the clothes on our backs."

Evie hesitated, uncertain whom her husband intended the scorn for, and considered her options. She could go on or not say another word. After a moment, she pressed on, the truth, however much it may hurt him, was important.

"At cards? You were decent but then you drank away most of your winnings."

"How do you know I cheated?" He slapped down his cards, his tone angry, raw. The storm outside intensified. The wind howled and the rain drummed against the canvas. "How do you know I wasn't just a skilled player?"

Her legs shifted, restless. She slowly picked up the cards he'd dealt, took her time arranging them. "There were a number of complaints made against you. The sheriff came by about those and to ask you some pointed questions."

"And you believed the complaints?" Ben demanded.

"No." All the pain born out of long ago shattered faith voiced in a single whispered word. "I knew you were having a hard time but I believed you were a good man. I trusted you."

Silence descended. They played the next few hands without exchanging a single word. Only the raindrops made sound as they splattered on the canvas stretched above.

Ben cleared his throat. "The sheriff changed your mind?"

"No. He warned you that he was keeping one eye on your 'activities' and left."

"Then why are you certain I was guilty?"

"The sheriff was interested in more than your gambling or possible cheating but all you said to him was that if he wasn't going to arrest you, he needed to leave. Rude but calm, unusual for a man who prized his honor and always vehemently defended it."

"Maybe I blamed the man for losing my horses."

"Perhaps," Evie put down the cards she held and looked out at the grey shaded world. The road remained empty. She looked back at her husband. "You wouldn't look me in the eye when I asked what was going on. You said it was nothing I'd want to know about and stormed out of the house. I knew then you were guilty of more than keeping an ace up your sleeve."

Her heart ached. Chilled in her damp, muddy clothing she shivered. Evie gathered up the cards and shuffled restlessly.

"Like what?"

"Look." The clouds had parted and scattered rays of sunlight illuminated the surrounding countryside. "I think it's stopped raining."

"Evie."

She'd always skirted around what exactly he may have done. Evie still nursed a tiny shard of hope that maybe she was wrong, a shard that could shatter if she voiced her suspicion. She chose to offer him another example of cheating.

"Well you sold a neighbor your last horse. He paid a good price for the well-trained animal you promised him. But Spice was only green broke and Mr. Talbert's son was thrown."

Her husband's expression became stone and his bloodless lips set in a hard line. Flat, emotionless eyes held her captive. "Is that everything?"

"No," with a heavy sigh, she answered. "There was another matter."

"Which was?"

"You folks okay?"

A voice from outside broke the moment. Evie looked out to see a couple of men peering in at them. Without a word to her, Ben crawled out. Evie followed her husband, stood at his side while he explained their situation. Several minutes later, with the young men's help, they freed the wagon from the mud.

After that, the strangers accompanied them for a few hours, trading stories with Ben. It was late in the afternoon before their company rode off. As soon as they were alone, her husband became withdrawn again. Throughout the evening, while they set up camp, Ben barely spoke. He gathered pine boughs and made their bed while she made dinner. Evie watched and worried as her husband tended chores. Pronounced lines of strain marred his handsome face. Her attempts to talk to him were politely but firmly rebuffed.

Stars winked in the sky when Evie crawled under the covers to wait for her husband. A nearby creek delivered the peaceful sound of running water. Ben slipped in beside her and she lightly touched his hand. He turned his palm up and clasped hers.

"Was he okay?"

Warmth flowed through Evie. She closed her eyes. That was the reaction she'd expected the first time she'd told him about

Talbert's son. To hear it now restored a little faith and brought hope that she could believe in her husband once more.

"He broke his arm but otherwise he was okay."

"Thank God." Ben gave her fingers a gentle squeeze then spoke with careful deliberation. "I don't know what happened to me, why I acted without scruples but my honor *is* very important. I'm determined to be a better man than my father was. Whatever possessed me to lose sight of that will not again."

"That's nice to hear."

Ben turned on his side, brought his hand up and brushed her cheek. "Why do I get the feeling you don't believe me?"

"I want to," her gaze locked on his while her ears rang with the hard pounding of her heart. "I really do."

"But?"

"What happens when you remember? When you remember why?"

Chapter Sixteen

"Is there something you're not telling me?"

"I'm just pointing out that you don't know what was going on in your mind, what caused you to abandon your quest to be a better man." Evie deflected his question. "And I worry that when you remember…"

There was a long silence. "Maybe it was something to do with James."

Evie stiffened. "Where did that come from?"

"I'd like to think the loss of our son would have impacted me more than the loss of some horses. Since I can't remember, it's hard to know. You rarely speak of our son."

Her hand moved down, rested on her lower belly. She blew out a breath. "Right after we lost James, he was all we spoke about. We cried. We grieved. Time passed and we talked about him less but there's *nothing* about our son I haven't told you."

"You've gotten over him."

"I don't think a person ever gets over losing their child but I've accepted it, we both did," her tone weary, hollow.

"It all seems unreal."

"Losing our son?"

"Everything."

Agitated she tried to move away but Ben put his arm around

her, kept her close. "That's why I worry that when you remember, when everything seems *real again*, it may change how you feel."

Ben kissed her forehead, "Whether or not I regain those memories, I'll never compromise my integrity again, I promise."

Absolute conviction burned in his voice, and made her want to believe him. His thumb brushed across her cheek. Ben raised her hand to his lips, kissed each finger.

"Do you hope I remember or wish that I don't?"

"Honestly?" A flush crept up her neck. "Both."

"Care to tell me why?"

Evie pulled her hand free. Her voice held worry, tension and a suggestion of challenge. "Does our marriage seem *real*?"

"You are very real to me."

"You don't remember me. Can you really care about us?"

"Yes I can."

Doubt rushed in, denying the answer she wanted to believe. "How can you? You don't know me."

"I know enough to like you, to admire your loyalty, strength of character and to be attracted to the way you smile.

"You've known me a few weeks, days really because at first you were in such bad shape." Restless she shifted and part of her wanted to pull away, run from the awkward, emotional discussion.

"More than enough time."

"Maybe you're just making the best of a bad situation."

"You consider our marriage a bad situation?"

Her teeth chewed her bottom lip a moment. "Sometimes."

"Ouch."

"I'm sorry."

"Don't apologize, I welcome the honesty."

"Still I didn't have to be so blunt."

"Its fine," Ben assured her though she could hear the strain in his voice. He tucked a few wayward strands of hair behind her ear. "And I do care for you Evie Rolfe."

"You barely know me."

"I know enough."

"Ben I—"

"I know you don't like early mornings but you get up and do what's needed anyway. I know I've done wrong by you yet you nursed me, took care of me and stayed with me. I know you're bright and compassionate. I know that, unless they're stealing bread, seeing a wild animal makes you smile. I know when I hold you in my arms you tremble. And I know when you're near, all I want to do is kiss you, touch you and give you pleasure."

Hope sparked within her.

"That's quite a list."

"And it's all true." His low voice packed with raw need, his breath caressed her lips as he moved closer. "Can I kiss you now?"

Evie set her worries aside. "Please."

Blood rushed through her veins. She held herself rigid as her husband brushed his lips against hers then pulled back. The tease of a kiss stole her breath. His thumb caressed the sensitive skin of her bottom lip. He kissed one corner of her mouth then the other.

"Please," her breath fast, her whisper a plea.

Ben claimed her mouth again and this time didn't stop. He deepened the kiss. His tongue tasted, demanded. Sensation shot through Evie. Her lips parted, allowed him further intimacy.

Passion soared as he probed the recesses of her mouth. She squirmed, whimpered and wrapped her arms around his neck. Her lower body strained to get closer. His hand moved down, grasped her hip and pressed her to him.

His mouth lifted, breath hard, voice rough, "I need you."

One hand moved up her body and cupped her breast. Evie gasped. He captured her lips again, hungry, urgent. She lost herself in the wave of passion her husband created for several long moments before he shifted. His arousal pressed against her thigh through their respective layers of clothing and icy cold reality clashed with the heat of excitement.

Torn, confused, Evie broke off the kiss, brought her hands down to his shoulders and started to scoot back. He halted her retreat with a firm grip on her hips. His lips found the side of her neck. He trailed hot kisses down to her shoulder. His teeth raked over sensitive skin. She couldn't breathe, couldn't think.

"Ben."

His palm moved over her hip to the soft curves behind. He pressed her against him, "Evie."

"Ben I—" His tongue ran over her collarbone. Her fingers dug into his broad shoulders. Thoughts scattered.

Voice husky, his head lowered. "Yes."

His mouth closed over the peak of her breast. Evie sucked in a breath. She arched her back, her body taut. Quilts slid down. His hand started to bunch up her skirt.

"No."

Ben stilled. After a couple of seconds, he lifted his mouth a hair's breadth. His hot breath fanned the damp fabric, stirring an ache deep inside her. It almost made her throw caution to the wind. Almost.

"No?"

"I...I..." She tried to slow her breathing, form a coherent thought. "I'm not...I can't."

Evie felt his heavy sigh all the way to her bones. Guilt added another thread in her tangled emotions. His hand released her skirt, moved to her mid back. Her grip eased. Ben shifted up and slightly apart. For some time that is how they remained.

Her breath slowed to normal as coyotes howled close by. The lonely sound felt like a reflection of her heart. Ben dropped a kiss on her nose.

"It's okay." His palm came up, caressed her jaw. Still torn between doubt and passion, she moved one hand down, over his chest then along his side. When her fingers brushed the bindings on his ribs, he sucked in a sharp breath.

"I'm sorry." Evie pulled away and this time her husband didn't try to stop her. Flat on her back, she stayed beside him.

Ben reached out and clasped her hand. "It's okay."

Clouds crossed the night sky and covered the bright moon. Her mood as dark as the inky black that surrounded them, Evie didn't respond. She felt the weight of his gaze but refused to look at her husband. After a couple of minutes, Ben squeezed her hand then released it. He pulled the covers up over them. His arm snaked out over her waist.

Anxious, Evie turned her head and stared at him. In the darkness, his expression was indiscernible. The knot in her stomach tightened.

"Stop worrying, Doll and get some sleep. It's all right." He kissed her hair. "Sweet dreams."

His voice rough, weary, rang with sincerity. Her tension eased. A measure of peace wrapped around her like a blanket, comforted her. Within minutes, emotionally drained, she slept.

Sunshine found its way into the shadowed area under the wagon and woke her the next day. On her side, Evie stared out into the world. Oaks dotted the hill beyond a giant pine. She yawned, stretched then turned over and discovered her husband gone.

His voice traveled to her on the light spring breeze as she tossed back the blankets. Evie couldn't make out his words but the cadence of his voice was soft, soothing. Curious, she eased out from under the wagon and found him a few feet away, brushing Sugar.

"Good morning."

Ben turned and dropped a kiss on her lips. "Morning."

"I...uh," For a second, Evie's mind blanked. "I'm going to the creek to get some water."

"Wait," He gave the mare a pat. "I'll come with you."

"It's just over there," her arm swept to the left.

"Where I can't see through the thick brush and trees."

A chill shot through her, "you think I'd be in danger?"

"I don't think so but we're in unfamiliar territory and should be cautious." Ben strode back to the wagon, reached up under the seat and pulled out the rifle.

"Oh," slightly more at ease, Evie walked past him to the tailgate. She grabbed the canteens, soap and a cloth. "Okay."

Side by side, they walked through tall grass to the shallow flowing strip of water. Ben helped her get water then leaned against a tree. With his hat low on his brow to shade his eyes, he watched Evie wash her hands and face.

"How are your ribs feeling?" She stood up, finished.

"They're there."

His dry response made her laugh. "Still hurt?"

"Only when I breathe."

Evie moved to his side, "I'm sorry, I thought you were doing better."

"I was."

It came to her in a flash. Her eyes closed for a brief second as she beat herself up for not noticing before. "You hurt yourself again getting the wagon free."

"Maybe," he shrugged and headed for their camp. "I believe these are blackberry bushes we're walking past."

"It's too early for berries."

"I know."

His wistful tone made her smile as they parted ways near the wagon. Her husband loved berries. While Ben made coffee, Evie searched her kitchen things until she located a particular tin. She mixed pancake batter then added what she'd found to it when he wasn't looking. Some minutes later, anticipation high, she handed him his plate. He noticed the blue dots right away.

A boyish grin spread across his face. "Evie, how?"

"We dried blueberries last year and had a few left."

"You're amazing." Ben put his plate down on the tailgate, pulled her into his arms and gave her a quick hug. "Thank you."

Ben strode off, fetched a fresh cup of coffee for her then turned his full attention to the task of cleaning his plate. Evie sipped the hot bitter brew, took care to keep her expression composed. The last of the honey had been drizzled on their breakfast but it was a small matter. The important thing was the smile on Ben's face.

Her husband went to hitch up Sugar, whistling, after they finished eating. His good mood infectious, Evie smiled as she cleaned up and readied herself for the day. She made their lunch while Ben packed up their bed then put out the fire. A short time later, they rolled out of the clearing.

Evie glanced up when they bumped onto the road. Dull grey clouds edged areas of blue. The threat of rain made her swallow a sigh. She left her bonnet on her lap, tilted her face to the sky, determined to enjoy the sun while it lasted. Ben reached down, gave her thigh a squeeze. She turned and smiled at him.

For a moment, it felt like they were the only people in the world.

Hoof beats shattered the illusion and Evie grimaced. All the traffic the bad weather must have discouraged the day before appeared out of seemingly thin air. From that moment on, other travelers were constantly within sight. She almost wished it would storm again.

They rounded a bend and the road started to follow a wide, deep blue river. She noted tilled fields and farm animals with increasing frequency as midday neared. Rain never materialized though the day remained overcast. The road, deeply rutted from heavy use, made the ride uncomfortable. Early afternoon, they arrived at a busy ferry with a sprawling city across the way.

The ride over the river was uneventful but crowded. Evie was relieved when they drove off into Ontario. Ben started to say something but a loud whistle drowned out his words. Excited to see a train, she looked in the direction of the sound and slumped. There were too many buildings in her way.

Ben smiled and snapped the reigns. Sugar picked up speed, kicked up a cloud of dust. With skill, he navigated around other vehicles. He found the station and pulled in the crowded lot by it as the train, a black metal beast, shuddered to a stop.

Buckboards and buggies littered the area around them. More than two dozen people crowded the platform and others gathered on the ground nearby. High-pitched squeals of excited children rang in Evie's ears. The chaos that surrounded them absorbed her attention for a few minutes.

"Seen enough?"

"Oh Ben, thank you," She resisted the urge to clap her hands like a child. "Could we stay for a few minutes?"

"We can stay as long as you'd like."

Evie impulsively kissed his cheek then without pause pulled out their lunch. "Thank you."

"First time you've seen one?" Ben leaned over. His lips brushed her ear as he spoke.

"No." Fascinated by the train, she hardly paid attention to her food as she ate. "You took me on a trip for our first anniversary."

"Did you like that?"

Her smile came slow then spread wide. "I loved it."

"So our life wasn't all terrible?" He mused aloud.

"Did I give you that impression?" Expression somber, Evie faced him. "No, it wasn't all dreadful. We had good times."

"I'm glad."

"Me too."

Gazes locked, silence ruled a moment. "Ready to move on?"

"Out of town?"

"Well we need supplies first but I was wondering if you'd like to spend the night in town?" Ben put them in motion.

"I'd love a break from the wagon's rock hard seat."

"Oh does my wife have a sore—"

"Mr. Rolfe."

"Yes my dear." He glanced at her. His eyes twinkled, his tone entirely too innocent as they drove down main street.

His teasing made her feel they were becoming a couple again.

Ben stopped and asked directions to the stable. Confident, her husband set a fast pace.

"You know, if you're hurting I could rub your—"

Evie swatted his arm, "stop."

"What?" The knowing smile he flashed at her sent shivers down her spine. "I just want to help."

Her lips parted to deliver her retort when Ben pulled up in front of their destination. She clamped her mouth shut. They arranged for Sugar's shelter. For a little extra, Mr. Jacobs, the stable master, allowed them to park the wagon next to the building. He promised their things would be secure under his watchful eye. The helpful man also gave them directions to a store in easy walking distance.

Happy to be on her feet, Evie enjoyed the short stroll to the grocer. They replenished their supplies in no time. Her husband flashed a grin at her as he added honey to the pile of basic foodstuff. A boy helped them carry the heavy load back to where Mr. Jacobs agreed to store their boxes, inside the stable.

"You okay?" His green eyes darkened with concern and they fixed on her as soon as the boy hurried away, his tip in hand.

"I'm fine."

"You're quiet."

Evie rubbed a hand over her eyes, "just tired."

"Yeah, me too," Ben put an arm around her shoulders and squeezed. "Let's go find someplace to put our feet up."

She leaned against him. "Sounds good."

"Hey did you hear what Jacobs told me?"

"He fed Sugar a measure of oats?"

"No, well yes but that wasn't what I meant. The river we crossed was the Snake." His expression worn, face a tad pale but his eyes shone with excitement. "You know what that means?"

"We're in Oregon."

"Yes indeed," Ben grinned. "And we're only a half day from the Bar 7 Ranch."

His fingers stroked circles on her upper arm. Their gazes locked.

Weariness forgotten, her lips parted ever so slightly. Everything, everyone but the man beside her faded from existence for Evie. Eyes half closed, her heart pounded as she anticipated his kiss.

"Daddy, did you see the train?" A young girl shouted as she ran by them. "I wanna ride on it. Please. Please."

Startled Evie jerked back and hit the brick wall behind her. She rubbed the sore spot on her head with one hand while she rested the other on Ben's shoulder for support.

"Are you all right?"

"It smarts but I'll be okay."

The girl, red-faced, returned, whispered 'Sorry ma'am,' then tore off down the street after her family.

"Something else I can help you with?" The stable master emerged from the building.

"Would it be possible to get a ride to a decent hotel?"

"Certainly," the older man nodded. "My son would be happy to take you anywhere in the city."

"Thank you."

Mr. Jacobs disappeared into the stables then came back with a strapping young man. Ben belatedly remembered to check their weapons with the stable master while Caleb hitched up a buggy and Evie fetched her bag out of the wagon. Minutes later, they drove them through the busy streets of Ontario. The city's constant noise made her poor head throb. Evie was relieved when they reached the hotel.

As soon as Caleb pulled up in front of the building, she got out of the buggy and hurried inside. Ben followed, carried her bag. When she hesitated in the large reception area, her husband moved past her. He crossed the room to the check-in desk.

"My wife and I would like a room."

The clerk looked down his nose at them. Travel weary, rumpled and dirty, Evie knew they didn't present an impressive picture. "Our rooms are expensive. Perhaps you'd like to try another place, more suitable."

Ben drew himself up ramrod straight. He fixed a glacial stare on the arrogant man before him. Evie swore the air around them dropped several degrees. After a moment of tense silence, her husband allowed his gaze to travel the length of the clerk.

"Perhaps you didn't hear me. We'd like a room."

The man paled at the cold fire in Ben's voice. He looked down at the open register book. Faced with her husband's stony expression, the clerk swallowed hard then turned around to pluck a key from the board behind him. Without a word, he turned the register around and as Ben signed them in, gestured to someone behind them. Evie started as a hand reached for her bag and jerked it away.

"Ma'am?" A boy, with an uncertain expression to match his tone, stood beside her. "Can I help you with your bag?"

Heat flashed across her cheeks, "Of course."

The bellboy stretched out his hand but kept a wary eye on Evie as she handed over her bag. The youngster, with a polite smile, gestured for them to follow. Ben climbed the staircase slow and steady, a tight grip on the handrail. His exhaustion was obvious by the time they reached their room. He sank onto a comfortable chair.

"Anything else?" The boy set her bag down by the wardrobe.

"Yes," Ben pulled a coin from his pocket and tossed it to him. "I'll give you another if you can get some food sent up and a bath for my wife."

"We don't have a tub sir, but I could haul up some hot water."

"That would be just fine." Evie assured him.

A broad grin covered the bellboy's face. "Yes ma'am."

Once the door closed, she crossed to Ben's side. "Are you sure we can afford this?"

"Likely not, but it's one night and I want to spoil my wife a little." He brought her hand to his mouth, kissed it. "Allow me this indulgence and I promise to be frugal forevermore."

"Forever?" She arched one eyebrow, her tone skeptical.

"Maybe not forever," His crooked smile charmed her. "But for a good long while."

Likely, there were cheaper places. She looked around the bright, clean room. In fact, they could save the entire cost by camping but something inside of her rebelled. It'd been a long, hard year with one crisis after another. One small extravagance sounded good.

"Okay but just for tonight."

"Just tonight."

Evie squeezed his hand then pulled free, and walked over to her bag. She dug out clean clothes then turned to ask Ben if he wanted to change as well. His eyes closed and face tilted toward the ceiling, it was clear the fast few days had taken their toll on her husband.

"Ben," She moved back to his side. "Are you okay?"

"I'm fine, just tuckered out."

His sleepy tone did little to reassure her. "We should get you into bed."

"Well darling I thought you'd never ask." Ben opened his eyes, exposed the laughter that danced in their depths.

"Ben."

"Evie."

Though she shook her head, Evie couldn't help but smile as she stepped away. She went to the far side of the spacious room and turned down the covers on the bed. Distinct thuds sounded on the pine floor. She looked over to find Ben leaned against the wall, watching her. The warmth in his eyes held her fast as he straightened then approached.

"You're lovely."

"I'm a mess."

"A lovely mess." He smiled down at her, touched her cheek.

Her face hot, Evie stepped back from the bed and motioned him toward it. "Come on you're dead on your feet."

Ben didn't hesitate. He sat down on the bed then, with a moan of utter relief, relaxed into its softness. His eyes shut and his breathing fell into the slow steady pattern of sleep in seconds. Evie smoothed the covers over her husband then stood, watching over him until a knock sounded at the door.

Before the noise disturbed Ben, she hurried to answer the summons. The bellboy and a maid stood in the hall. With quick, quiet efficiency, they delivered two steaming buckets of water, linens and a covered tray. The scent of freshly baked sourdough bread intoxicated her. The hotel staff exited with one of their precious few coins in gratitude.

After locking the door, Evie went to the long, low dresser and lifted the cloth off the food. Her mouth watered. Two cups of coffee, sugar, cream, sun yellow butter and a pot of strawberry jam surrounded a basket of still warm, thick sliced bread.

Her hands reached for a cup even as the thought crossed her mind. With a wishful longing for the honey she preferred, Evie stirred in a couple spoonfuls of sugar and a liberal splash of cream. She inhaled the aroma as the familiar sound of Ben's snoring started to fill the room.

Evie turned, gazed at her husband as she savored the rich brew. Her stomach growled. She looked back at the tray. *Just one.* She succumbed to hunger, spread layers of sweet butter and jam over a slice of bread and consumed it in a few bites.

Next, she turned her attention to the hot water. She stripped off her grimy travel stained clothes and indulged in a long sponge bath. When finished, she dipped her brush in the water then ran it through her loosened hair until the worst of the dirt and tangles brushed out. After, she donned her wrinkled but clean dress then pinned her hair up in a loose knot on the top of her head. Evie felt human again.

"Beautiful."

At the sound of Ben's husky voice, she spun around. Evie smiled at the sight of her husband standing by the bed, his hair adorably rumpled from his nap. "I think your vision is blurred but thank you, kind sir."

"On the contrary, I see you clearly." His gaze held hers captive as he crossed the room to join her. Ben trailed fingers down the side of her face. "You're beautiful." He dropped a kiss on her mouth, stole all her coherent thoughts. "I see the bellboy returned."

"Ah yes."

"Did you get a snack?"

"I ah..." His thumb stroked her jaw, distracted her. "Yes I did. I would've woken you but I thought you needed—"

Ben placed a finger on her lips, leaned in close. "I did need the rest."

"I should've waited."

"I don't want you to go hungry." His voice lowered on the last word and caused her lower body to ache. "Would you like more?"

"Yes," Evie breathed.

With a satisfied smile, he stepped back. "Let me wash up and we'll find a restaurant."

"Oh, okay," Cheeks hot, she went over to the window.

While her husband spruced up, Evie watched the activity on the street below. Several minutes passed before Ben announced he was ready. She turned around and stilled. His hair, slicked back from his face emphasized his strong features. The way his clean shirt clung to his broad shoulders begged her to touch him. The man riveted her.

"Is something wrong?"

Snapped out of her trance, Evie shook her head and walked to his side. "You look quite handsome."

"Thank you." His hand settled on the small of her back. "Shall we go?"

Even that casual touch fed the building fire of her passion. Seconds passed before Evie could nod her agreement and they headed out. They found a restaurant nearby and enjoyed a well-prepared, leisurely meal.

Hours later, they walked back in full dark. The moon shone bright in a star-studded sky. Her anticipation built with every step. *Tonight is the night.*

Her heart thundered as he held the door open for her to enter their room. The hour was late. In silence, they went about their nighttime routines then slipped side by side into bed.

Confidence high, Evie scooted close as her husband blew out the light. He drew her into his arms. Ben groaned, cradled her against his hard body. His lips brushed her forehead then he dropped a kiss on her nose.

Tension and excitement intertwined. Evie closed her eyes, raised her chin, eager for his kiss and waited. His breath fanned her mouth. A second passed. She hardly breathed. More time passed until she was unable to withstand the suspense anymore and she opened her eyes.

Moonlight streamed through curtains she hadn't closed and bathed her husband. He seemed to be sleeping. At first Evie rejected the evidence before her. She knew how fast, under any circumstances, Ben could fall asleep but he wouldn't do that to her tonight, not when she was finally ready. She touched his face. His mouth dropped open and he started to snore.

Hurt and discouraged Evie pulled out of his embrace, her gaze still fixated on his face. Pride kept her from acting on the desire to shake him silly. Part of her hoped her movement would stir him but that soon died. Ben slumbered on.

Evie threw back the covers and rolled out of bed. She stood, hands on her hips and glared at her husband for a long moment. Finally, with a growl of pure frustration, she stomped her foot then whirled around, marched over to the chair, flung herself down. Ben didn't notice a thing.

Chapter Seventeen

A smile on his face, Ben woke slowly, drifted up through layers of awareness. He reached for Evie and encountered empty space. Vision still blurry he stared at the pillow where her head should've rested. He blinked, rubbed his eyes, confused as his gaze swept the room. To his surprise, his wife sat in the chair, bundled in the deep brown coverlet from the bed, looking out the window.

"Evie?" When she didn't respond, Ben tossed back the blankets and got out of bed. In two long strides, he reached her side. "Evie?"

"Ben."

Her dull tone raised concern. He reached out, laid a hand on her shoulder. "What's wrong?"

"Nothing," Evie shrugged.

Puzzled, Ben was certain something troubled her but he was at a loss on how to handle the problem. Should he push or let her have space? The vast blank hole in his memory aggravated him the most at moments like this. He should know what to do.

"Are you hungry? Want breakfast?"

"I'm fine."

"That's good." Though he tried to keep it even, frustration edged his voice. "But I'm starving. Why don't we try another place this morning?"

"If you'd like," her flat response tried his patience.

"Or we could find a bakery."

"Whatever you want."

"I want to know what's wrong."

When Evie only shrugged again, he pressed. "I don't know how we handled things before but I don't like this at all. I'd appreciate it if you'd just spit out what's bothering you."

Again, she didn't answer. After a minute, Ben turned on his heel and went to where he left his clothes by the bed. He dressed with rough, jerky motions. Irritated, his boots hit the wood floor hard as he walked toward his wife then dropped down to sit near her feet.

A long moment passed while Ben gazed up at her. With resolve, he focused on his wife but said nothing and waited. Evie started to squirm. He remained, watched. Until she gave him an answer, they were going nowhere.

His unwavering gaze disturbed the comfortable numbness she'd gathered around herself like a cloak against a bitter wind. Withdrawing was easy, familiar, what she'd always done when her feelings had been hurt. Evie clutched the coverlet tighter. His presence a thorn, the silence became unbearable.

"You fell asleep."

"I fell asleep." He repeated. Evie looked down at him and nodded. Ben stared at her for a number of seconds before he spoke again, his tone incredulous. "You are upset because I fell asleep?"

"Yes."

"Why?" Ben drew out the one word as he leaned forward.

Unable to maintain eye contact, she looked away. Heat crept up her neck as Evie tried to explain. "I thought...I thought that we were..." Frustrated, she blew out a breath. "You didn't even kiss me."

"You're pouting because I didn't kiss you."

"No!" Put like that it sounded petty. "I'm upset because I was ready to be *affectionate* and you snored."

"I snored." He echoed.

"I felt rejected."

"I did not reject you." Ben didn't move a muscle, didn't raise his voice but his indignation echoed in the room. "Last night and the night before and the one before that, I wanted you. Hell, I've wanted you for longer than that." He got to his feet. "I fell asleep because I hurt and I. Was. Exhausted." His gaze blazed cold fire. "You keep going on about how I let you down, let myself down, how I lost faith in life, in myself." He leaned to the right, snatched his hat off the dresser. "I wonder what came first; my lack of faith or yours." He set his hat square on his head. "It seems to me you're ready at any perceived slight to find me guilty of some offense, as if you want to get rid of me." He crossed to the door. "I'm going to get the wagon. I'll send someone up to collect you."

His tone deflated her. His words barbed darts that pierced her heart and rendered Evie speechless.

Ben left. His careful closing of the door telegraphed far more than slamming it shut would have done. She buried her face in her hands and bawled.

Long moments passed. The sound of her sobs echoed in the room until at last Evie cried herself out. She shrugged off the warm folds of the blanket and stood. Her head throbbed. Weary she stumbled across the room to the washstand.

Evie poured water from the white pitcher into the matching basin next to it then splashed her face. She dared a glance at her reflection in the mirror above the stand and winced. The clock on the dresser chimed. She turned from the sight of her red, splotchy face to note the time.

Someone will be coming soon. Her gaze swung to the door then down at her rumpled nightgown. She quickly splashed more water on swollen eyes then got busy getting ready.

His words cycled through her mind.

The memory of how drained he'd been yesterday flashed as

she spread the coverlet over the bed. *I should've understood. I should've—*

A knock on the door interrupted her thoughts. She walked over and opened the door. The bellboy stood in the hall.

"Ma'am, Mr. Rolfe sent me up to fetch you."

Evie offered him a polite smile, "Let me get my bag."

"I'll get it for you," The boy wasted no time, slid past her and in a few quick strides, crossed the room. He palmed the handle of her bag. "Anything else ma'am?"

"No, thank you."

"If you'll follow me then?"

Evie nodded. She wiped damp palms on her skirt, picked up her cloak then on leaden feet proceeded downstairs.

"He's waiting across the street at Nell's." The boy waved an arm toward entrance. "Would you like me to walk you over?"

"No thank you," She pressed a coin in his hand, took her bag from him and stepped out the door.

Rain sprinkled from a sky strewn with dark, angry clouds as Evie exited the hotel. She tossed her cloak on, tugged the hood over her head then picked her way across the busy street to the where Ben was waiting. Framed in one of the large street side windows was the man she sought.

Mug in hand, her husband sat at a table near the door. Ben stood as she approached, pulled a chair out for her. A waitress appeared before Evie had the chance to speak. They ordered the special on the harried woman's recommendation. Alone again, he turned his attention to the world outside.

Her hands twisted in her lap. Evie struggled to find the right words, torn between the need to apologize and the strong desire to pretend nothing happened. "About earlier, I—"

"This isn't the place to continue that discussion."

The steady murmur of other conversations pierced her consciousness. Her face flushed.

Silence fell and persisted over the next hour. Preoccupied with thoughts of how to put things right between them, Evie took little notice of her meal. She picked at the eggs on her plate until Ben finished. Expectation made her heart race as they pushed back their chairs.

Eager to set things right between them, Evie stepped outside to wait by the wagon while Ben settled their bill. The day had darkened. A chill wind kicked up. She shivered as her hood fell back, hair whipped across her face.

As she tucked loose strands behind her ear, Evie glanced up. Clouds now almost completely covered the heavens but, for the moment, the rain ceased its steady flow of misery. She gave Sugar a pat and the passing traffic drove through muddy puddles without pause, splattered her cloak. She backed away from the street with a grimace.

Impatient, Evie stared at the doors of Nell's. As if in answer to her unspoken plea to hurry, her husband emerged from the building at last. He walked up to her. Without a word, he took her bag and shoved it under the seat.

His expression unreadable Ben helped her onto the seat then got up beside her. Silent, her husband snapped the reigns and they started down the street. Grassy fields dotted with cattle replaced buildings and scurrying people in a matter of minutes. As the city faded in the distance, the sky started to clear and huge sections of brilliant blue appeared above.

Sunlight caressed her face, warmed her skin. Ravens glided upon the gusting wind. Evie risked periodic comments of little consequence as the miles passed. His short, one-word responses kept her tension high.

Flat land surrounded them. It afforded no privacy from their numerous fellow travelers. However, traffic thinned the further they drove into the country where trees and wildlife became more common than people, wagons and acres of grass. By midday, they had an entire stretch of road to themselves but before she dared to offer an apology, Ben cleared his throat.

A shiver of foreboding went down her spine. Words she'd thought to say fled. Her eyes closed, shut out nature's beauty and swallowed hard. He reached over, covered her clasped cold hands with one of his.

"I'm sorry about this morning, I over reacted."

"No I'm the one who did," Evie opened her eyes, studied his profile, tried to gauge his mood. "And I'm the one who needs to apologize. I'm sorry."

Silence followed for a heartbeat. Ben glanced at her, his expression cautious, tone serious. "I'm not very good at being a husband yet."

"Because you lost your temper?" Her eyebrows furrowed.

"Because I'm not sure if I should insist on arguing with you about who's more at fault, if it'd be best to agree that we both were equally or just accept your apology."

His earnest tone caused her lips to twitch. A thread of warmth wove through her. Tension ebbed.

"I like the last one."

Her husband pulled up. His gaze locked on hers. "I want to be clear. I did not reject you but I'm very sorry about how I reacted to your hurt feelings."

"And I made a mountain out of a molehill. I truly am sorry."

His arms came around her, hugged her close. Evie shifted to lean her head on his shoulder. Relief rendered her boneless and she welcomed the peaceful moment. The sound of oncoming horses reminded her long before she was ready that they had stopped in the middle of the road.

Ben dropped a kiss on the top of her head. "Ready to go?"

At her nod, his arms dropped. He tightened his grip on the reigns as two riders stopped beside them. The older, weathered man chatted with Ben about the possibility of more rain and the condition of the road while Evie struggled to maintain a polite smile. The breeze carried an icy bite and she missed the comfort of her husband's heat.

Her face ached by the time the men headed on. Evie glanced up when Ben set the placid mare in motion. Clouds were few and scattered. The sun, bright and golden, shone. Within an hour, she shed her cloak and welcomed the wind's cool caress on her skin.

By unspoken agreement, they avoided emotional topics and passed the time with light conversation and easy silences. They pressed on through the noon hour. Ben produced ham sandwiches and a jug of water he'd bought in town. They ate as the wheels turned.

Late afternoon, Ben took an overgrown fork off the main road. The wagon swayed through tall grass and hidden rocks over a trail that twisted through a thick stand of trees. Soon it was as if they were alone in the world and Evie welcomed their isolation.

As the shadows lengthened, they parked beneath an enormous fir tree beside a lazy flowing stream. Evie climbed down, stretched then joined her husband in the routine of making camp. The busy work was a welcome distraction to the thoughts nagging at her.

Later, dinner eaten, fire banked, attraction bubbled to the surface as she sat on a blanket beside Ben. Evie leaned back and rested her palms on the ground behind her, studying the stars that sparkled above them. He wrapped an arm around her, pulled her close and tucked her head on his shoulder.

Her gaze wandered. Moonlight danced over the water beyond their feet. A deer, more shadow than form, crossed the meadow downstream.

"You were right."

"About what?"

"About me." She drew in a deep breath and a little courage then continued. "I didn't want to be wrong. I did jump on any little thing you did."

"It's okay."

"No it's not," Evie looked up at her husband. "But I promise I'll do my best to give us a chance from now on."

His hand lightly stroked her upper arm. "That's all I want, a real chance to make things right with you."

His husky voice stirred longing. Evie shifted, turned into him, brought her hand up onto his chest. Her heart beat faster.

"Do you remember me at all?"

"No," Ben spoke softly. "Not here." He pointed to his head then dropped his hand down, covered hers. "But my heart does. I love you."

Shocked, Evie started. She pushed against his chest hard. He fell onto his back, the circle of his arm taking her with him.

For a second they lay frozen, his startled expression the only thing she could see. Her nerve almost deserted Evie, and then his fingertips brushed the side of her face. She smiled. Warmth infused her and she snuggled against the length of him.

"I love you too."

One hand tucked under her jaw, Evie laid her head on Ben's broad chest. With deliberate slowness, she eased her free hand down the solid planes of his stomach. Her husband tensed. She felt his heart beat faster as he tightened his arm around her.

Evie traced lazy circles with her fingers, large and small, over worn flannel. The heat of his skin radiated through the soft fabric. She brought her hand up and opened his top button.

His breath caught. Encouraged, Evie opened another. She caressed his flesh. The contrast between his coarse hair and soft skin fascinated her. Slowly, one by one, she worked her way down until his shirt hung open.

Ben squeezed her upper arm then trailed his fingers up and down over her skin. Her breath quickened and she lifted up onto one elbow to watch his face. Reaching down, Evie pulled his shirt free of his pants and then spread the edges to expose a greater expanse of bare flesh.

A muscle in Ben's cheek contracted. His eyes closed. She laid her palm on his stomach above his belly button then moved it in a large arc until it rested just above the waistband of his pants. He sucked in a ragged breath. Evie smiled, pleased with his reaction.

Crickets started their night song. She eased her hand back up over his stomach and the bindings around his ribs. His eyes opened, dark green pools, as Evie tangled her fingers in the thick hair that covered his chest. Ben reached up to brush the hair back from her cheek. His fingers ran down the side of her neck then over her collarbone.

Without braking eye contact, Evie pulled back, sat up. Ben rose up on his elbows to watch spellbound as she unbuttoned the bodice of her dress. She eased it off one shoulder first then the other. His rapt expression emboldened her.

The thin straps of her chemise slid down, her undergarments fell, leaving her breasts bathed in moonlight. Evie pushed him onto his back again, followed his downward motion to lie on top of him. Her lips brushed over his as their bare flesh met. She teased, tasted and feathered her mouth over his repeatedly.

His hands roamed over her bare back. Evie flicked the tip of her tongue between his lips. He moaned. With one hand on the back of her neck, Ben pressed her closer.

Encouraged, she deepened her kiss. His fingers moved over her skin, restless, in a path over her shoulder, down her arm, across her side and up her back. Their intensity awakened a sliver of alarm. She broke off the kiss and sat up, her breath hard while Ben's hands fell to his sides.

Her heart thundered in her chest. Silent, they stared at each other, a taut thread of awareness between them. As Evie held her husband's gaze, his need for her apparent, a heady rush of power and desire, coursed through her. She reached down, clasped his hand and placed it on her breast.

Shivers raced down her spine. The roughness of his palm against her released a wave of sensation. Her fingers tightened for seconds then loosened his hand. Her husband's initial caress, a gentle touch, brought a whimper of pure pleasure to her lips.

Evie leaned forward and placed her hands in the dirt on either side of his head. Ben slid a hand along her side, up to her other breast, massaged it until she was restless with need. His hand shifted. Her sound of protest became a gasp as his lips closed over her nipple.

His tongue circled the hardened tip. Her breath became ragged as Ben shifted his attention to her other breast. Her arms quivered with the strain of holding herself above him. The stimulation soon overwhelmed Evie. She wanted him to stop and yet she never wanted him to stop.

Wary but intrigued she moved onto her side, next to Ben. The breeze teased the flesh his mouth had moistened. Passion crouched within her, hesitant but eager to unleash.

Her husband turned to face her and his smoldering gaze left Evie in no doubt of his desire. Yet he didn't reach for her. She brushed a few dark locks of hair out of his eyes with a hand that shook.

Impossible for her to ignore, her need for him demanded action. Evie wrapped her arms around Ben and covered his mouth over hers. The touch of his lips made her pulse race. She thrust her tongue into sweet battle with his and pressed closer, waist to chest, legs entangled.

His hands returned to her skin, moved from the curve of her hips to the slope of her shoulders. Evie broke off their kiss, her breath coming in swift, hard pants. Without pause, she scattered open mouth kisses down the length of his jaw.

Ben buried his face against the side of her neck. Evie felt his rigid arousal against her thigh and soon his fingers worked to unfasten her skirt as he nipped the sensitive skin at the base of her throat.

Yet again, Evie pulled out of his arms. She pushed to her feet, clutched loose fabric around her hips while Ben stared at her with singular intensity. Before doubt could take hold, she dropped her skirt. A heady sense of power rushed through her as her husband sucked in a harsh breath.

Emboldened Evie smiled. Slowly, she removed her clothing,

bit by bit, savoring his riveted attention, until only moonlight covered her ivory skin. She looked down the length of him, inch by inch, then back up, an eyebrow arched, to meet his gaze with one full of challenge.

Her husband responded with action. Ben peeled off his open shirt, tossed it aside. Evie knelt then stretched out on her side and watched him unfasten his pants. She leaned closer, allowed her bare breasts to brush his skin. He swore under his breath. Her smile widened. The flustered man needed a minute before he could kick away the last of his clothing.

As soon as Ben turned to face her, Evie stroked one hand down his side, over his hip to caress his thigh. She then molded her curves to his powerful body. When she trailed kisses over his chest, her husband moaned, low and guttural.

His response encouraged Evie. She worked her way down his body tasting and teasing him with her mouth and tongue, stopping at his hips to repeat the process back up to his chest. Ben cupped her jaw, tilted her face so he could capture her mouth in a hot demanding kiss. One hand twisted in the hair at the base of her neck while the other explored her body.

For a second Evie almost forgot to breathe. Incoherent sounds passed her lips as his mouth left hers to blaze a path down her neck to her breasts. As he kissed and sucked, Ben continued to caress every inch of skin within his reach until she ached with need and writhed against him.

Her thighs clenched together. Ben nudged them apart. When he rested one of her legs against his own hip and touched her intimately, Evie gasped. His fingers trailed over her silky damp curls. Within minutes, she arched against his hand. Her fingernails dug into his shoulders while he continued to arouse her.

"Dear God," her hoarse cry silenced nature's creatures.

His mouth sucked hard on her nipple as one finger pleasured her intimately. Evie couldn't handle the assault on her senses anymore. She had to have control. With both hands, she pushed with all her strength against him.

Unprepared for her action, Ben fell onto his back. Evie followed, straddled him. For a heartbeat, courage threatened to desert her. She stared at the man beneath her while he trailed fingertips down her sides, waited.

Desire soon coiled tight within her and she couldn't wait another second. Evie rocked her hips and slid over his erection. Ben groaned. His hands moved to her thighs, assisted motion as she rubbed against him again. Need built to a persistent demand.

"Please."

"You sure?"

"Yes."

Ben grasped her hips, raised them just enough to position himself at her entrance. His gaze locked on hers, he eased Evie down his length slowly. Joined, she cried out with pleasure. He pulled her hips forward and started a rhythmic dance to completion.

Their bodies moved together, driven by need, faster and more frantic every moment that passed. Suddenly Evie clenched around him. Her muscles relaxed for a second then she arched hard against him. Rocked by a series of intense contractions, she threw back her head and screamed.

His fingers dug into her thighs while her release pulsated around him. The incredible sensation drove him to the edge. He thrust up into Evie once, twice then with a hoarse shout, poured himself into her.

Languid she collapsed on his sweat slicked chest. Minutes slipped by. Breathing slowed. Triumph and satisfaction mixed, a fog of contentment clouded her mind.

Words refused to form. After some time, she pressed a kiss over his heart then shifted off her husband. Evie stretched out on the blanket. Ben laid an arm over her waist and kissed the tip of her nose. She smiled as her eyelids drifted shut.

"It's time to wake up."

His persistent voice pulled Evie out of a deep dreamless sleep. Her eyes opened slightly. Bright sunlight was torture, she groaned.

"Come on Doll, we're burning daylight."

With a grimace she sat up, pushed hair off her face with an impatient hand. "I don't care."

"Well good morning sunshine."

"Morning," Evie mumbled, frowned in the face of his grin.

"It's a beautiful day."

"If you say so."

"I do indeed."

Uncertain, shy in the light of day with areas of her body that hadn't ached in this manner in ages now aching, Evie felt out of sorts. "If you don't stop being so blessed cheerful, I'm going to kick you."

"You'd hurt me after I slaved over a hot fire for you?" He clapped a hand to his chest as his expression morphed into one of fake indignation.

Her eyes rolled. "Please tell me you didn't cook."

"Afraid my darling?" Unperturbed by her grumpy tone, his smile returned, broader than before. "Don't worry I made you something you'll love."

A rich aroma pierced her morning fog. "Coffee?"

"Yes ma'am."

"With honey?" Evie dared to dream.

"It's out and waiting for you."

"Well then," she snagged her clothing out from under the blanket and started to dress. "You're forgiven for waking me."

Ben bowed, his eyes danced with laughter. "That's most kind of you—"

"Would you excuse me?" Personal needs urgent, Evie needed him to leave so she could dress quicker and dash into the brush.

"Of course." Her husband didn't hesitate. He leaned down,

kissed her thoroughly, scattered her thoughts then walked away.

Bemused, Evie stared after him for some seconds before she at last finished dressing. She attended her needs, splashed her face and hands with frigid stream water. With the strong lure of fresh, hot coffee, her fingers made a few impatient attempts to smooth her tangled hair then gave up.

Evie glanced up as she turned to face their camp. Endless light blue painted the sky above and her mood lightened. Eager to join Ben fireside, her gaze dropped, sought her husband as she stepped forward. A firm grip halted her progress.

Cool metal caressed her cheek. Her blood chilled. A bead of sweat dripped down along her hairline. Her lips parted but Evie couldn't make a sound. She stared at her husband's back, only a few yards away and willed him to notice.

With grim irritation in his tone, the man who held a gun to her head spoke and sent shivers down her spine.

"I should just shoot you now."

Chapter Eighteen

Confusion hovered at the edge of her thoughts. Evie recognized the voice. She knew one of the men who'd followed them from Cedar Ridge held her now but it didn't make sense. Those men should be in jail.

"What do—"

The barrel dug into her skin. "Call out to him."

"Ben," Evie croaked. Fingers squeezed her arm hard then he moved his arm up, across her throat. She tried again, louder, "Ben."

Her husband turned. The smile on his face died. His gaze seared as he took a step forward, drew the pistol, aimed.

"Let her go."

"Stop there." She heard the man pull back the revolver's hammer. His arm tightened against her throat, sent a wave of pure terror through her. "We've come for our money."

Ben narrowed his eyes. "We?"

The cocking of a rifle, a distinct sound, came from her left. Saliva gathered in her mouth as metal rubbed her temple and her stomach churned. Evie barely dared to breathe.

"Yeah, now toss over our money before I make a mess out of your pretty wife."

"Harm a hair on her head and I'll hunt you down like a dog." Ben's voice was low, controlled and full of menace.

"Hand it over now," the man's tone cold, hard, resolved. "Or we'll just dump you both and find it ourselves."

"I don't have it."

Dead silence filled the air for a long moment. The smell of his unwashed body filled her nostrils. His arm moved for a split second and Evie thought he was going to release her. Instead, his fingers spread over her throat the threat implicit as he squeezed. She gasped. Ben cursed.

The man didn't make a sound. His hold eased. She felt a second of relief then his hand moved downward, settled over her breast. Slowly his grip tightened until tears streamed over her cheeks.

"If you want to play games," his sour breath wafted over past her face, "there's only one that amuses me."

"I'm not playing," Ben bit out.

The man crushed Evie against him. his fingers pressed her flesh with bruising strength. She whimpered.

Her husband growled, "I don't have your money."

"If you blew it all on hotels and restaurants," His teeth closed on the soft skin where her neck and shoulder met. Evie froze, horrified. "I guess we'll have to take it in trade."

"No!" Fierce, Ben's voice sounded almost feral.

"Then cough it up now."

"I don't have it."

"Too bad." The man started to drag Evie in the direction of his companion. She made an incoherent sound of protest.

"Stop." The look in Ben's eyes was so cold it sent shivers down her spine. He pulled a small bag out of his pants' pocket with his free hand. "I have some money."

Her captor halted. "Pitch it here."

"Let her go."

Heart in her throat, Evie watched Ben inch closer. A scowl darkened his face. Her breath audible, strangled, she fought for a semblance of calm.

"When I have the coin."

"Not until you let her go."

"Billy could shoot you right now we'd have the money and her."

"You'd have neither." Each word dripped venom. "You'd be dead."

Their standoff continued for a number of minutes. Nerves stretched to the breaking point, Evie stared at her husband as she waited with complete faith that he'd rescue her.

"Throw it close and I'll let her go."

With a soft thud, the bag landed a few feet in front of Evie. The man shuffled them forward. As soon as the money was within reach, he thrust her from him. She hit the rocky ground hard and cried out.

In an instant, Ben was beside her. With his solid presence between her and the man, Evie sat up. Her husband reached down, touched her shoulder, a brief contact that comforted. A shaky breath passed her lips.

"This isn't enough. Where's the rest?"

"That's all we have."

"What else you got?"

"Nothing of value."

"We'll see."

The thin, raggedy dressed man headed to their wagon. He jumped up on the tailgate, kicked off the little honey pot then flung back the loosened canvas. In horrified fascination, Evie watched him rummage through things, toss clothes and dishes out on the ground. She flinched when the box with James' bootie and their wedding picture cracked open on the hard earth.

Cold as ice, she got to her feet. Evie held her head high, pushed fear aside. Time crept by. In the end, the man pocketed a watch and an old silver comb then hopped down, stomped through the mess he'd created.

"Pathetic," he scoffed. "The old lady had better stuff."

"You done?"

"This was a waste of time." The man smiled his contempt

as he put his fingers to the brim of his hat in a mockery of the respectful gesture. "Until we meet again, it was a pleasure ma'am."

His sneer stiffened her spine. The man slipped into the stand of trees where his companion hid. They heard them ride away a moment later. Her shoulders drooped in relief.

"You okay Sweetheart?" Ben smoothed hair off her face.

Tears clouded her vision. Evie locked her gaze on his as the events replayed in her mind in vivid detail. Tremors rocked her. She wrapped her arms at her waist.

"Oh my God."

"It's okay," Ben wrapped an arm around her and held her to his warmth. "They're gone, it's okay."

"They could've killed us."

"But they didn't." His hand rubbed her upper arm.

Her gaze scanned the area. "They could come back."

"It's possible but I doubt it."

"Why?"

"Right now, there's nothing left they want."

"I guess," doubt filling her tone. Branches creaked as the breeze picked up a little force. She shivered. "That marshal said he caught them."

"I know."

"Then how could they have..? "

"I don't know. I don't think we'll ever know."

"What are we going to do? They took all our money." Her voice sounded hollow, defeated.

"Not all, you have some."

"A couple of pennies in my pocket."

Ben wrapped one arm around her and she leaned against his side. "We'll be all right."

"How?"

Wind ruffled his hair as he shook his head. He held her gaze steady, expression serious. "We'll be at the ranch soon with my family."

Evie drew in a deep breath, considered his words a moment then nodded. For several minutes longer, they stood together, silent, and watched the tree line. Nothing stirred except for some birds. After a time, Ben relaxed his stance, shoved the gun back in his belt.

The instant he eased his vigilance, emotion seized her and Evie lost what little control she had. Ben ran a comforting hand up and down her back. A low keening sound escaped her lips and she wilted against him, and wept like a child.

Sobs spilled forth, ripped from her depths. Her husband wrapped his arms around Evie and gently rocked her. She buried her face in his shirt, clung to him. Her distress soon dampened soft brown flannel. Untold minutes passed. Her ribs ached when at last she'd cried herself dry.

Afterwards, drained, she still couldn't relax. The awful man's smell filled her nostrils. Revulsion crawled over her skin like an army of red ants. She could feel his touch.

"I need a bath."

"That'll have to wait until we get to the ranch."

"I want to wash now." She all but whimpered.

"Evie I don't think they'll come back but I can't be sure."

Her stomach knotted. "Okay," her tone subdued, she pulled away from her husband. "Sorry."

Her braid had come apart. Long strands of hair poked her eyes, stuck to her lips. She wiped her face with the palms of her hands, felt her eyes puffy and raw.

"You're fine." Gentle but firm fingers cupped her chin and tilted her face up. "Just fine," his voice subdued. He brushed a thumb across her cheek, wiped away a stray tear. "Come on, let's get something to eat."

"Just a second."

With her husband close behind, she walked over to their scattered belongings. Evie picked up the little wooden box that she'd stored her precious things in. Tenderly she put the baby bootie safely back inside, shut the cracked lid then set it on the tailgate.

Evie let him escort her to the fire although her appetite was nonexistent. Tiny flames flickered among the coals. Her husband reached down and cut her a piece of charred, crumbly cornbread as she filled a mug. She took a sip of the lukewarm brew, grimaced, and then bit into her breakfast. Immediately she gulped bitter coffee to wash the taste out of her mouth then tossed the rest out for the grey jays that hovered near.

In silent accord, they abandoned all pretence of enjoying a meal. Evie doused the coals with the last of the coffee while Ben fed the rest of the bread to the birds. Dishes in hand they headed to the wagon. Working together, it didn't take long for them to gather their things off the ground and repack the bed.

They were back on the well-traveled road headed west an hour later. Jittery, Evie placed her hand on her husband's rock solid thigh. The simple contact gave comfort. Love, powerful and strong, swept through her. Lovely memories from the night came up and chased out dark thoughts about the morning.

"Do you think we'll reach your cousins' place today?"

"Yes."

Ben didn't say another word after that. Flat land evolved to fir tree covered hills as the day advanced. A narrow, muddy creek started to run along the left side of the road. Her dress clung to sweat damp skin, as the day's heat grew uncomfortable despite the breeze. Although Evie found her husband's silence odd, she didn't prompt conversation again. It was enough just to be together.

After a time, she reached down into the bag by her feet and pulled out her brush. She took her time, worked out tangles and braided her hair. In deference to the bright sun, as soon as Evie finished, she put on her bonnet.

Around noon, they reached Fir Mountain where Ben convinced Evie to wait in the wagon while he reported the hold up to the sheriff and got directions to the Bar 7 Ranch. Over an hour from the small town, they rounded a stand of pines and arrived at their destination. The two men by the barn cast curious glances in their direction as they pulled up in front of the sprawling log home but neither approached. A stout middle-aged woman with a faded apron over her dress answered Ben's knock on the door while Evie once more stayed with the wagon.

Her husband returned a short time later. "They're gone."

"Your uncle and his family? They moved?"

"No, apparently my aunt and uncle are on a trip and my cousins are out moving the herd. Alice, the housekeeper, expects them back in a few days."

"Oh." worry knotted her gut. "What will do until then?"

"Alice isn't comfortable with us in the main house. She doesn't know us, but since I've the look of a Rolfe," Ben arched an eyebrow, "we're welcome to stay in the old homestead cabin."

Evie smiled with relief. "That's nice of her."

"Yes it is."

An odd note in Ben's voice troubled her but just then one of the ranch hands came over, told them he'd show them to the cabin and the opportunity to express concern was lost. The man led them down an old, mostly overgrown pathway. As they rolled between clumps of skinny oaks and over countless rocks, the main ranch buildings disappeared from sight. Several minutes passed before they pulled up in front of a snug house set back in a clearing. Their guide showed them the spring, the outhouse and where some split wood was stacked then left them to settle in.

A grin slowly spread across her face as Evie stepped inside the structure. The home, though small, was larger than the one they left behind and had an actual bedroom. She walked around a table and chairs to touch the cook stove with reverence. It'd been well over a year since she'd cooked on one and the prospect thrilled her. Hope displaced angst. She finally believed her husband's claim that this would be the start of a new and happy life together.

"Here," Ben walked in, handed her a wadded piece of linen.

In the cloth, Evie found two sad looking blueberry muffins and four squished boiled eggs. "Where'd this come from?"

"I got it in town."

"And then forgot to tell me?" Hungry, her stomach growled.

"Sorry, had a lot on my mind."

Evie studied her husband a moment. His behavior seemed a bit off. She couldn't pinpoint what worried her but the only thing that made sense was that the early morning standoff still bothered him. With a mental shrug, she decided to let it go.

"Thank you, it was thoughtful."

His expression distant, Ben nodded. He took a seat at the table as she divided the bounty onto two plates. They ate in silence while her gaze wondered the room, planned where she'd put things if his relatives let them to stay awhile. Wrapped up in her musing, Evie didn't notice how quiet her husband remained until he got up and started to bring things in from the wagon.

An uneasy feeling tightened her gut as Ben ignored her plea to wait for her help. He brought in their dishes, bedding, her bag, their food supplies and the box that held their special items all before Evie finished her last bite. All he'd left for her to help with was the pallet.

After they lugged it inside, Ben went back outside to move the wagon around to the lean-to behind the cabin. She made up the bed, proper, in a matter of minutes. Her step light, she re-entered the main room and started to unpack a few things. As she worked, Evie discovered an old washtub in a corner. Her gaze returned to it repeatedly and the desire to wash away any trace of the outlaw's scent grew.

"Evie I—"

"Oh Ben," she turned to face him. "There's a tub." Her palms rubbed together, her tone eager. "Would you fetch some water so I can bathe?"

For a long moment, her husband simply looked at her, his expression unreadable. The sense that something was wrong came back. Her eyes narrowed. She took a step toward him.

"Ben what's—"

"Sure."

"If you're tired or hurting it can wait."

"It's fine."

"I'll try not to be so bath obsessed after this its just—"

"Evie," his voice tightly constrained Ben grabbed a large pail by the door. "It's fine."

"But—"

He paused by the door, looked back at her. "We'll talk after your bath."

"But—"

"After your bath."

His firm tone caused Evie to shake her head as he walked away. Her husband was more stubborn than a mule and when his mind was set, almost nothing changed it. Impatient to hear what troubled him, she had Ben dump each pail directly into the tub.

When the container was a little less than full, she started to strip. Her husband immediately marched back outside. Evie exhaled hard as she dropped her dress onto the rough-hewn wood floor. With a sliver of rose scented soap in hand, she stepped into the bath. She stood, shaking, as her fingers dipped into the icy water, worked over the bar until lather foamed. Her skin a carpet of goose bumps, she washed quickly then hurried to put on clean clothes.

"Evie?"

His hoarse voice made her pause in the act of fastening the last button on her long sleeved blue shirt. She turned to find Ben in the doorway, his expression sent worry tumbling through her. Her numb lips had trouble forming words.

"What's wrong?"

"It's my fault."

The self-disgust in his voice made her gut tighten. Cold pierced her heart. Apprehension heightened.

"What is?"

"This morning, those men," Ben stepped close, eyes stormy with turmoil. "You could've died." His fingers trailed down the side of her face. "I need to go. You're better off, safer without me."

"You insisted on waiting until after I took a bath to announce that you're leaving me?"

"It was important to you after...this morning."

"Yes but..." Words escaped her.

"And I didn't want you to haul all that water yourself."

"You didn't want me to haul water?" She shook her head in disbelief. "What do you think I'll be doing if you leave?"

"My cousins will be back soon. You'll be fine."

"I will not."

His fisted hand unclenched to lay flat on his thigh. The stubborn set of his jaw spoke of his conviction. "You could've died because of me."

"You aren't responsible for those lowlifes."

"I think I am actually," Ben scowled. "And that puts you in danger."

"What are you talking about? You kept me safe."

"Those men tracked us all the way from Cedar Ridge. They found us where we'd camped off the road twice, and escaped that marshal to come after me again. Don't you find that odd?"

"What are you trying to say?"

"You said I started drinking and gambling after I lost faith, believed there was no point in being good."

"Why are you bringing this up now?"

"I think you know why. What haven't you wanted to tell me?"

"Ben—"

"What was Sheriff Green asking me about?"

She shook her head, wouldn't look at him.

"Evie please, I need to know."

Her words came forth slow, reluctant. "There had been a series of robberies for some time all in or within a day's ride of Cedar Ridge."

"I thought it was something like that. And he thought I was

responsible?"

"Why does that matter now?" A wealth of emotion rang in her response. "We're here to start over, this is our fresh start."

"Do you think those men would be so persistent over so many miles for a couple of dollars?"

"I don't know, maybe."

"I did some hard thinking this morning. I think I did take their money, likely their shares from a robbery. Could I have hidden some in any of our things?"

A bad feeling settled over her. "Sheriff Green asked me something similar."

"What did you tell him?"

"I said no, there wasn't any money. But...I did see you with a bag of coins the morning a few hours before the attack. After he brought Sugar home the sheriff said he checked, all your bags were empty."

"So you don't think I hid it?"

"I can't think of anywhere you could have."

"Then those who beat me up got a bonus."

"What does all this have to do with you leaving?"

"Those men still believe I have their money. They aren't going to give up, not for long. They'll be back unless," Ben averted his gaze. "I lead them away."

"That's ridiculous." Spine stiff, her edgy tone seemed to echo in the room. Minutes ticked by before green eyes at last met blue.

"I need to go." Expression closed, his tone held a note of conviction that alarmed her.

"I believed you, believed you meant your promises." Tears threatened as she pleaded. "I love you."

"And I love you," expression hard, eyes over bright, voice stern, "very much."

Acid burned her throat. "So much that you're leaving?"

"Exactly," he asserted with force.

Anger crystallized. "Deserting me won't protect me. It'll just leave me, facing trouble alone, again.”

“I’ll protect you. I won’t let them near you, I promise.”

“You can protect me by staying here by my side like you promised.” Stress tightened a band around her temples as silence stretched between them. Nausea rolled in her stomach. “How will I survive? Beg from your relatives?”

“I’ll find work, support you.”

“So you’ll pay my way but won’t stay with me, hold me at night, share my life or love me.” Bitter scorn laced her tone.

“You’re not listening.”

“I’ll be happy to listen to you any time you want to start making sense.” Aggravated, Evie sucked in a harsh breath then released it slow. “You love me and I love you. We should spend the rest of our lives together.”

“I have to go. You need to accept that it’s for the best.”

“You...” Evie threw her hands in the air, exasperated.

“Someday you’ll understand.” He muttered through clenched teeth and half turned, back rigid, presented a profile carved in stone. His hands worried his hat a moment before he put it on.

The words, shards of ice, pierced her heart. Her poise strained to the point of shattering, held, barely. She glared at his shadowed face, frustrated and spoke soft but with a bite.

“Don’t dress this up as something noble.”

“Evie please I—”

“Just go.” her words sounded hollow, emotionless then with a hard shake of her head, she turned her back on him.

Tension held her upright. Silence ruled a moment then the door slammed shut with an awful finality. Evie stared at the stone fireplace dry-eyed even as a whirlwind of emotion raged within her.

Hurt and anger melted together and burned like lava in her veins. Her throat constricted. She reached out, gripped the high back of the nearest chair hard. Every breath required effort. Her heart longed for the man who’d walked away even as righteous fury pulsed through her.

Seconds later, agitation seized control. Evie paced the length of the room until her head throbbed so bad she couldn't ignore it. Hands visibly shaking, she dismantled the remains of her braid in a couple rough motions then sank down onto a chair, deflated and drained of fight. She closed her eyes and covered her face with both hands. Over time, the headache lessened to bearable and, restless, she stood up.

The next hour passed with irritating slowness as Evie found things to do. She put her food and cooking necessities on the two shelves by the stove then stacked the emptied boxes next to the door. As she scanned the room, looked for what to do next, the small box on the table caught her eye. Her gaze fixated on it. With slow, dragging steps, she crossed over and opened the lid. Her hands shook as she pulled out their wedding picture.

For some time Evie stood and stared at the photograph. Her heart ached. Tears stung her eyes but didn't fall. She already missed Ben, his wit, warmth, kisses, even his stubbornness. Her movements those of an old woman, she shuffled to the bedroom and lay down, the picture held to her chest. Weary, she closed her eyes, tried to sleep but the silence itself tormented. Without her husband's dreadful snores rest eluded her.

Evie eventually gave up. Chilled to the bone, she wrapped a quilt around herself and walked into the main room, looked out the window. As she stared outside, the nugget of hope that Ben would come back died. An endless, bleak future stretched before her. Tears welled up, streamed down her cheeks. Sadness sapped her spirit; she couldn't muster the energy to wipe her face.

Suddenly something deep inside of her snapped. Her mixed emotions morphed into cold hard resolve. Without her husband, nothing else mattered. She wouldn't let Ben go this easy.

Determined to track him down to at very least continue the argument, Evie threw off the blanket and stomped outside. The setting sun painted the clouds burnt orange. Liquid gold bathed the distant hills. Full darkness would soon arrive, but she dismissed fear.

Evie made her way to the lean-to, tired yet energized. The mare stood inside a small corral next to the shelter. It took a few minutes to find the saddle still in the wagon. In the low light, she stumbled and dropped her heavy burden. When she bent over to pick it up her fingers brushed over a piece of knotted leather and she froze.

Her mouth dry Evie opened the secret pocket her brother had created. She swallowed hard then felt inside. Her fingernail struck against the tightly packed coins. Tears filled her eyes. She couldn't wait to tell Ben about her find. They could give the outlaws their money and live the rest of their lives in peace.

"Are you all right?"

Evie sprang up and whirled around with a gasp. "Ben?"

"Were you expecting someone else?" Her husband stood a few yards away, just beyond the reach of a large pine's shadow.

"No, of course not." Her heart sped. She drew in a calming breath then marched up to him. A thousand different things to say danced through her mind. Evie seized one of his hands with both of hers and spoke before she lost courage. "I missed you."

"We've only been apart an afternoon," Ben stared at her, his eyes dark with intense emotion.

"One of the longest afternoons of my life, I missed you the minute you walked out the door."

"And I you," he gave her hand a gentle squeeze. "I couldn't stay away even though I still believe you'd be better off without me."

"I don't agree."

"Even if my presence puts you in danger," his voice rumbled with a strange note she couldn't place.

"Even if," Evie inched closer, studied his expression for a clue about what he was thinking. "Isn't that why you came back, to be with me, do you want that?"

"I want that more than anything."

Evie slumped as tension fled. "Thank God."

"But I need to—"

"Ben." nerves frayed, she struggled to remain calm, certain he was going to say something she wouldn't want to hear. "Please I—"

"You don't know everything yet."

"Pray, enlighten me…" Although she'd promised herself she wouldn't lose her temper, worry on top of raw emotions had her on edge.

Seconds felt like hours as she waited his response. She placed her hand on his chest, impatient and implored him with her gaze. At last, Ben spoke.

"I remembered something."

That was the last thing she expected him to say. "What?"

"I'm an extremely flawed man who loves you beyond reason."

"That's a memory?"

"No, that's a statement of fact. I remembered leaving after we argued on the day I was attacked."

"I told you about that," her tone revealed impatience.

"I know," Ben confirmed. "But I also remembered being on the road to our old place, seeing men ride up to me."

"You remember the attack?"

"Only that flash," disappointment haunted his tone.

"Well that's good." Evie tried to sound excited about it even though she was concerned with the issue at hand. "Maybe it will all come back soon."

"I hope so, but that's not what's important right now."

"What is?" Hope laced her whisper.

"I was headed back Evie. I was headed back."

Confused, she shook her head, "I don't understand."

"That day, like right now, I headed back for you."

The sweet implication flooded her mind. Her lips parted yet she couldn't make a sound. Evie dropped his hand and took a half step back. Her legs threatened to buckle. She swayed on her feet, sank to the ground and stared up at her husband, mute.

Ben lowered himself down to sit beside his wife. Her eyes swollen, skin mottled, the evidence of her tears shamed him. He took her hands in his.

"I'm definitely not good enough for you." When Evie started to object, he shook his head and she quieted. "However, I'm far too selfish to stay away. I love you, Doll."

"You were headed back to me," her voice incredulous.

"Yes I was." Ben paused. "I wanted you to know that first."

Dread crept in. "First?"

"When we were in town, I told Sheriff Marston everything."

"You did what?"

"I told him everything."

"Why?"

"It won't be a new beginning if I'm always worried that my mysterious past can creep out from the shadows and snatch it all away."

"Are you going to jail?" Her lips trembled.

"I don't know. Maybe. It depends on what evidence the good sheriffs discover. I can't confess to crimes I don't remember committing but, Sweetheart, it was the right thing to do."

"What about those other men? Do they just get away while you..?"

"No, the sheriff said he'd wire the marshal from Elk Bend and learn what he can. I'm sure he'll be actively hunting for them. Evie, if I go to jail—"

"I'll wait for you."

"Does that mean I'm forgiven for earlier?"

"Do you think I should?"

"Have mercy on me Sweetheart," he continued without pause, pleading his case. "Being without you would kill me." Ben cupped her chin and turned her face so he could look into red-rimmed eyes. "I need you in my arms every night and to wake up every morning beside you." He put gentle fingers over her lips when she started to make a sound. "I can't promise I won't behave like a jackass again, but I'll love you like no other."

"Ben," her soft sigh feathered his hand.

"Please honey. Once I figure out all this outlaw stuff, I'll find work, buy us land and build you a nice cabin, big enough for a family. I'll give you your dream."

Evie took hold of his hand, pulled down so she could speak clearly. "All I want is you."

"Does that mean..?"

"I should make you work harder to persuade me."

His lips brushed hers then Ben framed her face with his hands, his gaze held hers. "You are my life."

"I love you," Evie melted against him, unable to resist.

"So you'll forgive me? Give me a second chance?"

Her hand came up to rest her palm on his cheek, "Yes and—"

Her husband whooped, jumped to his feet and tossed his hat in the air. The loud unexpected sound spooked Sugar. The mare leaped over the rickety fence and took off. He shook his head, fell back onto the soft grass next to his wife and laughed.

"Ben—"

"Guess I shouldn't have done that."

"Probably not," her tone indulgent, Evie smiled even as she shook her head. "I need to tell you—"

"How much you adore me?"

"Yes I do but Ben in Sugar's—"

"Don't worry about the mare. She won't go far." He reached over, toyed with the long loose locks of hair that tumbled over her shoulders.

"That's good but—"

His fingers caressed the side of her neck. "We'll track her down in no time."

"Okay but—"

"Have a little faith in your husband."

"I do I just need to tell you—"

"Does it involve imminent danger?" He stroked her cheek.

"No but—"

"Then it can wait. I've something more important to attend to."

Her lips curved, hinted at a smile. He was right. She had plenty of time to tell him about the money.

"Tracking down Sugar?"

"We'll go after the mare in a minute or two."

A sparkle in her eyes, Evie leaned closer. "Why not now?"

"Because," Ben tugged her onto his lap. "I need a taste of my wife." He captured her mouth in hungry possession and kissed her senseless.

The End

www.ingramcontent.com/pod-product-compliance
Lightning Source LLC
Chambersburg PA
CBHW010634100726
47900CB00011B/2826